Breaking the Cowboy
Cowboys series from

M000215194

*Be advised, this novel contains discussions and issues
regarding infertility.

BREAKING THE COWBOY

THE COLDIRON COWBOYS SERIES

Breaking the Cowboy is a work of fiction. Names, characters, businesses, places, events, and incidents are either the products of the author's imagination or used in a fictitious manner. Any resemblance to actual person, living or dead, or actual events is purely coincidental.

Copyright © 2021 by Mina Becket

ebook ISBN: 978-1-7327051-8-0

Print ISBN: 978-1-7327051-9-7

Published by CurtissLynn Publishing

Cover and internal design by Shiver Shot Design

Editing by The Killion Group, Inc.

Rescuing love is never easy.

Veterinarian Dr. Louisa Coldiron comes from a long line of hardworking, rough riding, straight-shooting cowboys. Her father and brothers are cowboys and nearly every male in the small town of Santa Camino, Texas, is, was, or will be a cowboy. And experience has taught her that when a cowboy gets thrown into the mix, something gets broken.

Falling in love with the horses she helps to rescue is easy. Pretending she isn't falling for the sexy cowboy who teaches them to trust again…?

Not so much.

After years of roaming, Brody Vance feels he's finally found a home at the Promise Point Horse Rescue Ranch and a woman he could easily love. But he knows a wounded heart when he sees one. Louisa has more in common with her patients than she's willing to admit.

Coaxing Louisa's skittish heart into letting him take the reins of passion will take Brody's tender expertise.

Thank you to Jax and Sarah for letting me ask those hard questions and for letting Brody and Louisa tell your story.
Your marriage, love and commitment have inspired me.

BREAKING THE COWBOY

A COLDIRON COWBOYS NOVEL

MINA BECKETT

CURTISSLYNN
PUBLISHING

CHAPTER 1

LOUISA COLDIRON COULD BUY HER OWN DRINKS, SADDLE her own horse, and drive herself to the chapel without any assistance from a cowboy.

Yet she desperately needed one to ride to her rescue.

The fully restored, midnight black 1979 Chevy truck was her baby and she loved it. But right now, she wanted to roll it into the weeds and let it sit until the tires dry rotted.

She'd always wanted a vintage truck, something classy and sexy, so she'd traded her little sports car for a practical work vehicle when she'd started her veterinary internship.

But as she felt under the hood for the release handle, she realized that her purchase had been based on a zealous and impractical wish from her adolescent years, not a pragmatic decision for her career. After finding the handle, she gave it a squeeze and then raised the hood. Placing her boot on the front bumper, she hoisted herself up to get a better look at the engine.

She fidgeted with the battery cable, hoping a loose connection might be the problem. *That can't be it.* If it were, the headlights and dash gages wouldn't work. Too bad, the truck didn't have all the bells and whistles a new vehicle had to warn her when something wasn't right under the hood.

Normally, she wouldn't have needed them. Having been raised on a cattle ranch with two older brothers and a father who insisted she be self-sufficient had given Louisa a common knowledge of basic automotive care and taught her how to notice telltale signs of engine trouble. When she was twelve, McCrea let her help change the brakes on one of the ranch's flatbed diesel trucks, and thanks to Jess, she could change the oil in any vehicle. But neither of those lessons would help her now.

There hadn't been anything wrong with the truck's performance last night on the way home from the wedding rehearsal or this morning when she'd driven it into town to have her hair and nails done. That meant whatever had gone wrong had done so after she got home.

The problem could be something simple, a loose wire or bolt or just a faulty part. There was no need for her to worry. Engines failed, vehicles needed upkeep and repairs. Just because her truck wouldn't start didn't mean there was foul play afoot. Still, she couldn't shake the familiar uneasiness stirring inside of her.

She stepped down from the truck, slammed the hood closed, and dusted her hands, careful not to chip a nail. After climbing back inside the cab, she held her breath as she gave the engine one more desperate crank.

Nothing, not a sound nor a click, just silence.

Frustration bubbled up her throat, rousting a sharp, ear-splitting scream that frightened a nest of scrub-jays from a nearby tree. A frenzy of fluttering wings and squawks rattled the air as the birds took flight.

She gave the steering wheel a couple of hard yanks for good measure, then snatched her phone from the seat beside her. Using her thumb, she scrolled down her list of contacts to find the only uncalled one on her list.

She stopped when she came to the photo assigned to Brody Vance's personal cell phone number. He had collar-length, chestnut hair, assertive blue-gray eyes that glittered when he smiled, and a cleft chin that did crazy things to her stomach.

Louisa remembered, in detail, the hot summer day she'd taken the photo. Brody had been working in the paddock with a rescued colt. He'd been covered in dirt and grim, sweaty and shirtless, she'd wanted to enjoy the moment longer than the seconds it took for her to pass from the veterinary clinic to the horse stables. So, like a teenage girl stalking her first crush, she'd darted behind the head-high bales of hay stacked to the side and hoped to secretly capture a few shots when he wasn't looking.

But Brody had swung around to look directly at her just as she snapped the picture. She'd been mortified, of course. He, on the other hand, had loved every minute of her red-faced excuses and salty curses as she'd lost her balance and pitched forward into the hay bales. They'd tumbled over and she'd been caught standing with her proverbial pants around her ankles. He'd chuckled and given her a wide, sexy grin before she'd hurried inside the clinic.

In a few hours, she'd be holding onto the arm of Mr. Hot Ass himself as he escorted her down the aisle. They'd be close, their bodies touching like they had been last night at rehearsal.

How was she going to make it through this wedding without melting into a puddle?

Damn the man for making her feel out of sorts and damn her truck for leaving her stranded. Unwilling to throw in the towel and make the call to Brody, Louisa scrolled up and hit the call icon beside her friend Violet's name.

Louisa was four months into her veterinarian position at the Promise Point Horse Rescue, a non-profit organization her brothers had started six years ago. Not only did the Rescue save horses, but its equine therapy program had helped hundreds of veterans suffering from Post Traumatic Stress Disorder.

It was immensely rewarding to know that she was saving horses and helping to make a difference in the lives of people. And it felt so good to be home with her friends and family. But so much had changed in the years since she'd left home for college. Three out of four of her closest friends were either married or involved in a serious relationship. Eleanor, her best friend since the second grade, had married McCrea two years ago and they'd recently welcomed their second child. Last Christmas, Sage announced her engagement to Carter McDermott. Today, everyone in the small town of Santa Camino, Texas, was piling into the Tall Oaks Winery for Mallory and Jess's wedding.

She and Violet were the last remaining bachelorettes of their five-member sisterhood, and right now, Violet was her only alternative to Brody. "Come on, Vi. Please, answer your phone."

But Violet didn't pick up. Like a dozen times before, her phone rang three times and cut straight to voicemail. "Howdy, this is Vi. Leave a message."

Groaning, Louisa flipped the phone face down and planted her face in her hands. She was not calling Brody for a ride.

Nope.

No.

Ah-uh.

She'd just sit here and wait.

Lifting her head, she drew in a steadying breath. When her family realized she was late, they'd check their phones, see her missed calls, voice mails, and text, and call her back. She just needed to relax and be patient.

"Right," she mumbled.

Blowing a stray strand of hair from her eyes, she settled against the seat and waited for her phone to ring. Minutes ticked by and like her truck's engine, there was nothing. No ring. No vibration or message alerts, only silence, and the longer she waited for someone to call, the later she'd be.

The auto repair shop in town wasn't open on Saturdays, and no one was answering the phones at the new tow truck service.

Whether she liked it or not, Brody was her last resort for getting to the wedding. Gritting her teeth, she flipped the phone over and scrolled back to his number.

Heat swept over her body, causing Louisa to inhale a shaky breath before hitting the call button beside Brody's number. It was June in the Texas Hill Country. When she'd carried her things to the truck, the outside thermometer had read seventy-five degrees, but she hadn't felt the rising heat until she'd started thinking about Brody.

As his cell started ringing, Louisa wedged the phone between her shoulder and her ear and began fanning her face with a coloring book she'd snatched from the dash. At seven, her niece, Sophie, was infatuated with anything remotely related to fairytales and princesses. *Aladdin* was one of her favorite stories.

She slid from the truck and headed towards the cool comfort of her air-conditioned Airstream travel trailer, thinking that if she could magically summon Brody like a genie from a bottle, it would spare her the task of asking him for a ride. Simply rub the lamp and her wish would be his command.

A snarky grin pulled at her lips when she thought about her chaps-wearing nemesis as a mythological shapeshifter.

"Imagine that," she said and snorted through a laugh.

Brody Vance popping out of a lamp riding a magic carpet, ready to grant her three wishes. No way. If that cowboy popped out of anything, it would most likely be a bottle of whiskey, and he wouldn't be sitting cross-legged on a rug. That was too tame for a cowboy like Brody. He'd be riding a wild stallion.

His chest, tantalizingly tan and smooth with a well-groomed spread of dark brown hair covering his pecs and abs, would be bare. Her daydream deviated to naughty as she stripped those dusty chaps from his firm, sculpted thighs. There Brody stood in all his magnificent male splendor, completely naked in her mind's eye.

Holy Moses.

Nearly tripping at the bottom step of the trailer, Louisa tried to remember how many rings had passed since she'd dialed Brody's number. She'd lost count but knew he should have answered by now. Two more rings and she started to worry. He always answered when she called.

Always.

The next ring was interrupted by a deep and winded, "Hello."

That single word spoken sensually jerked the air from her lungs. "T—there you are."

"Here I am." The husky tone of his voice intensified the burn that was gathering between her thighs.

"W—what were you doing? Wait." She grimaced and was hit by a nauseating surge of jealousy in the pit of her stomach. She'd suspected that Brody was secretly entertaining a woman on his mysterious weekend trips out of town. But she'd never had a shred of proof to back up her claim.

So, had Brody brought his lady friend to Santa Camino? Had she caught them in the middle of something? And did she want to know the answer to either of the above?

No, she did not. "Forget I asked. I assumed you were alone."

"I am alone," he drawled, his voice velvety soft.

Her nausea eased and another hot flush rushed over her skin as her mind latched on to an activity a man like Brody might be doing alone. Something that would leave him breathless. Flustered and aroused, she spoke in broken syllables. "Oh…I, ah. That is…I…"

"Shame on you," he scolded, his voice dipping lower. "For thinking of me doing that."

"How'd you kno−" She stopped in mid-sentence when she realized he'd tricked her into confessing her dirty assumption. "Damn you, Brody."

That deep laugh of his, the one that made all her lady parts applaud and whistle, rumbled up his throat. "Don't clutter your innocent mind with such thoughts of me. I'm not a five-finger, one-handed kind of guy."

Louisa's mind was far from innocent and the mental picture of Brody's wide hand fisted around himself had her nearly taking a bite out of her bottom lip. "Can we just stop the bullshit and get back to why I called?"

"Okay, sweetheart." The tender humor in his voice made her want to hang up and walk the twelve miles to Tall Oaks. "What can I do for you?"

Louisa hadn't been intimate with a man in quite a while, and after that little stroll down Dirty Lane, her body was more than eager to jump in with a long and detailed list of what Brody could do for her.

But this wasn't a wicked fantasy where sex wouldn't have repercussions. This was reality and that sexy voice on the other end of the phone belonged to a man with a sensibility and gentleness about him that had made Louisa want to reconsider her rule about dating cowboys.

That unsettling fact, plus Brody's mysterious trips out of town every other weekend, had her throwing up barriers left and right. Experience had taught Louisa that cowboys weren't worth the risk. Wild and reckless, they often left a trail of shattered hearts behind as they rode off into the sunset in search of another naïve heart.

Having been that credulous conquest six years ago had given Louisa a proactive and unsparing attitude towards shooting down Brody's advances. "My truck won't start. Can I catch a ride to the wedding with you?"

"Let me guess." There was a short pause for effect. "No one else is answering their phone?"

Brody had a real gift for reading horses. It was like he knew what the animal was thinking. It's what made him such a good trainer. But he also had an unnerving knack for reading people as well. Body language, eye movements, and hand gestures were all like signals to him.

Not that a guy had to be gifted or psychic to know when Louisa was giving him the cold shoulder. She was damn good at pushing men away. But nothing had worked on Brody. She'd tried every way in the world to detour him, but nothing seemed to affect his determination. He simply sauntered past or sidestepped whatever she threw at him. Angry words and sharp-tongued insults were nothing to the man. His course was fixed on her and so far, nothing had slowed him down.

Brody had been the Rescue's horse trainer for nearly two years, so she'd known before accepting the veterinarian position that they'd be coworkers. She'd told herself that she could handle the attraction, and it was only a matter of time before he lost interest in her and moved on.

Boy, oh, boy, had she been wrong.

The cowboy was as persistent and patient as he was handsome, which was the most disturbing part of all. Because when Brody Vance wanted something, he got it. And it was no secret to Louisa or anyone else that what he wanted was her — in his bed.

Trying hard to dismiss the images that thought provoked, Louisa added an extra layer of iciness to her voice. "How'd you know?"

"Oh, just a hunch." He laughed, unoffended that he'd been her last resort. "I know you'd rather eat the rattlers off a snake than ask me for anything."

You got that right. "So, are you comin' or not?"

"Yeah," he answered. "Give me time to shower and change and I'll swing by and pick you up."

CHAPTER 2

Nearly an hour later, Louisa had planted herself in front of the small window above her one bowl kitchen sink so she could watch for Brody's truck.

Her stomach had worked itself into a tight knot that wouldn't ease until the wedding was over and she was back home and away from Brody.

Her little private war with that cowboy had started the day they met, the day McCrea hired him. Long, muscular thighs clad in faded Wranglers, a clean, freshly pressed chambray shirt and a corduroy jacket, he'd dressed to impress. And Brody had. Doffing his Stetson, he'd greeted Louisa courteously and with a gentlemanly smile.

If the attraction she felt towards him had been merely physical, she would have dismissed it and him without a second thought. But something inside of her had changed the instant she locked eyes with Brody on that first day. She'd felt a silent yet cosmic big bang inside her chest. And over time, the sensation had grown into a painfully sweet temptation to truly connect with him.

That had been one of the most terrifying and unexpected experiences of her life, so then and there, she'd set out with only one goal in mind. Break the cowboy, show his true colors and send him running. Because back then, she'd been one hundred percent sure there were only two things a cowboy like Brody was up for granting her. A hard time and a quick roll in the hay.

Louisa had taken the hard time because quarreling with him helped to keep those barriers she'd built between them cemented in place. Though she was tempted to tip-toe closer to that roll in the hay, she feared that Brody might be the embodiment of an old ghost and a mistake she vowed never to repeat.

But lately, she wasn't sure her opinion of Brody's cowboy ways was entirely fair or accurate. And the war she'd waged was becoming harder and harder to fight.

She and Brody ate together and three or four times a month they traveled hundreds of miles together on rescues. She spent more time with Brody than she did her family, which was another problem she hadn't counted on. And her family adored him. Her mom set a plate for him at the family table every Sunday he was in town, and he'd become her dad's regular fishing buddy. McCrea and Jess were not only his bosses, they were also his best friends.

The man was in every part of her life, save one.

How had that happened?

Gazing out the window, she tried shifting her thoughts from Brody to the vast open fields of Coldiron land and her future. Fifty acres of that prime Texas Hill Country ranchland was hers, left to her by Granddad Wade in his will. She'd been in college when he died, so rather than let the hay go to waste and the fields become overgrown, her dad had agreed to maintain and utilize the land for their family's cattle ranch.

She rode out here last summer with her dad, and

they'd spent the whole day talking. The hum of tractors and diesel ranch trucks fitted with flatbed trailers had echoed in the distance until late that evening. Together, they'd sat up on the ridge and watched the ranch hands load the last round bales of Bermuda grass. The smell of fresh-cut hay had clung to the fields well after the sun disappeared into the horizon.

They'd talked about different things but mainly her career plans once her internship was over. Joining the Promise Point team hadn't been her only option. Thanks to her family's connections with a few big-name horse breeders, she'd had an offer from a veterinary hospital in Lexington, Kentucky, working with a bloodstock agent. The money was good, and the hours were great. But spending her days examining racehorses and reading x-rays to determine an animal's future performance wasn't what she wanted to do with her career.

Doc Tolbert had been with the Rescue team since its inception, and split his time between it and his own veterinary practice. When he'd announced his retirement last year, her brothers had asked her to consider taking his place at the Rescue.

Three weeks ago, Doc had approached her about filling in for him at his practice two days a week, making it clear that the position would inevitably lead to her taking over his clientele after his retirement.

Louisa hadn't committed to anything yet, but the offer was never far from her mind, especially now that she felt she was losing her battle with Brody. Her brothers wouldn't like her decision to leave the Rescue, but they'd respect her wishes, as would her mom and dad.

But she'd have to make her decision soon.

She shifted her weight to her other hip and let her gaze drift across the land. For as long as she could remember, it had been enclosed by black, four-rail wooden fences and metal cattle gates. But the weathered barrier had been removed months ago for a road. A shady spot near a grove of cottonwoods had been leveled off for her travel trailer.

Louisa envisioned a house just past the curve. Nothing extravagant, something small with a guest bedroom and a garden tub. She missed long soaks in a bathtub and having breakfast at a real table.

In the evenings, the sun splintered into a thousand golden rays across the sky as it drifted down past the horizon. The view was why she'd chosen this spot. It was quiet and peaceful, and she loved it here.

But sometimes, she felt as empty as the unfenced acres in front of her. In the quiet confines of her small trailer, a heavy, bemoaning sigh emerged from her throat. The sound echoed out then vanished into thin air, amplifying the bareness inside her. Tears accompanied the deep sadness that overtook her. One by one, they rolled down her cheeks.

You have a wonderful life, she reminded herself. *A blessed life.* She was grateful, really she was, but sometimes it was so hard not to dwell on how empty she felt when everyone around was falling in love, getting married, and starting a family.

Like a hundred times before, the pain of her past crept over her; it blocked out the happiness she'd felt earlier. She was stuck in the guilty mire of a past she couldn't change and a future she wanted but couldn't have.

The distinctive crunch of tires as they gripped gravel caught her ears, drawing her thoughts away from her unfenced fields of regret to the cowboy rolling up the drive to rescue her.

Sighing heavily, she walked the short distance to the tiny bathroom and checked her makeup in the mirror.

Using a tissue, she patted away any evidence of tears from her cheeks and stepped to the bedroom for her bridesmaid's dress. She looped a hand through the bag containing her boots and makeup and waited until Brody was halfway up the drive before she opened the door and stepped outside.

This was only the second time Brody had been to her little domicile. The first time, he'd dropped by to help Jess and McCrea set up the electrical outlet for her trailer.

It was a nice gesture, something friends and neighbors did for each other. But Louisa hadn't said thank you or offered him so much as a bottle of water for his kindness. Instead, she'd stubbornly crossed her arms, swiveled around on her boot heels and walked inside without a word. That had hurt him. She'd seen it in his eyes right before she'd turned away.

It had felt wrong to shun him like that, but when he'd opened the truck door and stepped out, that hollow feeling inside of her — the one that felt acres wide – seemed a lot smaller.

How could a man fill a hole that enormous just by planting his boots in her drive? Tossing the dress over her shoulder, she assumed a glare.

Dust churned up by the Dodge's tires trailed up the road after it and settled to the ground as Brody let off the gas. The truck came to a crawl and then to a cautious halt in front of her, producing a very sexy Brody Vance.

He gave his damp tousled hair a comb through, leaned across the seat and opened the door. Dressed in a white t-shirt, a pair of well-worn Wranglers and his work boots, the man looked good enough to eat. Rays of the midday sun sliced through the truck's windshield, painting his dark brown hair with gilded highlights. He'd shaved, probably just before he'd showered, but there was already the trace of a five o'clock shadow spreading across his lower jaw and chin.

Louisa gulped down a moan as the knot in her stomach slid lower and tightened.

Damn, damn, double damn...

"You're late," she bit out, applying her usual grace to the situation.

Brody smiled, skewing the stubble-covered cleft in the center of his chin to one side. "Get in and we can argue on the way."

Arguing shouldn't make a woman feel all warm and tingly inside, but God help her, it did. She stubbornly held her ground, refusing to make a move towards the open door. "I could have walked to Tall Oaks by now."

Brody shrugged a large shoulder. "Okay, I'll let everyone know you're on your way." He eased off the brake and the truck rolled forward, slamming the door closed.

Louisa lifted a fist in his direction and yelled, "Brody! Get your ass back here!"

The truck stopped, shifted into reverse, and began rolling backward.

She reached for the handle as he hit the lock button. "Unlock the door."

The window came down a few inches. "Nope. I offered you the front seat and you turned it down."

"I did not! I was just making a point."

"And that was?"

"I called you over an hour ago."

He rubbed a hand of his over his jaw. "I told you I had to shower."

"It's only a fifteen-minute drive from the Rescue to here. How long does it take you to shave, shower, and get dressed?"

"Maybe I wasn't at the Rescue," he stated patiently. "Maybe I was working at the Twisted J today."

He'd purchased the old Johnson ranch back in December and hired Carter and his subcontractors to repair the house. Brody was always there in his spare time, clearing the land and installing new fences.

But she'd been so annoyed about asking Brody for a ride that she hadn't considered he might be there instead of his cabin at the Rescue. The Twisted J was at least a thirty-minute drive from her place. That plus the time it took him to shower and change ...

"Oh − ah, well," she said, feeling a little guilty for nearly biting his head off. "I guess that explains it."

"I guess it does," he said but didn't unlock the door.

"So, what? You're going to leave me stranded?"

"I'd never do that," he said, frowning slightly with a hint of mischievousness in his eyes. "Just apologize for being rude and ungrateful and the front seat is all yours."

It wasn't that she was too prideful to right her wrongs. She could say "I'm sorry" to anyone, even Brody. But she feared apologizing to him might soften things between them, shift the foundation of their relationship, and cause cracks in the barriers she'd worked so hard to build.

She couldn't risk it, so she planted her fisted hand on her hip. "I'd rather be a hood ornament than apologize to you."

Squinting against the sunlight, he sighed, then turned his eyes towards the fields and pointed a thumb over his shoulder. "Then there's plenty of room in the truck bed."

She let out an audible gasp. "Do you know how long it took me to get my hair styled like this?"

His gaze wandered back to her. As his eyes moved over her hair and face, they darkened to a sensual shade of metallic blue. There wasn't a man on earth that looked at her like he did.

Not one.

"A while, I suppose," he said.

"Three hours, Brody," she seethed. "Three grueling hours at the Red Door Beauty Salon listening to Bertie Petry spew out gossip like Old Faithful."

"Don't worry," he said, a slow smile spread across his face. "I'll drive slow."

"Drive slow?"

He winked at her. "Anything for you, Lou."

She wanted to scream. "Nearly everyone in the county is going to be at this wedding. If people see me riding in the back of your truck, I'll be the laughingstock of the town."

"We wouldn't want that, now would we?"

"No, we wouldn't."

His roguish grin made her stomach feel like it'd been hurled off a ten-story building. "Did Bertie mention the new rumor about us?"

He didn't try to hide his attraction for her or downplay the town blather that they were already lovers. He was as immune to gossip as he was to her angry tone and razor-sharp tongue.

"No, she didn't," Louisa said, assuming a bored expression. There wasn't anything unprofessional about Brody's behavior while they were working. He took his job and hers seriously. He respected her as a woman and as a veterinarian. But when they weren't on the clock, he was like this.

Baiting. Flirty. Irresistible.

He wrapped one arm around the other and did a weird thing with his fingers. "It was about the new sex positions we're trying out."

The attraction between them was always there,

building like an electrically charged storm. A storm that had recently kept Louisa tossing and turning with lucid dreams of arousing foreplay and earth-shattering orgasms, so she did not want to think about sex positions with him, new or otherwise. "Open the damn door, Brody."

He broke into laughter and hit the unlock button.

CHAPTER 3

Louisa set her bag in the seat between them and climbed in, making sure her plastic-covered dress was out of the way before she shut the door.

Brody circled around her trailer and headed out the drive to the main road, tilting his head towards her truck as they passed. "What's wrong with it?"

"I don't know. Maybe a dead battery."

"I can take a look at it when I drop you off after the wedding," he offered.

She knew his intentions were good, but she didn't want to give him an excuse to bring her home, and she sure didn't want him under the hood of her truck. He was a fair mechanic, she supposed. But seeing Brody covered in grease and sweat would rouse her curiosity to an unbearable level. "That's not necessary. I'll catch a ride with Violet and call a tow-truck in the morning."

"Tomorrow is Sunday," he reminded her. "Sam won't be in the shop."

"Then I'll call him Monday."

He stopped the truck at the end of the drive.

She assumed it was to wait until traffic cleared. When Brody didn't pull out after a car passed, she glanced his way and found him staring at her. "What's wrong?"

His eyebrows inched closer together in a slight frown. "Have you been crying?"

Caught off guard by his question, Louisa made a pfft sound. "No."

Brody lifted a finger to a spot near the bottom of her jaw. "Then what's this?"

The sensation of his calloused forefinger grazing her skin sent goosebumps over her skin. She flipped the sun visor down and turned her head so she could better examine the spot he'd pointed out. A single tear stain cut a white line down her cheek and through her makeup.

She worked to quickly smooth the blemish away. "It's just a smear."

"Look," he said, his voice softer than before. "I'm sorry about taking so long, but I was in the middle of something when you called."

She hated that she made him feel culpable for something he hadn't done. But it was either let him assume blame for her tears or tell him the truth. Somehow, she felt like she owed him that honesty and she didn't know why. Maybe it was because he was a decent man who deserved more than her. Perhaps if she told him the truth about why she'd been crying, he'd give up on her. That was, after all, what she wanted.

Wasn't it?

"Lou?" Brody's concerned voice gently nudged her.

But there was no way she could tell him the truth, so she brushed aside his apology like she had her tears and let him misread her silence for irritation. That was easier than trying to explain her conflicted emotions about her mistakes. "You should have thought about that something before you volunteered to be a groomsman in my brother's wedding."

The moment the words left her mouth, she regretted them. Because after weeks of her mom shamelessly asking every available man in town to be a groomsman and escort her down the aisle at this wedding, Brody had been the man to say yes.

Laying one wrist across the wheel, he shifted sideways in the seat and gave her one of his long considering stares.

Holding on to the remnants of her pride, she avoided his eyes and the obvious and concentrated on adjusting her bridesmaid dress so that it lay flat across her lap. "We're late. Drive."

Unwilling to be anything other than a gentleman about the whole groomsman situation, he turned his attention to the road before easing off the brake. "Were not late."

Technically, they weren't. The wedding wasn't scheduled to start for another hour and twenty minutes, but Louisa liked being early. It made her feel prepared.

"And in my defense," he went on to say. "I had plenty of time to finish that something, but you called and expected me to drop everything because you needed to be somewhere an hour early."

It hadn't taken Brody long to notice her anxiety-producing phobia about being late. He'd picked up on it a couple of days into their first week of working together. It wasn't a big deal, she told herself. There was nothing wrong with wanting to be punctual or prepared. "I've been told I'm a handful by more than one man. You don't need to restate it."

"Well," he gave her a quick wink and went back to looking at the road, dismissing those accusations like they were nothing. "Lucky for you, I have big hands."

Louisa dropped her gaze to the hand resting on his

thigh. A jagged but superficial cut, red and healing from a recent tangle with Shorty Turner — a hot-tempered cowhand who had been a long-standing employee of the Coldiron Ranch until a couple of days ago — ran the length of Brody's knuckle.

She turned her head to stare out the window as she remembered how that day had gone from bad to worse without warning. She'd driven to Dallas early that morning for her appointment with her gynecologist, Dr. Heinz, then she'd numbly climbed back into her truck and made the trip back to Santa Camino on autopilot. In desperate need of comfort, she'd gone to her parents' ranch instead of home to her lonely little trailer.

His favorite broodmare had given birth to a colt and she'd promised to stop by for a look-see. She'd stepped out of her truck, grabbed her bag, and headed for the barn where she knew her dad would be, her thoughts on the results of her exam and the facts that never changed no matter how badly she wanted them to.

Shorty and a few of the other ranch hands had been taking a break on the corral fence. As she'd passed by them, he'd said, "Watch out, boys, she'll screw you hot and leave you cold."

Low jeers and snickers had followed. It wasn't the first time Shorty had cast a nasty comment her way or tried to sully her reputation among the other cowboys. Louisa had wanted nothing more than to arm herself with a pitchfork, march to the fence and dethrone Shorty from his high and mighty position. But reacting to him would only feed his vengeful behavior, so she'd pretended not to hear.

After passing the corral, she followed the covered pathway leading to the barn and nearly jumped out of her skin when she saw Brody step from the shadows. Mortified he might have overheard Shorty's comment, she opened her mouth to explain. But he'd quickly silenced her by pushing a forefinger to his lips. Then he'd opened the barn door for her and quietly disappeared back into the shadows.

Puzzled but unwilling to call attention to his covert actions, she'd gone about her business of examining the mare and foal. The sheer, ingenuous excitement on her dad's face had helped ease her sadness and she'd soon forgotten about Shorty. But then they'd heard a ruckus outside. After hurrying to investigate, they'd arrived at the corral just in time to see Brody's large fist plow into Shorty's jaw.

The right hook had knocked the foul-mouthed cowboy to the dirt. With blood and spit oozing from his mouth, Shorty had grunted and cursed as he slowly rolled to his knees.

Brody had grabbed Shorty by the collar, yanked him to his feet, and swung him around. The man's dazed eyes went wide when Brody's large hand had viced around his throat and pinned him to the barn wall with a promise to do more than loosen a few teeth the next time he saw him mistreating another horse.

No one, including Shorty, doubted that.

Her dad hadn't been as lenient. He'd drawn Shorty's wages and sent him packing within the hour.

THE SILENCE BETWEEN LOUISA AND BRODY CONTINUED AS he drove. It made the fifteen-minute drive to the vineyard feel like an eternity. She breathed a sigh of relief when the Tall Oaks sign came into view.

Nestled in the middle of the vineyard, was a Tuscany-styled mansion. Its sprawling vista views, quaint chapel, and elegant ballroom made it the perfect venue for weddings.

"You're awfully quiet," Brody said as he flipped on the signal light and slowed the truck to make the turn into the vineyard.

"I have nothing to say."

He laughed. "Really?"

"Yes, really."

"I don't believe that. You always have something to say about what I say."

Biting her tongue, she hooked a hand through the dress hanger and grabbed her bag from the floorboard. She was ready to make a quick exit and leave Brody behind, at least until she had to walk down the aisle arm and arm with him.

But she wanted to rebound with a snide comment about how tacky pickup lines didn't work on her and that she was too smart to be conned into bed by a cocky cowboy who loved the sound of his own spurs. After all, that was the way everyone, including Brody, expected her to handle situations like this.

But her smart mouth and cutdowns were partly to blame for her unpopularity among the cowboys around Santa Camino. They were also one of the reasons no man, other than Brody, was willing to be paired with her for more than a couple of hours.

However, the other half of that blame lay with Shorty and though she'd had nothing to do with him losing his job, she knew it would help fuel her cowboy-hating reputation. Thanks to Shorty, gossip around town was that the new vet for the Rescue had an intense dislike for cowboys but indulged in licentious acts with one every night.

It didn't matter that neither of those two juicy bits of gossip was true. They mixed like oil and water and formed a bitter taste in locals' mouths - her future clients if she took over Doc Tolbert's practice. It also made Louisa feel like a hypocritical harlot.

Brody drove around back to where the wedding party had been instructed to park. "Come on," he jeered softly. "I thought you'd have something to say about my big hands comment."

Louisa knew if she didn't say something, he'd say she was pouting and she hated it when he poked at her with that adolescent remark. She never pouted. "Does that line ever work?"

He maneuvered the truck into a spot, shifted it into Park, and killed the engine. "That wasn't a line, sweetheart," he said, holding up his hands as proof. "It's a fact."

That it was. Long, fingers, stout knuckles and broad palms with prominent tendons and veins, Brody's hands looked as though they'd been carved from solid marble and were a remarkable representation of the man. Masculine, rigid, and capable with the right amount of kindness and sensitivity. They were powerful, intriguing, and sensual. More than once, she'd caught herself wondering how those big hands measured up to other parts of his body.

Holding back a lustful sigh that would surely give away her thoughts, she glared at him coldly. "Knock it off, Brody. We both know where this is going and if I've told you once, I've told you a hundred times. I don't date cowboys."

He shook his head, confounded by what she'd said. "But what you haven't told me is why."

Her granddad Wade used to say that cowboys had a code written across their hearts. One that directed their lives and set them apart from other men.

Cowboys take pride in their work and their brand. They keep their word and they always put their family first. You remember that young lady.

Oh, if Wade were here now, she'd tell him a thing or two about how not all cowboys lived by that honorable creed. Some cowboys were weasels wearing Stetsons.

It was because of one weasel that she'd single-handedly managed to alienate herself from nearly every cowboy, present company included, in the county. That hardly seemed fair to good men like Brody or showed maturity on her part.

But it was what it was.

Maybe if she let the tears flow and cried on Brody's shoulder while pouring her heart out about the "why" behind her rule, he'd finally understand that he didn't stand a chance with her. But she wasn't going to allow him privy to her past to justify her dating rule.

That mistake was a thousand miles away. Chris Keegan owned a horse ranch in Oregon, was married to a gorgeous model, had three beautiful children, and produced his own television show with a substantial financial portfolio to boot. He didn't have one damn use for her anymore, and she was damn happy about that.

She never had to lay eyes on the man again, and no one had to know what love had cost her. "Why I don't date cowboys is none of your damn business, Vance."

CHAPTER 4

A SMART MAN WOULD HAVE WALKED AWAY THE FIRST TIME Louisa Coldiron took a bite out of him. But Brody had never claimed to be intelligent, only good with horses.

Dropping an arm on the back of the seat, he twisted around to get a better look at Bertie's handiwork.

Louisa's cocoa-colored hair had been highlighted with subtle blonde shades, curled and styled into a messy but sexy updo at the base of her head. A band of tiny mauve flowers dotted the underside while wispy strands of hair framed her oval face.

"So you've said, many, many times," he said, wrapping one of those silky strands of hair around his forefinger.

Her dark mahogany eyes, still harboring traces of red from the tears she'd denied, were outlined in amber and dusted with an antique shade of gold. "If you know I won't answer the question, why do you keep asking it?"

Facial traits passed down from her Native American ancestors—Comanche, Brody thought he'd heard her say once — were more prominent in the Coldiron men. Still, traces of that beautifully strong heritage could be seen along the smooth ridgeline of Louisa's brow and the delicate slant of her wide cheekbones.

She only wore makeup and styled her hair on special occasions. Around the office and in the field, her hair was usually hidden beneath a straw Stetson or twisted and bound by a plastic clasp. Her face was normally bare, natural and beautiful. Brody liked her that way, but this... this was nice and so was having her this close.

"What? No answer?" she playfully returned his mockery.

Her eyes were like mood rings, betraying her with shifting colors that gave away her true feelings. When she was up in arms like she was now, they were deep, dark pools of umber, intent, focused, and on point.

He held the strand of hair between his finger and thumb, caressing the smooth silkiness of its texture. "I guess maybe I'm hoping one day your answer will be different."

Her eyes momentarily searched his before they dropped to her lap. "It won't ever be different, Brody."

He gave the strand of hair a gentle tug, prompting her gaze back to his. He made his smile faint but challenging. "You sure about that?"

Gathering her bottom lip between her teeth, she swallowed before whispering, "I'm positive."

There were other times, rare times when her eyes transformed to a dusky sienna that reflected both affection and vulnerability. The color reminded Brody of the canyon where he and Allison had played when they were kids. He should feel like a damn fool for associating the color of her eyes with something so special when most days she didn't take the time to say hello or even offer him a friendly smile.

But he held on to the faith that he was making progress towards chipping away the hard personality she'd crafted around the true Louisa. The smiling, soft-spoken, unassuming woman she was when she thought he wasn't around.

The change in her eyes usually happened when she was tending to one of her patients or playing with her nephew, Tucker, never while she was talking to him. His heart yearned for the day when her eyes would hold that beautiful warmth for him—the day when she'd drop her shields and let him closer.

"I'm not." He moved his hand to cup her jaw and brushed the pad of his thumb over her cheek. When she didn't pull away, he added, "I think that one day you'll see just how much I care for you."

"Brody …"

The way she whispered his name hardened his body to a painful ache. Easing his hand under that messy bun at the base of her head, he inched his lips lower. "Trust me, sweetheart."

Indecision pleated her brow. "I—"

"Let me in." Desire pounded through him. "And I swear to God, you'll never regret it."

The tip of her tongue slipped along the outer edge of her bottom lip, painting it with a glossy sheen of temptation. "I can't."

"Yes, you can. Let me show you…"

His plea triggered something. Hunger mingled with the vulnerability in her eyes. Shiny sparks of copper fired through her irises as she raised her chin.

Brody's heartbeat kicked into full race mode as he anticipated the possibilities of this moment and beyond. Using his other hand, he cupped her jaw and leaned closer. His lips were centimeters away from brushing hers.

Finally, after two longs years, he was going to kiss Louisa.

But just before his lips brushed hers, she planted her palm in the middle of his chest. "Where were you the weekend before last?"

The blissful buzz inside his brain fizzled. "What?"

"You leave town every other weekend." Her voice had a tremor to it, an uncertainty that made him think those tears she'd lied about earlier might return. "Where do you go?"

Brody had wanted to tell Louisa about Riley when he was first awarded custody, but he wasn't sure how she'd take it. So he'd waited, thinking that once their relationship had developed into something more serious, he could break the news that he had a son.

But he couldn't blurt that out now. "Have dinner with me tonight and I'll tell you."

Her lips quirked to a sideways grin and her eyes shifted to rebellious. "Mmmm... Dinner. You sure food is all you have in mind?"

Hell, no. Food wasn't on Brody's mind, but eating was. All she had to do was say the word and this wedding would be short a bridesmaid and a groomsman. He'd drive her back to that tin can she called home, strip her body bare, and feast until they were both satisfied.

That wasn't going to happen until she allowed herself to trust him. And that wasn't going to happen until he answered her question. But he worried that telling Louisa about Riley and the circumstances surrounding his son's conception would only reinforce her low opinion of him.

Disappointment replaced the desire coursing through his body, and Brody knew the tender moment was over. He could feel her retreating and he knew from experience that if he didn't back off, they'd be embroiled in a full-blown, Louisa cursing argument right here in the parking lot of Tall Oaks. So he forfeited, dropped his hand, and settled back into his seat with a heavy sigh. "It's just dinner, Lou. You, me, talking, eating, and getting to know one another."

"We have dinner all the time."

"I meant a nice sit-down dinner with plates, silverware, and wine glasses. Not greasy cheeseburgers and fries from a fast-food joint on the way back from a rescue."

She ignored his clarification. "As co-workers, we know all we need to about each other. Anything else would be personal." Smiling sweetly, she gave the handle a hard yank. "And technically, a date."

"With a cowboy," he threw in, frustrated they were back to her ridiculous dating rule.

She jumped out. "You got it."

"I'll leave my hat at home and wear a suit," he said with a dull smile. "How's that?"

The keys hanging from the ignition clamored loudly when Louisa slammed the door behind her. Brody watched her cut across the parking lot and hurry to the sidewalk, those firm breasts and round hips bouncing to the beat of her boots.

Sarcastic, intelligent, headstrong, and fearless, Louisa was like a fast-moving tornado to most men. A squall they stayed clear of. But Brody knew that at the heart of every storm was a quiet place. A place she protected at all costs.

He'd been in love with her for nearly two years and done everything short of writing it in the sky. But she'd refused to see his gentle efforts. He wanted desperately to stand in that quiet place with her, touch her heart, and show her that his love was nothing to be afraid of.

But sometimes, he wondered if that was ever going to happen. Loving someone without having that love returned had a way of grinding a man down and Brody's persistence was near the bone.

Blowing out another long, troublesome sigh, he

reached into the back seat for the Stetson he'd bought especially for today, situated it on his head, then grabbed the box with his new boots inside. After getting out and locking his doors, he jogged to catch up with her. They walked around the building to the side door without speaking.

"It's about time you two showed up," Jess said with an amused expression.

"Do any of you jackasses know how to answer a phone?" she seethed, stopping shy of the door to shoot him and Dean a hot glare.

Jess dug into his pocket for his phone. "Six missed calls and three voicemails."

Dean didn't bother checking his. "What happened?"

"My truck broke down." She jerked her head in Brody's direction and reached for the door handle. "So I had to call him for a ride."

The door swung open and McCrea stepped out as she was about to grab the handle. She shoved past him, knocking him off balance and nearly down.

Holding his Stetson by the crown, he yelled, "Hello, to you too!"

"Cumbubble. That's a new one." Jess laughed and hit the next voicemail. "Check your phone."

"Why?" he asked cautiously.

"Louisa's truck wouldn't start," Brody explained. "When no one would answer their phone, she had to call me for a ride."

McCrea held his phone to his ear. "Shitpouch, twat-waffle and," he closed one eye and rolled the other skyward. "What's a knob monger?"

"You don't want to know." Grinning, Jess nodded towards Dean. "Your turn."

"I'll pass." Dean's face held tight to the coldness that

served him well as a criminal defense attorney. "Jesus, Brody, how do you put up with that woman?"

Brody shrugged, thinking Dean should be used to his cousin's impudence and creative cursing by now. "I love a challenge."

Dean pulled cigars from his jacket pocket. "Then Lou is certainly the woman for you."

It seemed everyone but Louisa knew that.

Brody opened the door and stepped inside.

Louisa's dad, Hardin, was already dressed for the wedding and deep in a conversation on his cell phone. He paced back and forth in the small entryway as he talked.

Brody held up his hand, silently offering him a greeting.

"I think it's a great idea." Hardin acknowledged him with the same gesture then gave the person on the other end of the line his full attention. "Yeah, yeah, she's back home and working at the Rescue." His smile went wide with pride. "Oh, yeah, she's a damn fine veterinarian. Damn fine."

Hardin's mention of Louisa tweaked Brody's interest.

"No," Hardin frowned. "I think I can help with that. Yeah. I know she'll love seeing you again. We can all have dinner and catch up."

Brody placed his boots in the corner out of the way and stepped back outside. He waited until the door was closed before he said anything. "Who's he talking to?"

McCrea shrugged. "Don't know. He's been on the phone for over an hour."

"Did y'all see that big article in the Santa Camino Tribune about Dean and his latest win?" Jess's grin was wily, a clear indication Dean was about to get a hard-core ribbin'.

"I'm so proud." McCrea reach over and took hold of

Dean's jaw, then gave it a rough shake. "It does my heart good to see a good ol' boy on the front page of our small-town newspaper."

Dean bucked his head back, breaking free from McCrea's hand. "Fuck off."

His bawdy dismissal rousted hearty laughs.

"Mike Warner is a pompous windbag." Dean was quick to give his opinion on the editor-in-chief.

"Ah." Jess propped a hip against the railing. "Mike's alright."

"The article is garbage," Dean gruffed, his face dead-pan. "Mike wouldn't know good reporting if it bit him on the ass. He made me sound like some 1950's black and white TV lawyer who gets the job done by way of his shady side-kick private eye."

Jess threw his left foot sideways and crossed it over his right ankle, shifting to a more comfortable stance against the railing. "So you're telling us you don't have a shady side-kick dick helping you solve cases?"

Dean withdrew a shiny silver cigar case from his pocket and handed each of them a cigar. "My shady dick is none of your damn business."

More laughter followed.

Dean was a cigar aficionado, having a compact, wafer-thin cutter tucked away in his pocket at all times. After making what he professed was the perfect cut, he passed the tool around.

Since his employment at the Rescue, Brody had come to appreciate the simple pleasure of enjoying a fine Cuban cigar with his friends.

He wet the end and made the cut, careful not to pene-trate too deeply into the cigar and handed the cutter to McCrea, then he struck the wooden match and waited for the sulfur to burn off. He angled the cigar, careful not to let the flame touch it, rotated it, and slowly puffed until the foot began to burn.

With shaking hands, Jess tried three times to strike a match.

"Damn, man. Are you that nervous?" McCrea asked.

Jess's sun-darkened completion paled slightly, but the jovial expression of a man in love held strong. "As a long-tailed cat in a room full of rockin' chairs."

"Keep your mind on the honeymoon." McCrea took the matches from him, successfully striking it to a flame. "That's how I got through my wedding."

Jess pulled in a smooth puff once the cigar was lit, his expression veering towards strained. "We haven't had sex in a month, and Mallory wants to wait until we're in Paris before we consummate the marriage, so I've done nothing but think of the honeymoon."

"No second thoughts?" Dean questioned as he lifted his chin and crafted a smoke ring in the air.

"Oh, hell, no." Jess was quick to answer. "Mallory's the love of my life."

Before Mallory arrived in town, Jess had spent most of his time behind a desk at the Rescue, wallowing in misery over the loss of his rodeo career. A near-fatal fall had shattered his leg, leaving him with a bad limp and a severe case of unhappiness.

But nowadays, Jess was never without a smile. With help from the mayor and several town council members, he and Logan Gates, Violet's older brother, had organized Santa Camino's first rodeo. Though small compared to others around the state, the event was expected to be a huge success.

Mallory had been by his side, encouraging and supporting him every step of the way. He'd done the same for her when she announced she wanted to open an art studio. They were a fantastic duo who deserved happiness, and Brody was glad they'd finally found it.

"Jesus," Dean swore and blew another smoke ring. "The single men in this family are dropping like flies. I guess Brody and Lou will be next in line for the altar."

Brody wanted nothing more than to be one of those flies, dropping dead in love on his way to the altar with Louisa. But he was starting to think he was fooling himself. He tossed the cigar to the sidewalk, crushed it out with the toe of his boot, and answered with a dismal smile.

Dean hit him on the shoulder. "Same here. I'd rather be castrated with a thin wire than sleep with one woman for the rest of my life."

Jess's legs turned in at the knees. "Damn, Dean."

"Yeah," McCrea agreed, wincing. "Damn."

CHAPTER 5

Dean checked his Rolex. "Forty-five minutes until showtime."

After the cigars were in the trash, they all headed inside to the groomsmen's suite. It was a long rectangular room and like everything else at Tall Oaks, the décor and furnishings were luxurious. Six walnut-stained marble top dressing tables sat around beige walls. Nickel framed vanity mirrors hung above each one and were fitted with matching frosted lights.

The bathrooms were separate and they each had a dressing booth. It was a ranch-style wedding but with a flair of fancy thrown in. The groomsmen's outfits were dark blue jeans, deep brown sports jackets with white shirts, and birch-colored vests.

McCrea and Dean picked theirs from the clothes rack and took the first two booths. Jess grabbed the hanger with his clothes on it and motioned Brody down to the last two booths at the end of the room. They were far enough away that whatever was said between the two of them wouldn't be heard.

After tossing his dusty hat onto one of the dressing tables, Jess stepped inside a booth. "How are things between you and Lou?"

Brody set his new Stetson on the table and took his clothes into the booth next to Jess's. "About the same."

"I've known you long enough to know when something's bothering you."

Brody yanked his t-shirt over his head and flung it into a corner, unable to put the state of his frustration into words.

Jess darted a glance over the thin, paneled wall that divided the booths. "Did you two argue?"

He shoved his jeans to his ankles and kicked them onto the shirt. "All we do is argue."

"Well, arguing ain't necessarily a bad thing. Me and Mallory argue all the time."

"I've heard the two of you argue." Brody slid his arms into the dress shirt and straightened the collar. Jess and Mallory's arguments were a type of foreplay that most likely involved hot makeup sex afterward. "It's not the same with Lou and me. We aren't lovers. Hell," he cursed and kicked his legs through the new blue jeans. "You know that. She won't even let me close enough for a kiss." He measured an inch between his thumb and forefinger. "We were this close in the truck."

"But?"

"She asked me where I was the weekend before last."

"Oh, man," Jess groaned. "You haven't told her about Riley?"

He took the vest and sports jacket with him as he went out of the booth. "No, and I'm not sure I will."

Jess opened his door and stepped out too. "What are you going to tell her when he comes to live with you?"

He saw Riley's face and his chest tightened with the

memory of their goodbye two weekends ago. The boy's small, bottom lip trembling, tears spilling down his chubby cheeks and Allison holding him close as Brody had driven away.

It damn near ripped his heart out every time he had to leave. But now, he wasn't so sure that bringing his son to Texas was the right thing to do. Colorado was Riley's home and Allison was the only mother he'd ever known. Uprooting him seemed selfish.

Some days he thought about taking Allison's job offer as a guide at the True Line. Leading tourists through mountain trails wasn't exciting or fulfilling like working at the Rescue, but it was steady work.

And Riley wouldn't have to leave home.

If he accepted the job, he'd have to give up on his dream of having his own home, at least for now. He'd always wanted his own spread—a ranch with livestock and a nice home for his wife and kids. The Twisted J was every-thing he wanted.

A sharp stab hit him in the chest when he thought about that home not being here in Santa Camino and his wife not being Louisa. But after two years, he was starting to give up hope. He could put the Twisted J back on the market and, with the improvements he'd done to the house and the land, come out with a sizable profit. There were other women he could fall in love with. "He may not be coming to live with me."

Jess propped his hands on his hips. "What? Why? What happened?"

"Nothing happened. But I've thought that maybe I don't want to stay in Santa Camino anymore."

"Two years ago, you were all about putting down roots here," Jess said, not buying his thin excuse. "Something had to have happened to change your mind."

"That's just it, Jess," he admitted as he sat down on the padded bench and unboxed his boots. "Nothing has changed and I'm tired. Tired of arguing and tired of fighting with a woman who's never going to have feelings for me. And most of all, I'm tired of hoping for something that's never going to happen."

"You know how it is when you get hurt," Jess said, coming to his sister's defense. "Learning to trust again takes time."

Brody had been through hell and back with a woman he hadn't loved and tried to settle down for the sake of his son. In turn, Heather had left him in the middle of the night and led him on a wild-goose chase over half of the southwestern United States. She'd taken his unborn son and injured him in ways he never thought possible, so yes, he had been hurt. But not the way Jess was referring to.

And Brody's experience with Heather hadn't jaded him towards other women. "I learned from my experience. Now, I can spot a woman like Heather from a mile away. Louisa's known me for two years, but instead of judging me by what she's seen of my character, she keeps drop-kicking me into the same category as the cowboy who hurt her. She has since the first day we met."

"Yeah, but you're the only man who recovered and came back for another kick."

"Jesus, man," he groaned. "This ain't funny."

"I didn't say it as a joke."

Brody dropped his elbows to his knees and stared at the floor, thinking as he often did about a concerning similarity between Louisa and some of the horses he helped to rescue. "I've dealt with abused horses long enough to know that sometimes the damage is so deep trust can't be regained."

"Yes." Jess adjusted his shirt as he talked. "My baby

sister is stubborn and cantankerous like a jackass sometimes, but she's a woman, not a horse."

"You know what I mean."

Jess nodded that he did. "I think deep down, Lou knows she can trust you."

Brody wanted to believe that, but his faith was weakening. The first few months after he was hired, Louisa had gone out of her way to avoid him. She sat at the other end of the table at Sunday dinner and had kept a good three feet between them anytime they were together. The only time he'd ever gotten close to her was the day Jess was thrown from a horse.

She'd been in such a fragile state. Her tears had broken Brody's heart. He'd held her and tried his best to comfort her and she'd let him. He'd thought for sure that had brought them closer.

But after they learned Jess had escaped major injury with only a few superficial cuts to his head and a broken arm, Louisa's aloofness towards Brody had returned, double-fold until she'd started working at the Rescue.

That three-foot distance was hard for her to maintain now that they were co-workers. They were a team, whether she liked it or not. At the clinic and in the field, she was a force. She jumped into action without hesitation to save her patients and argued her side of every case without flinching or backing down. She was fearless, assertive, strong in spirit, will, and body.

Louisa was everything Brody wanted in a woman and more.

"She doesn't know I said anything, does she?" A disconcerting frown furrowed across Jess's brow as he began buttoning his shirt.

"No. Louisa doesn't know I know anything."

Jess hadn't gone into detail about the cowboy Louisa

had met while in her second year of college, only that she'd brought him home and Hardin had given him a job at their ranch before their relationship fell apart.

Brody put his vest on and went back to the booth for his tie, thoughts going to Riley and the decisions he soon had to make. When he brought his son to the Twisted J, all aspects of his life had to be stable. He didn't need to be involved in a relationship with a woman who couldn't trust him, and he didn't need to be chasing after one who, most of the time, acted like she despised him.

What kind of example would that set for Riley as he got older?

Carter's subcontractors were in the finishing stages of the remodel. Brody had ordered furniture and appliances that were scheduled to arrive anytime. With the help of Allison's color and accessory skills, he'd purchased comforters, curtains, linens for each of the bedrooms, towels for the bathrooms and pots and pans for the kitchen.

Last week, he'd gotten excited when the FedEx driver delivered his new Crockpot. Everything he'd dreamed about when he'd moved to Santa Camino was finally happening. Everything except Louisa falling in love with him.

Disappointment knotted in Brody's throat like an undercooked camp potato. There was still time for him to walk away, mostly unscathed. There was time to build a life with his son at the True Line.

He walked back to stand in front of the mirror, whipped the tie over his head and looped it into a knot. "I've, ah…" He paused to clear his throat. "I've been offered a job in Colorado."

Jess stopped shoving his shirttail into his jeans, surprise dropping his jaw.

"I know," Brody said, feeling bad for waiting until

today to tell his boss and friend that he might be leaving. "I should have told you sooner."

"I—I don't know what to say." Jess rested his forearm along the back of a chair. "This isn't about money or you being unhappy with the position, is it?"

"No. I love my job at the Rescue, but something's gotta give, man." Brody raked both hands through his hair and dropped his gaze to the floor. "I hate leaving Riley. I hate seeing him cry for me. I miss my son, Jess."

"I don't have kids, but," Jess blew out a short breath, "I get it."

"It's time I stopped waiting on Louisa and made a decision. I work side-by-side, day after day with her, and I can't touch her. I don't think she'll ever believe that I'm not like that asshole who hurt her."

"Her mind believes," Jess said. "It's her heart that's having trouble. Maybe she just needs more time."

"She's had six years," Brody said and then asked the question he feared the most. "You don't think she's still in love with him, do you?"

"No," Jess answered without hesitation.

"Then what's the holdup?"

"She was nineteen, Brody." Jess's voice edged lower with anger. "Too young to be involved with a man like Chris."

It was the first time Jess had dropped a name into Louisa's past. "Chris?"

Jess's mouth thinned to a hard line. "I shouldn't have let that slip."

"But you did, so spill it."

Sighing, Jess raised his hand to his face and made a long pass along his bottom jaw. "When Lou brought Chris to the ranch, he was just a down-on-his-luck cowboy who needed a job. He said he'd been cowboying his way across Oklahoma and wanted to try his luck in Texas."

After Heather skipped town, Brody had spent months driving from state to state, trying to find her. He'd picked up ranching jobs here and there to help pay for a private detective. When one job ended, he moved on to the next town. He'd had a few opportunities to stay on full-time, but he'd turned them down. It was a drifter's life and something he hadn't minded at the time.

But it was hard.

The work was rough, the days were exhaustive, and the nights were lonely. There wasn't always a hot meal or a warm bed waiting for him at the end of the day. Often, supper was a bag of peanuts or jerky, and he'd spent the night sleeping in the cab of his truck. "I've lived that life. It ain't an easy road to travel."

"It was for Chris," Jess said. "They met outside a bar that was just down the street from campus. She was walking by. He was walking out and didn't see her —"

"And they conveniently bumped into each other," Brody interjected. "Classic but uncreative way to introduce yourself to a woman. Go on."

"How many college bars did you visit when you were cowboying?"

Bars had never been high on Brody's entertainment list, even while he was earning his degree. "None. Those places are too noisy and overcrowded with kids who are just old enough to legally drink but not old enough to know a damn thing about real-world consequences."

"Exactly." Jess's face was stone-cold. "I think Chris was Lou's first lesson in real-world consequences."

"Meaning?" Brody wanted the whole story, not just bits and pieces.

Jess finished tucking his shirt into his jeans, buttoned

and zipped them, and then reached for his belt. "I'm not sure. Chris told me how they met, and I figured the rest out on my own. She's never talked to me about him or what happened. I only know there was a change in her after he left and that's about the time she swore off on dating cowboys."

Brody had more questions but knew the answers needed to come from Louisa, not Jess.

"Do yourself a favor." Jess threaded his belt through the loops of his jeans. "Tell Lou what you just told me. Tell her everything. Tell her about Heather —"

"God, no," Brody said, flinching hard at the mention of Heather's name.

"Yes," Jess answered back. "And everything that happened. Take Lou to Colorado or have Allison and Riley come for a visit. Lay everything out in the open for her."

He didn't know if he had the strength for that, not now when he felt so broken and discouraged. "Then what?"

"I don't know. All I do know is that you may not get a second chance if you screw it up." Jess buckled his belt. "Can I be blunt?"

Folding his collar over the tie, Brody turned to face Jess. "Sure."

"Tell Louisa everything before you sleep together."

"If I tell her everything, there's a good chance we won't be doing anything together."

"And if you wait until you have, you won't be any better than Chris in her eyes."

"What's that supposed to mean?"

Jess held up a hand, indicating he wasn't going to say any more about the man. "See what happens and if you still want to leave, you do so with my blessing. Just promise me you'll wait until I get back from Paris before you make any decisions. Can you do that?"

Brody nodded, silently giving Jess his word he would.

"Christ Almighty." Dean burst out of his booth laughing. "Who's responsible for the pink ties?"

"My bride picked them out." Jess snagged his tie from the hanger.

"See," Dean told McCrea, who had also just emerged from a booth. "He's not even married yet and she already has him by the balls."

"Shut up and put the damn thing on," Jess ordered, not taking anything his cousin said to heart. They all adored Mallory and didn't care what color the ties were.

McCrea whipped his over his head and began tying it in the mirror. "It's her day. She gets what she wants. He's just here for the vows."

Jess took a spot in front of the mirror next to him. "What he said."

Brody wasn't sure he could keep his promise to Jess once he told Louisa about Riley, but he wasn't going to spend the day worrying about that now. This was a joyous occasion, a celebration of love and commitment for his friends.

"Let me tell you how it went down," Brody said, joining the lighthearted jeering as he grabbed his hat and slipped an arm into his jacket. "Mallory said, and I quote: the only way you're getting the cannon is if you and your groomsman wear pink ties."

McCrea let out a hearty laugh. "That's exactly how it went down."

Jess looped the end of his tie through the knot. "Says the man who had donkeys at his wedding."

"Skeeter and Muffin are practically family," McCrea defended, sliding his tie into place.

The two donkeys were permanent residents at the Rescue. The children loved them, but Eleanor hadn't been sold on the idea of including them in her wedding. Brody suspected there had been a similar deal made between the bride and groom at that wedding too. "As I recall," Brody said, walking to the door. "The ties at your wedding were purple."

Dean groaned. "By the balls."

"Kiss my country ass," Jess rebounded, barely holding back laughter.

McCrea gave Dean a scathing scowl. "What he said."

CHAPTER 6

STANDING BEHIND THE CHANGING SCREEN IN THE BRIDAL suite, Louisa fought back the tears. Her heart was pounding so hard she felt like her chest might explode.

She'd burst through the door flushed and out of sorts with all eyes glued on her. After explaining that her truck wouldn't start and that she'd had to hitch a ride with Brody, the room had gone uncomfortably quiet.

"Are you okay back there?" Belle asked.

"Um, yeah," she answered her mom and silently blew out a shaky breath, thankful they couldn't see her face. "I'm just annoyed that my truck picked today to break down."

"Lucky for you," Sage added, "Brody was there."

"Yeah," she agreed, sniffing. "Real lucky."

If there were such a thing as providence, Brody would have given up his pursuit, found himself a woman he could have a future with, and let her be miserable in peace. But instead, he was whispering sweet nothings in her ear despite all she'd done to dissuade him.

Trust me, sweetheart.

Louisa had told herself that she wasn't the least bit interested in trusting Brody or any other man ever again.

Cowboy or not.

But Brody made her feel things she hadn't with any other man, even Chris. A man she was supposed to have been in love with.

Let me in and I swear to God, you'll never regret it.

She fought back another wave of tears.

You would regret it, Brody. And so would I...

"Did you say something?" Eleanor asked.

God, had she said that aloud? Wincing, Louisa tried clearing the emotion from her throat as she thought of something to say. "I... was just talking to myself."

"Oh," her mom replied. "I thought you said something about Brody."

"Me too," Mallory pitched in.

"Nope. Y'all must be hearing things." She wiggled her hips into the mauve curve-hugging bridesmaid dress and tried to pull herself together.

Eventually, the chatter that was going on before Louisa had entered the bridal suite resumed. As the women talked about the wedding and reception, it dawned on Louisa that Violet's voice was missing from the conversation. "Where's Violet? I called her a hundred times and her phone went straight to voicemail."

"She's walking Archie," Mallory said.

Having Mallory's floppy-eared basset hound as a ring bearer was a colossal mistake in Louisa's opinion. The pup was full of energy and unable to follow simple commands. He'd jumped and barked through the rehearsals, leaving everyone uneasy about how the rings might be delivered.

But since Mallory loved the pup so much, they were all willing to give chase if he ran astray during the ceremony.

"There you go, honey," Sage said, prompting Louisa to

glance around the changing screen just in time to see Sage turn Sophie around for her mother's inspection. "Doesn't she look pretty, Mommy?"

A halo of dusty-pink baby's breath adorned Sophie's dark brown hair and a bright smile — minus one missing front tooth — spread over her little face. She twirled around for her mother's inspection. The tulle bottom of her candy pink princess-style dress lifted and whirled around her, causing her to giggle with glee.

Eleanor smiled at her daughter. "Beautiful."

"You know," Louisa said, hoping a little lighthearted teasing would help to brighten her mood. "I still think having Sophie drop dog treats instead of rose petals is a good idea."

"Dog treats!"

Louisa ducked her head behind the screen, chuckling mutely at the shock on Sophie's sweet face.

"Mommy, do I have to?" Sophie's voice was pleading.

"No, honey," Eleanor answered, laughing. "Aunt Lou was just spouting off."

"Can you imagine what Pricilla would say about dog treats?" Sage snickered.

The Rescue held their annual charity bachelor auction at the winery and Donna Eaton, the event coordinator, was fantastic at making things run smoothly. But she was on maternity leave, so Pricilla Grainer was filling in.

Pricilla tried to be a professional but was easily excitable. When Mallory told her that she wanted Archie at the wedding, the woman had nearly had a meltdown. Dog treats would probably give her hives.

"Come to think of it," Belle said, a thread of concern in her voice, "Violet should have been back by now. Maybe someone should check on her."

Archie tended to roam. When his keen nose picked up

on the scent of something he liked, there was no stopping him. Violet might end up in the next county before Archie lost interest and found his way back home.

The thought of him dragging Violet through the grapevines made Louisa smile. It would be sweet revenge for leaving her to hitch a ride with Brody. "He's a puppy. What could go wrong?"

She eased the delicate lace-covered bodice over her breasts and shifted each of them so that they were even. The sweetheart neckline was a little too revealing for a woman with C-cup breasts and the skimpy bra she'd bought wasn't holding them in place. Reaching to the base of her lower back, she struggled to move the zipper more than a couple of inches. "Mom, can you finish zipping me up?" she asked, stepping from behind the screen.

As always, her mom was quick to help. Belle had worked countless hours helping Mallory and Jess plan the wedding without complaining and had done the same for Eleanor and McCrea.

Midway of her back, Belle slowed the pull.

Louisa glanced over her shoulder. "What's wrong?"

"It's a little tight, Louisa. I'm surprised Sue didn't make adjustments at your last fitting."

She straightened her posture and tried rearranging her breasts again. "I missed my last fitting."

"That explains it," Belle said, with an exasperated sigh as she carefully eased the zipper past the tension spot and to the top. "I'm not sure it'll hold, so just be careful and keep your wrap close by."

The lace bolero Mallory had chosen to accessorize the bridesmaid dresses wouldn't cover her breasts if the zipper gave way, but it might help save her modesty.

"Missing that last fitting wasn't my fault," she defended, remembering the unexpected trip she'd taken a week ago.

"Brody dragged me out to Darby Center's place on a rescue."

"Bull." Eleanor looked up from adjusting Mallory's chapel-length veil long enough to cut her a skeptical glance. "I doubt Brody dragged you anywhere."

"I agree." Belle moved to the stand holding Mallory's bouquet and straightened a pale pink peony with her brow raised high. "It was more than likely the other way around."

"Why are you so hard on that poor man?" Sage asked, shooting Louisa a chastising glare.

It irritated her that her friends and family were always quick to jump to Brody's defense and slow to raise a shield for hers when the shoe was on the other foot. Why couldn't they take her side just once?

"I've never really understood why you treat Brody the way you do." Mallory glanced up at Louisa, her lovely face adapting a puzzled expression. "He's a good man who obviously cares about you."

Mallory was Eleanor's half-sister and a talented artist who had a gift for capturing details. Her life-like paintings of Tucker and Sophie were amazing. But Mallory was a tad naïve when it came to Brody.

Mallory had arrived in town last summer when she'd brought their mother's ashes back to be scattered on the Mackenna family ranch. That meant she'd known Brody for about two seconds, so Louisa didn't take much stock in her soon-to-be sister-in-law's opinion of the man or his feelings for her. "Care is such a loose word and not at all convincing."

"Denial looks ugly on you." Leave it to Sage to say what no one else would. "You know he likes you, yet you rake him over the coals every time he comes near."

That wasn't true, her conscience defended. Brody had

been very near in the truck, so near that his breath had brushed across Louisa's lips with the warmth of a lover, soft and inviting. And no raking had occurred.

"Might I remind you that like and care aren't the same, especially where romance is concerned," Eleanor added.

"Oh, lord, here we go," Louisa moaned. Because she and McCrea had had a rocky start, Eleanor felt obligated to share her wisdom on love and romantic relationships even when it wasn't wanted.

"El's right." Mallory twisted around on her seat. "I like cheese pizza. But I care for Jess."

Louisa squinted one eye as she tried unsuccessfully to find logic in what Mallory had just said. "Did you just compare my brother, your future husband, to a cheese pizza?"

"You should have gone with chocolate cake," Sage said, amusement twitching at her lips. "It's sweeter and more decadent than tomato sauce and Italian seasonings."

"God," Mallory's shoulders fell. "Now I want chocolate cake and pizza."

"Brody is sweet on you," Eleanor announced as if her opinion were the gospel truth.

But Louisa wouldn't give in. She couldn't, not for a second, try to examine the scope of feelings Brody might have for her. If she did, she might lose what composure she had left, so, grinning wickedly, she flicked her tongue like a snake. "He's sweet on something, but it ain't my charming personality."

Belle's face crinkled with distaste. "Must you make everything sound tawdry and lewd?"

"It is what it is, Mom," she said, brushing aside Belle's disapproval. "What Brody wants is sex."

"His affection for you runs deeper than physical gratification, Louisa." Belle's voice changed to the mom lecture tone. "And you know it."

What she knew was that no matter how much she wanted to entertain thoughts of Brody's affection for her, she couldn't. Because sometimes, in order to live a normal life, one had to make decisions based on facts, not on wild flights of fancy.

"She's right," Sage agreed. "Any man who puts up with you has to have a strong constitution and be motivated by more than lust."

Louisa sat down on the arm of the sofa, feeling somewhat dented by their remarks. They made her sound like a cold and callous monster who verbally abused Brody daily. "Puts up with me? What's that supposed to mean?"

"Come on, Lou," Sage said. "You know you're tough on Brody."

"Sure, there are times when I'm a little rough with my words —"

"It isn't just your words, Louisa," Belle cut in. "I've never seen you give anyone the cold shoulder like you do Brody. You're rude, obnoxious, and downright mean to the man."

It was hard for Louisa to deny what her mom had just said. She couldn't count the times she'd been all those things and more to Brody. But she had her reasons.

"We all care about him," Belle continued. "And watching you take a piece out of him every time he comes near you is…"

"Awful," Mallory supplied.

"He tries so hard to be your friend," Eleanor said. "I can't think of anyone in Santa Camino, aside from you and Shorty Turner, who doesn't like Brody."

Around the room, heads bobbed up and down in agreement.

That ruffled Louisa's temper. "Don't you dare put me in the same category as that leech."

"You put yourself in it," Belle said sternly.

"I have not!" she replied. "And just because you've all witnessed me taking a bite out of Brody a time or two doesn't mean I'm a monster. We aren't always at each other's throats. We have a great work relationship and most of the time, we go through the day without having a single argument."

"Or a single conversation," her mom said.

Louisa crossed her arms over her breasts and cocked her head to one side. "We talk."

Sage raised her eyebrows. "Oh, really? About what?"

She felt like she was on trial for a crime she hadn't committed. "I don't know. Horses, the rodeo, and a hundred other things." Sage wasn't impressed, so she added. "And we had lunch together twice last week."

Sage narrowed her eyes. "What was on the menu?"

"Menu?" She frowned. "What menu? We grabbed two tuna sandwiches from the Gas & Go on Tuesday and on Wednesday, Brody brought a batch of his homemade chili."

"Brody's chili is so good." Mallory glanced up at Eleanor and licked her lips. "He adds a can of beer to it and cooks it in the slow cooker."

"Oh, I know," Eleanor agreed. "He could win contests with that chili."

"Horses and the rodeo," Sage scoffed. "Tuna and chili. That's all so romantic."

"It isn't supposed to be romantic," Louisa snapped. "Brody and I are co-workers."

"What I can't figure out is why you're so mean to him," Mallory cut in.

"I know why," Belle added.

"We all do," Eleanor mumbled under her breath.

Louisa was more than happy to let them entertain the reasons, knowing they'd never get close to the truth. The women in this room were her closest friends, her mom included, so she usually didn't bother with hiding things from them.

Chris was the exception.

Eleanor had gotten pregnant with Sophie the night she and McCrea broke up, and lived in Austin when Chris was hired on as one of her dad's cowhands. Sage had been in Dallas dealing with a new baby and an adulterous husband. Poor Violet had just buried her dad.

Louisa had introduced Chris to her parents as a good friend who needed a job. He'd insisted they keep the nature of their relationship a secret from them, so her mom was also clueless about what had happened. Chris had said he wanted to prove to her dad that he was more than a ranch hand and worthy of his daughter.

It had all seemed so romantic and adventurous. But when it ended, Louisa had weathered the heartbreak alone. She'd spent fall break at her small apartment near campus recuperating by herself and had told her family it was the flu.

No one knew the details of what had happened. Though Jess had dropped hints that he knew about the affair, Louisa hadn't confided in him about what had ended it. Not that she couldn't trust her brother to keep her secrets, she could. But she was too ashamed to admit that what had happened was because of her own blind stupidity.

No one knew about Chris or what their affair had cost her and she wanted to keep it that way, so if she had to make up silly rules about dating cowboys and occasionally douse Brody with coldness and mean words to keep that hidden, she would.

"Brody is a big boy," Louisa said, adding another layer of icy resistance to her cause. "Not some teenage kid who shows up at my doorstep with roadside wildflowers and cheap chocolate. He can take anything I dish out."

"He's a mature man who respects you," Belle reminded Louisa in a way that made Brody seem like an endangered species. "He's kind and gentle −"

"Ugh." She threw up her hands. "Here we go. Singing Brody's praises — again."

"Every solid inch of him," Sage embellished while cleaning up the brush and leftover baby's breath from the table, "is masculine, strong, sexy, and experienced."

Louisa dropped her hands to her hips and looked askance at her friend. "Aren't you engaged?"

Sage's eyebrows went high again. "A woman doesn't go blind just because she falls in love. Brody is hot."

"A man like Brody doesn't need to show up at your doorstep with flowers or chocolate," Eleanor went on to say. "He just needs to show up, like today."

"When you need him," her mom, added.

"Can we stop talking about food?" Mallory whined.

Sage shoved the brush into the makeup bag near Mallory and leaned her backside against the edge of the dressing table. "I think you're afraid you might fall for that cowboy if he gets too close."

Having her fears yanked out and strewn across the room for conversation wasn't going to help her get down the aisle with Brody, so Louisa refused to acknowledge, deny, or discuss Sage's comment.

"Y'all are blowing this way out of proportion," she said, trying to sound as barky as she usually did when she was being pressed about Brody. But she was struggling to keep a lid on her emotions. Her voice sounded weak and uncertain.

"All we're saying is," this time, Belle's approach was much more subtle, "why not give him a chance? See what happens. He's already proposed once."

Word of that proposal had spread like wildfire and added gasoline to the town bonfire that she and Brody were lovers. She'd been in Sage's real estate office when Brody finalized the purchase of the Twisted J. She'd confronted him about the rumors that he was buying it for a woman. He'd answered her with a toe-curling remark about how she was the woman and that he was waiting on her to help pick out paint colors for their nursery.

Crossing her arms over her breasts, Louisa dropped her focus to her bare feet. She'd tried over and over to block out the image of Brody's face as he'd said those words. But the deep longing in his eyes still haunted her. It had been the sweetest, most adoring proposal, but it was years too late.

That was the root of her conflict. So while her heart had screamed yes to his offer, her mind had quickly stepped in and taken control of the situation. Because as tempting as Brody's proposal was, the outcome would end in disaster for both of them. Brody wanted something she couldn't give him. "That wasn't a proposal, Mom."

"Yes, it was." Sage's smile looked like one of those suction cup cats on the back of car windows. Wide, obnoxious, and impossible to ignore. "I was there. Picking out paint colors for the baby's room?"

"There is no baby!" There never would be. Suddenly, those tears Louisa had been holding back broke free. Swinging around so that her back was to them, she hurried over to the changing screen and began stuffing her clothes into her bag. "And despite what everyone thinks, nothing is going on between us that would produce a baby!"

"So you're saying the two of you aren't lovers?" Mallory asked.

"No. Absolutely not. The whole notion that we are is… is…ridiculous."

"Why is it ridiculous?" Sage asked, not knowing the pain she was inflicting by pressing the issue.

"I'll second that question," Mallory said.

She saw Eleanor's hand shoot up. "Third."

Silence returned to the room as they waited for her to answer. She heard her mom walk across the room, pull out a chair, and sigh as she sat down. "Were all ears, Louisa."

Louisa had to come up with an excuse and since answering truthfully was not an option, she did what everyone else in Santa Camino did when the truth wasn't readily available.

She relied on good old-fashioned gossip.

Aside from their so-called flaming hot affair, one of the things that made natter about Brody so alluring was that people in town knew little to nothing about him, his family, or where he was from. It was like he'd just dropped from the sky. "We've only known Brody for a couple of years and you people want me to marry him and bear his children."

"I don't think that sounds unreasonable," Mallory said innocently.

Eleanor and Sage let out a round of giggles.

"Seriously," Mallory said, affronted by their laughs. "Brody is kind, sweet, longsuffering, and God knows, patient to a fault. You know all you need to about him."

"No, I don't," Louisa rebounded, stepping around the screen to plant herself on the couch. "I mean, Brody could have a whole other life outside of this town."

"Oh, Louisa," Belle chastised.

"He paid cash for the Twisted J." She narrowed her eyes at Sage. "We all know he doesn't make that kind of money."

"Maybe he won the lottery," Mallory suggested.

"Or came into an inheritance," Sage supplied another explanation.

Rolling her eyes, Louisa scooted to the edge of the couch and flung a hand towards the drive. "The man leaves town every other weekend. Where does he go?"

"You could ask him," Belle offered.

"I have."

Wide-eyed and speechless, the women drew in a collective breath and held it.

"What?" Louisa asked.

"Ah—" Belle attempted a weak smile. "We're just curious about what his answer was."

Her mother had earned a law degree and worked at a firm in Dallas before she'd married her dad. He often bragged about how his wife had gone up against some of the biggest lawyers in the country without flinching.

Under that quiet composure, stylish short hair, and perfectly applied makeup was a tigress who, when riled, could tear a man to shreds with a few cleverly chosen words.

The woman was also cool under pressure and could wear a passive face to keep a secret when she had to. But Louisa had learned to read her mother's expressions, so this face, the one that said Belle knew more than she was letting on, was more than a little unsettling.

"That he'd tell me if I'd have dinner with him." Louisa cocked her head to one side and crossed her arms over her breasts. "What are you not telling me?"

"Nothing," Belle said while the others exchanged subtle glances at each other.

"So," Sage proceeded cautiously. "Are you going to have dinner with him and find out?"

She let out a snort. "Hell, no. I don't date cowboys."

Multiple groans echoed around the room.

"I give up," Eleanor said.

Belle threw up a hand. "I think we all have."

Relieved they'd ended the distraction about the possibility of Brody having another life, Louisa snagged her boots and slipped them on. "Those rumors circulating around town last year about how Brody might be a criminal wanted by the FBI might be true. He might be a bank robber. That would explain the money."

"Good grief, Louisa." Belle made a clicking sound with her tongue. "The FBI? Really?"

Eleanor pointed the comb in her direction. "I'd believe you were wanted by the FBI before I would Brody."

"Me too." Mallory snickered.

Louisa didn't believe the ridiculous FBI rumors any more than they did. But the other tales — the ones about him buying the ranch for a woman – left a sour taste in her mouth.

Sage pushed away from the dressing table and straightened her skirt. "I think most of us expect to see your photo on a wanted poster in the sheriff's office anytime now."

Belle edged a pinky finger around her lips as she checked her makeup in the mirror. "Finn is still looking for the vandal who graffitied that colorful penis onto the side of the county's search and rescue helicopter last month."

Sheriff Finn Durant's father, Clayton, owner of Durant Resources, a multi-million-dollar drilling corporation, had donated the second-hand helicopter to the sheriff's department for a tax write-off. The county was grateful, but some people in Santa Camino thought Clayton's donation was an under-the-table buy-in to his son's office. There were speculations that the graffiti was a backlash from individual members of the community who might not be supporting Finn in the next election. But because the vandals had used washable paint, Finn had quickly dismissed it as a tasteless prank.

Louisa held a hand over her heart to mock her mom's accusation, delighted that the conversation had moved from serious questions about her and Brody to these ridiculous yarns. "You can't possibly believe that was me."

Before she could answer, Sophie gave Belle's dress a tug. "Grandma, what's a penis?"

Belle's face flushed red. "Oh, dear."

Everyone burst into laughter and the subject of Brody, babies, and the FBI were dropped.

CHAPTER 7

Mallory's ivory off-the-shoulder silk gown clung tastefully to her curves. The airy skirt billowed around her bare feet as she sat in front of the large vanity mirror.

The gossamer sleeves gave the gown an ethereal quality. The setting, the decorations, and the gown were a bride's dream come true.

Over the last year, Louisa had developed a close friendship with Mallory, and there wasn't a doubt in her mind that she and Jess were made for each other. Her brother was finally happy, and she was ecstatic about that.

Louisa stepped closer so she could catch Mallory's gaze in the mirror. "You look stunning and I am so jealous of you right now." And in a way, she was. Not for the gown or how beautiful Mallory looked, but because despite her friend's troubled past, she was still able to love wholeheartedly. Mallory and Jess had taken a chance on love and each other and won.

Sage propped her chin on Louisa's shoulder and stared dreamy-eyed at the bride. "Divine."

Mallory's dark caramel-centered eyes were glossy with

anticipation and happiness. "Thank you." She pressed a hand against her midriff and let out a shaky breath. "I didn't think I'd be this nervous."

Louisa wasn't a bride, wasn't about to take vows or fly to Paris for an extravagant honeymoon with a man she adored and loved. She was just a bridesmaid, walking down the aisle with a man she worked with. That shouldn't be a stomach-churning event.

But it was.

And with the previous conversation looming over her head like a dark and stormy cloud waiting to burst, her stomach was still in knots.

She grabbed her bag and began searching through it for the antacids she'd bought before the rehearsal dinner last night. After popping two in her mouth, she set the bottle on the dressing table in front of Mallory. "Here."

"She doesn't need antacids," Belle said, snatching the bottle away from Mallory. "It's just pre-wedding jitters."

"Every bride has them," Eleanor assured her sister and gave the veil a final adjustment. "Those jitters will disappear the moment you see Jess."

Mallory smiled brightly and took one last at herself in the mirror. "You're right. It's just jitters. Nothing to worry about."

Suddenly, the door to the suite burst open and in charged Archie, barking baritone and lunging for his water bowl with Violet behind him.

The pink flowers Bertie had meticulously placed in her hair looked like swatted mosquitos on an old screen door. A long strand of hair had dislodged itself from the bobby pins and now swung loosely around her face. Her knee was scraped and bleeding, and there was a smudge of what Louisa hoped was mud down the right side of her face.

Violet collapsed on the sofa. "I love you, Mallory, honey, but never, ever again. That dog is a beast."

"Aw," Mallory crooned, reaching down to rub the pup's head. "He's just a baby."

The dog had grown considerably since Jess had gifted him to his bride-to-be at Christmas. Though he was still a pup — with short, crooked legs, an elongated body, mud-flap ears, drooping lips, and a wrinkled forehead — Archie bore the heavy-boned appearance of a full-grown bassett.

"He's a beast," Violet started again, propped her left boot on the small table in front of the sofa, and slung one arm over her eyes. "I'll be picking gravel out of my knee for a month."

Louisa felt awful. Sure, in her mind, Archie dishing out revenge seemed funny. But poor Violet looked like an old, wet saddle blanket that had been ridden for days and then draped across a rail to bake in the hot sun. "El, don't you keep antiseptic ointment in Tucker's diaper bag?"

"There's a first aid kit in the left pocket," she answered.

Since her nephew's arrival, Louisa had learned that a diaper bag was a survival pack. Everything a person needed to sustain life for weeks at a time was in that yellow duck decorated bag.

She dug into the pocket, pulled out the kit, and tore open an alcohol wipe.

The first swipe of sterilizer brought a hiss and a jerk from Violet. "Ow!"

"Oh, hush, you big baby."

Violet rose, gripping the edge of the sofa with another wince. "Some doctor you are."

She applied ointment. "I've never had a patient to complain."

"Let me be the first to state that you have a horrible bedside manner. Damn, that stings!"

When the adhesive strip was securely in place, Violet moved her foot to the floor.

"There, all done." Louisa closed the first aid kit and yanked the front of her dress up.

Violet held a hand over her left eye.

"What's wrong with your eye?" she questioned, concerned the pup had done real damage to her friend.

"Nothing. I lost a contact lens when I fell. This helps me to focus."

"Oh." Louisa looked down at her breasts, the target of Violets stares. "I know." She tugged at the top again. "The dress is a little snug."

"Snug?" Violet's lips snarked up at a corner. "One wrong move and those jewels are going to explode out of that dress like an inflatable raft."

Louisa gave Violet's scrapped knee a not-so-gentle pat.

"Ouch!" Violet's explosion prompted Archie to raise his head and bark, slinging drool and water over his tri-colored coat and the floor.

"Oh, God," Belle groaned, reaching for the baby wipes in the diaper bag.

Archie barked again, rolled onto his back and batted his sad brown eyes, begging Belle for a belly rub.

"Not a chance," Belle told him and ordered the dog to the side.

After slipping the first aid kit back into the diaper bag, Louisa wadded the adhesive strip package into a ball and threw it in the trash. Snagging her wrap from the screen, she walked over to the large oval mirror and tried adjusting it so it would hide her breasts.

But it was no use. Violet was right; one wrong move and they'd come bouncing out of there. Not only was she walking down the aisle with Brody, but she was doing so practically bare-breasted.

Wonderful.

"Everyone decent?" The question was followed by a knock on the door.

They all recognized Ed Tubs' craggy voice.

"Come on in, Ed," Belle answered.

Eleanor had grown up without knowing who her father was, but after she came back to town two years ago to sell her grandparents' ranch, she and Ed had found each other. She had recently become a partner in Tubs' Roadhouse, and they were both looking forward to running the business together.

Holding Tucker with one arm, Ed stepped inside the suite. The whiny baby shoved a tiny fist into his mouth and grunted a cry.

Smiling at his grandson, Ed winked. "I think he's hungry, Mamma."

Eleanor held out her hands and the baby made a dive for his mother. He showed robust Coldiron features at only nine months and had a stubborn streak just like his daddy.

When Ed saw Mallory, his eyes clouded with adoration as he bent to hug her. "Honey, you look radiant. Your mother would be so proud."

She returned the hug, sniffing back tears. "Thank you, Ed."

Mallory and Ed had grown close. They weren't blood relatives, but he showed her the same love and affection as he did Eleanor. Since her real father was a horrible man and now awaiting trial for a long list of criminal charges, Mallory had asked Ed to walk her down the aisle.

He had gladly accepted.

"Dad, don't make her cry," Eleanor scolded softly and handed Mallory a couple of tissues.

"Sorry." He rose with a smiling sniff and dried his eyes

with a thumb. "It thought I'd warn you that Pricilla is headed this way."

"Here," Belle said, handing Archie's leash to Ed. "Give him to McCrea. He's responsible for the rings if the pup won't cooperate."

"Belle." Pricilla's nervous screech echoed down the hall.

Their mother had a contingency plan for everything and was always calm during stressful situations. But Pricilla's voice was chipping away at the root of her mother's diplomacy and patience. Belle closed her eyes and whispered something under her breath before turning to face the woman with a well-mannered smile. "Yes, Pricilla?"

Pricilla's hand trembled as she pointed a finger towards the window. "Why is there a cannon on the south lawn?"

Everyone but Mallory rushed to the window.

Sure enough, there it was, Moss Pemberton's four-pound Alamo replica cannon Old Hellzapoppin', bold as brass and parked next to the winery's elegant Tuscany fountain.

Louisa held a hand to her mouth, trying to stifle the laughter brewing inside of her. She'd overheard Jess and McCrea talking about a cannon last week, but she had no idea it would be part of the wedding celebration.

"I thought they dismantled that thing after Moss died," Violet said.

"No," Louisa answered. "Didn't you hear? His son Wyatt donated it to the historical society."

Violet looked surprised. "I didn't know Moss had a son."

"He has three," Ed said, joining the women at the window.

"Huh," Violet mused. "You never know about people."

"I haven't met the other two, but Wyatt came by my office a few weeks ago to discuss putting Moss's place on the market." Sage used both hands to fan her face. "The man is one tall drink of water."

"Again," Louisa frowned at her friend. "Aren't you engaged?"

"Again," Sage answered, grinning. "Not blind."

"Belle," Eleanor whispered. "Did you know about this?"

Belle was co-chair of the Santa Camino Historical Society. "No," she said dismally. "It was supposed to be in storage until we could find a place for it."

"It was Jess's idea." Mallory volunteered with a sheepish smile. "I didn't think it would be a problem."

"It's a cannon," Pricilla said through tight lips.

"Yeah, but," Mallory's left shoulder lifted. "It's a small one."

"Pricilla, I—I'm sure," Belle stuttered in mid-sentence to find words. "I'm sure it's just for decoration. It probably doesn't even fire anymore."

"Well, actually," Mallory started to explain as the music began piping through the building's sound system.

"It's time!" Pricilla exclaimed.

"Not quite." Belle took her by the arm and led her to the door. "Remember? The warm-up music is just a prompt, letting us know that we need to get ready for the lineup. Take a deep breath."

Pricilla did as she instructed.

"That's it," Belle said, smiling. "Now, why don't you go and see if the groomsmen are ready."

Pricilla nodded and hurried down the hall.

Belle shut the door and went into action. "Eleanor, if you're going to feed that baby, do it now."

"There's a bottle of breast milk in the kitchen." Eleanor handed Tucker to Louisa. "I'll be right back."

The baby belted out a cry. "No, no, little man," she said, bouncing him at the risk of spilling her jewels.

Belle lifted the fallen strand of hair from Violet's eyes. "Sage, be a dear and do something with her hair."

"Come on, Vi," Sage motioned her towards one of the dressing tables. "Let's see if we can't clean you up."

When Tucker wasn't appeased by the bouncing, his cry turned into a high-pitched shriek that mimicked a hot teakettle. Archie barked a couple of times, then launched into a low, lonely howl. Soon the room became a cacophony of panic and wailing.

"Ed." Belle tried raising her voice over the noise. "Will you please get that dog out of here?"

"Oh, yeah, right," Ed said, wrangling Archie out the door.

Louisa slipped out behind him and waited until Archie's howls were a faint echo before she tried shifting the baby lower into a cradling position against her breasts. His tear-filled eyes kept her under close watch.

She never dreamed that she'd be an aunt twice over or that McCrea would be such a wonderful father. Her brother had been so dead set against being married and having kids, but the child in her arms was a testament to how love could temper a wild and fearful heart.

Tucker flattened a chubby hand against her breasts and snuggled closer. Louisa savored the moment of holding a small and precious miracle that was, for her, so far out of reach.

Using the tip of her forefinger, she traced the outline of Tucker's eyes, his cheeks, and his chin. It was a soothing technique she'd learned from Eleanor. More than likely, the baby would fall asleep and stay that way until she handed him off to Sage before the wedding started.

Repeating the motion, she slowly made her way down

the hall. Hoping that, in some way, the technique might help to soothe her as well. But it didn't. Feeling those soft, silky strands of the baby's dark hair graze her finger was bittersweet. The emptiness she'd felt earlier returned, leaving her with a hollow chest and an aching heart.

Chatter from the guests in the chapel grew louder when she neared the end. Pricilla was now causing havoc in the groom's suite and the catering staff was working in the grand ballroom, preparing for the reception. The only quiet place left was the tasting room adjacent to the ballroom. The kitchen was three doors down, so she could catch Eleanor on her way out.

She rounded the corner and stopped when she saw Brody standing just outside the tasting room near a window, with his shoulder propped against a frame.

He was wearing new dark denim jeans, a cream-colored Stetson, and matching hand-tooled leather boots. The sports jacket Mallory had picked out for the groomsmen added to his shoulders' girth and made them appear twice as wide.

Louisa's first reaction was to turn around and walk the other way, but she didn't often see Brody all gussied up. Not that his everyday work clothes weren't nice. They were, in all the ways that mattered for an estrogen-producing female. Sweat-soaked t-shirts clinging to his pecs, and well-worn jeans that were snug around his muscular thighs...

She'd learned that most evenings after the workday was over, he liked to unwind on the front porch of the cabin; shirtless and barefoot with a cold beer in his hand, he'd sit on the railing with his back against a post watching the sunset over the lake. While he stared at the water, she'd stare at him through the thin sheer curtains of her office window at the clinic. Thanks to those low-riding jeans and phenomenal chest muscles, that flex when he lifted the long-neck to his lips, she now had a stack of overdue paperwork two-foot high sitting on her desk.

She reminded herself that t-shirts and jeans were standard work attire for ranchers and workhands. But Brody was anything but conventional. When he dressed up, a woman couldn't help but stop, stare, and drool. The man was gorgeous, formed to perfection from the top of his head to the soles of his feet. There wasn't anything about his body that wasn't attractive.

A little too turned on by denim and dirt, she was ready to quietly backtrack and head in the opposite direction. But then she noticed something odd.

Brody was a big man every inch of six-three without his boots on who naturally stood with his shoulders square and his chin set in confidence. Not overly proud, just content and ready to take on whatever life threw at him.

But in the two years Louisa had known him, she'd never seen him stand like this, with his shoulders sagging under the weight of something heavier than his always cheerful disposition. He seemed so sad and alone, almost broken. The angle of his head allowed her to see his profile. A stern frown pulled at his brow. The muscles in his face were tense and contracted as he stared out over the grounds of the vineyard.

What — in the world of Brody Vance — deserved that much thought? What could be that troubling to a man as carefree as he?

He removed his hat, raked a big hand through that thick brown hair of his, and let out a long sigh. The width of his broad shoulders expanded beneath his jacket's fabric, and his large form filled the window. The movement and shift of light caught Tucker's sleepy attention, causing him to stir and let out a whimper.

Brody's gaze shot from the grounds to her and the baby, a smile replacing the bracing movement of his jaw.

Louisa was used to fending off that slow, churning burn that centered itself in the pit of her stomach and spread downward when his eyes locked with hers.

But after what happened in the truck — with him almost kissing her and his softly spoken belief that one day she'd see how much he cared for her — there was now something deeply intimate about that blue-gray gaze of his.

His focus moved from her eyes to her mouth, then down to her breasts. "That's," he paused to clear his throat, "some dress."

CHAPTER 8

Louisa's skin burned from Brody's near tangible scrutiny of her breasts.

"It's a little snug in places," she said, her cheeks burning with embarrassment.

Sensually raking his top teeth over his bottom lip, he grinned. "A little."

A sharp, body-piercing sensation hit Louisa between her breastbone and arrowed down. "Well, that's your fault."

He raised one eyebrow. "How so?"

Those two words, spoken with the gravelly undertone of his deep voice, vibrated over her skin, heightening her feminine senses. "I missed my last fitting appointment with Sue because I was with you at Darby Center's place."

"Ah," he said, accepting blame without argument as his grin turned mischievous.

Without the hat shading the upper part of his head, she noticed a spot near the top of his right ear. That side of his head had been away from her in the truck, so she'd missed it then. "You — ah," she pointed at the spot. "Have something on your ear."

He made a swipe. "Did I get it?"

"No. It's near the top."

He swiped and missed again.

Shaking her head no, she moved closer and he bent to give her better access. Touching his warm skin generated an odd sensation in the tips of her fingers. When the spot wouldn't rub off, she flicked it loose with her fingernail. "It looks like paint."

"Probably. I was just finishing up when you called. It must have dripped from the roller."

Disappointment settled into her chest like a thick, slow-creeping fog. "You were painting?" Without me? she wanted to add.

"Carter's crew is nearly done." His voice was much more profound than it had been the first time they'd talked about paint colors. He glanced down at his hat, his face donning that same strained look he'd had when he was staring out the window. "I can't keep waiting, Lou."

Oh, Jesus, Brody. Please, don't.

"Ah — yeah." She tried faking a smile. "I guess you're anxious to get moved in."

He gave her a slight nod. "I was when I first bought the place, but now the house seems so quiet and lonely." He lifted his gaze to hers. "It needs laughter and little feet running through its halls."

Her mind cut to a sweet but tormenting scene of a child's hands wrapped around Brody's fingers, laughing happily as it waddled down the hall, learning to walk.

That bittersweet ache in Louisa's heart, the one she'd felt when she held Tucker, intensified as if it burned a hole through her. She'd chosen not to pick paint colors with Brody because filling the Twisted J's empty rooms with their babies would be nothing short of a miracle for her. But the thought of him fathering a child with another woman was killing her.

She quickly pulled her gaze from his to that flake of paint clinging to the end of her finger, the sting of unshed tears clouding her eyes. It was blue. It wasn't a neutral color meant for either sex. If Brody had painted the nursery blue, then he already knew those little feet belonged to a baby boy.

Anger swept over her, filling that emptiness with resentment and hurt. Brody was as persistent with his advances towards her as he had been the day they met, so if there was another woman, the mother of his child…then she was the "other" woman again.

Louisa fought back the wave of nausea as that scenario skimmed across old and unhealed scars caused by Chris's betrayal. Her heart wanted to believe that Brody was different, but proof that he wasn't was right in front of her. She wanted to launch into a dead run in the opposite direction and never look back. But running from Brody and the truth, whatever it was, wasn't an option. She'd face him and his answer head-on.

She'd worked too hard to surrender her life in Santa Camino because of a two-bit Lothario. She steeled herself for what was to come. "This is a lively shade of blue," she said, trying hard to assume a casual expression as she asked, "What room did you paint?"

Brody held her eyes as if he were deciding what to say. Had she caught him? Was he going to confess there was another woman and that he was the daddy of a baby boy?

She held her breath, not knowing what she would do or how she would react if he did.

Moments of grueling silence passed, then his mouth transformed into a tired smile. "I didn't. Gerald Bixby is repainting his little boy's room. He was in the hardware store yesterday when Lenard was mixing my paint. I must have grabbed Gerald's paint by mistake. Now my kitchen has a streak of little boy blue through the center of it."

Relief slammed into her. "Oh, well," she said, expelling the breath she'd been holding with a laugh. "That's too bad."

"It was my fault for picking up the wrong can and for not paying attention to the paint when I poured it into the pan." Brody shifted his weight from one foot to the other, looking embarrassed by his mistake. "How could I have not noticed that the paint wasn't antique beige?"

"You have been a little preoccupied lately."

"Yeah. I guess I have." He scrubbed a hand over his face. "So, are you and Tuck planning an escape?"

"No." She smiled down at the baby, who was gumming two fingers. "He's hungry, so we followed El to the kitchen and are currently waiting on a bottle."

Brody pointed his hat at Tucker. "A man's gotta eat, right Tuck?"

Tucker's fussy reaction was to bypass Louisa's lace bolero, snag the top of her dress, yank it to his mouth, and bite down hard.

"Oh, no, little man. Don't do that. My zipper is hanging on for dear life." She tried prying the material away from his mouth, but the baby refused to give up the fight. She was one tantrum jerk away from mortification.

Brody set the hat on his head and stepped over to assist. She would have rather toted the baby down the aisle with them than have him come closer. But it was too late to protest.

He carefully took hold of the baby, allowing her to use both hands to free her dress. The baby wasn't happy about letting go and protested by crying as he crammed a hand into his mouth.

"It's okay, Tuck," Brody soothed and cradled the baby in the crook of his arm as he reached into his back pocket, pulled out a white handkerchief and offered it to her. "Here, it's fresh from the pack."

"Thanks," she said, noticing the monogrammed initials B.J.M.

"They were a gift," he explained. "From my sister, Allison."

Brody had a sister?

"Oh, well, um, I don't want to get baby slobber on it," she said, reaching it back to him. "I'll get a paper towel from the kitchen."

"Nonsense," he said, brushing his lips against the baby's forehead in a tender display of affection. "A little slobber won't hurt it."

She gave the dress a few swipes and decided that it was no worse for wear. The wet patch would vanish quickly, but the effects of Brody's sensitive side would be harder to dismiss.

Tucker squirmed and rubbed a wet fist over his eyes, growing more agitated by the minute.

"Momma will be here soon, little man," she said, handing the handkerchief back to Brody. "I'm sure he'll pass right out after his belly is full."

Before he could slide it back into his pocket, Tucker grabbed it, shoved it into his mouth and bit down hard.

"I doubt it," Brody said, chuckling. "An empty belly isn't the worst of Tuck's problems. He's teething."

He'd stunned her again. "And just how do you know that?"

"I pay attention," he answered, in a matter-of-fact manner. "El's been giving him breast milk from the bottle more and more instead of nursing him and his gums are red."

Louisa had noticed the baby's gums were red but hadn't attributed it to teething or his fussiness. "How'd you —"

"Thanks, Mary." The kitchen door swung open, and Eleanor rushed out with a baby bottle in one hand and a blue elephant teether in the other. She stopped in mid-step when she saw them. "Did Belle send a search party for me?"

"No," Louisa answered. "We — ah, kind of bumped into each other in the hall, that's all."

Eleanor's eyes bounced from Brody to Louisa when she realized she'd interrupted something. "Sorry I took so long. I had to heat the bottle and then Mary caught me on the way out."

Louisa leaned closer and tickled the baby's belly. "We made do, didn't we, Tuck?"

The baby answered with a growling sound that rousted another husky chuckle from Brody. "He's a heavy rascal. Let me carry him back."

"Be my guest," Eleanor said and handed him the bottle.

Laying Tucker in the crook of his arm, he eased the handkerchief from the baby's mouth and inserted the bottle.

Brody and Eleanor walked towards the bridal suite. Louisa followed, dazed at what had just happened. Seeing him with a child in his arms wasn't anything unusual. Sophie always made a beeline for him when he walked through her parents' door, and he often volunteered to help with Tucker when McCrea and Eleanor were at the Rescue. He also helped Kara, the Rescue's administrative assistant, with the kiddy tours and educational classes for area elementary students. The man was as comfortable around children as he was around horses.

But the easy way he'd handled Tucker's fussiness and the teething... How had he known?

As they started around the corner, Tucker squirmed, and the handkerchief floated to the floor.

Louisa crouched down and picked it up. Since when did a single man with no kids handle a baby like a seasoned pro or make such keen observations regarding breastfeeding and teething?

Using two fingers and her palm, she straightened the indentation of Tucker's slobbery bite on the otherwise stark-white material. Maybe his sister had a baby. Maybe Brody was an uncle and that's how he knew about teething. That would explain his nurturing side, but not why he'd looked so troubled when she'd found him at the window. Or maybe she was reading too much into this.

She traced a finger over the dark blue embroidery of the initials B.J.V. with her forefinger, questions firing through her mind like bottle rockets. Brody never talked about his family, so why had he suddenly announced he had a sister? Her mind jumped from one hypothetical question to another.

Had he been thinking about Allison or his nephew at the window? Maybe someone in his family was ill or in trouble. That would explain why he left town every other weekend. It would also explain her mom's odd behavior in the bridal suite a few minutes ago.

Dread settled into her stomach. But if that were the case, why hadn't he just told her?

"I've never seen you give anyone the cold shoulder like you do Brody. You're rude, obnoxious, and downright mean to the man." Belle's voice bounced in to knock on her conscience. *"...you take a piece out of him every time he comes near you..."*

"He tries so hard to be your friend."

Was that why Brody had mentioned his sister? Because at that moment, he'd needed someone to talk to? Someone to listen and help bear the weight of what he was going through?

A friend.

Oh, God. Louisa's heart sank with guilt as she recalled all the times Brody had gone out of his way to be a friend to her. Her mind floated back to last year when Jess had been bucked off and knocked unconscious by a horse. Watching her brother being catapulted into the air and crash into the metal railing had been a horrific replay of the night he'd nearly lost his leg and his life at the National Rodeo Finals years ago.

She'd felt so helpless and scared. But Brody had been her stronghold. He'd held her tight when there was nothing but tears and fear controlling her. He'd watched her lose all composure and quietly beg God not to let her brother die. He'd driven her to the hospital and waited with her until they knew Jess was okay. Then she'd done what she always did where Brody was concerned.

She'd shoved him away, figuratively, with her words and stone-cold attitude.

Louisa hated that Brody had witnessed that shattered side of her. But more than that, she hated that she'd let him walk away without so much as a thank you.

She prided herself on being a good friend and she hadn't been, not to Brody. She'd turned her back on him so many times. Today, he'd gone out of his way to give her a ride and escort her down the aisle.

He'd never once failed to be there when she needed him and in return...?

Louisa closed her eyes and leaned against the wall as the truth about her behavior hit home. She was a horrible person. She'd dealt with her fears and insecurities about Chris by shooting down Brody's kindness and generosity in the cruelest, most selfish ways.

Thankfully, Brody had a tough hide and he'd never once stumbled when she shoved, though one day he might. And if he did? What would happen? He might never talk to her again or worse. He might pull up stakes and leave town.

No, she assured herself. Brody's life was here, in Santa Camino, at the Rescue and the Twisted J. He wouldn't leave because of her.

She pushed herself upright and set out for the bridal suite, determined to make things right. Brody wanted more than friendship from her. But protecting herself from another painful relationship didn't give her the right to hurt him. She could be his friend because there were different degrees of closeness that didn't require a heart investment.

CHAPTER 9

Brody didn't often get sidetracked by breasts. But the vision of Louisa's in that low cut dress and lacy jacket ensemble made the simple task of putting one foot in front of the other hard.

It made other things hard too.

He shoved his hands into the front pocket of his jeans and transferred his weight from one foot to the other, trying to inconspicuously shift his erection to a less noticeable angle.

Those breasts were now seared into his permeant memory. He'd spent the last fifteen minutes fantasizing about what might have happened if his little buddy Tucker had jerked the top of Louisa's dress down a few more inches.

Now, standing with the other groomsmen outside the bridal suite, he was battling to keep his mind focused on his part of the ceremony.

Fortunately, this was the fourth one he'd attended since moving to Santa Camino, so he could probably walk through it blindfolded.

"Okay," Pricilla forced the word out using a weak smile. "Just like we rehearsed."

Archie responded with a deep bark that sent her back a few steps.

McCrea gave the pup's leash a gentle tug. "Settle down."

Pricilla pressed a hand to her chest. "How can we be sure he won't jerk from the leash and run off with the rings?"

"We can't." He patted the breast of his jacket. "Which is why I have the real rings here."

"Good." Breathing out a sigh of relief, she turned on her heel and walked quickly down the hall towards the chapel.

"If one of us farts, that gal is going down like a fainting goat," Dean decided.

Hardin clamped a hand over his nephew's shoulder and lowered his usually boisterous voice. "No farting in the chapel. Your Aunt Belle will disown you."

Bored and full of pure pup play, Archie growled and sank his teeth into McCrea's jean leg. Frowning, he tried shaking the dog free as he spoke. "That was a long phone call."

"Is everything okay?" Jess asked.

Hardin shook his head, indicating there was nothing to worry about. "I'll tell you all about it later."

McCrea and Jess knew they weren't getting more information about the mysterious phone call until their dad was ready.

Hardin clamped a hand around Brody's neck and gave it a squeeze. "Are we on for tomorrow? I've got a new topwater lure that'll drive the bass crazy."

Tall and impressively built, Hardin Coldiron could outwork men half his age. He was as strong as an ox and as ornery as a bear when he was pissed. But he had a heart of gold. And he treated Brody like a son. "Bright and early."

"Good, good." Hardin patted his shoulder then pointed to Jess. "Can we have a word?"

"Sure," Jess said, letting his dad lead him down the hall for a private moment.

Hardin smiled as he spoke in low, inaudible words. Jess's head dropped and he nodded as if to say, "I know, Dad. She's mine now and I'll be the best husband I know how to be."

Brody knew it was one of those talks because he knew Hardin and the kind of relationship he had with his children. He loved them and wasn't shy about showing it or offering his wisdom.

The talk ended with a long hug, broader smiles, and a firm handshake that brought back painful childhood memories for Brody. His dad would never have that talk with him. That moment and a thousand others had been lost the night Jameson drove away from the True Line with a fifth of whiskey in his hand.

Pricilla returned, waving Jess towards the side door of the chapel. Once he was out of sight, she opened the door to the bridal suite, and everyone began taking their places.

Typically, the best man waited with the groom at the altar. But since McCrea was in charge of Archie and the rings, everyone thought it best if he walked in the procession with the matron of honor.

Muttering what sounded like a curse under her breath, Violet limped out of the bridal suite and took her spot next to Dean.

Dean gave her a once-over, examining her squinting eye and bandaged knee. "What happened to you?"

"Archie took me for a walk." She switched her bouquet

from one hand to the other, shifted the wrap around her shoulders and roughly looped her arm through his. "I lost one of my contacts and now everything's blurry."

"Jesus," Dean taunted her with a rare half-grin. "You're a mess."

Stiff-chinned and eyeing him with disdain, she pointed a deadly finger at him. "I don't care if you are some high-priced criminal lawyer, Dean Coldiron. I will trip you halfway down the aisle if you don't wipe that smug grin off your face."

Dean's smile waned, but the humor in his eyes stayed. "Just know that if I go down, I won't go alone."

Violet said nothing after that.

Brody waited without his bridesmaid. Standing there all alone, watching McCrea and Eleanor steal quick kisses and lavish each other with adoring smiles made the aching loneliness inside of him worsen. It also brought a significant point to his mind.

When he'd attended their wedding year before last, he'd gone without a date because he'd been new in town. Since then, he'd become acquainted with almost everyone in Santa Camino, and he'd had plenty of opportunities with women ranging from serious relationship potential to just straight-up no-phone-calls-the-next-day sex.

But he hadn't pursued any of them because none of those women made him feel the way Louisa did.

Irritable and hopeless? Or the lowest form of cowboy crap on earth?

Brody usually didn't listen to the voice of his frustration, but it was getting harder and harder to resist its logic. He'd thought telling Louisa he had a sister would open the door for questions and conversation and perhaps lead to Riley. Then maybe the moment when he could finally tell her he loved her. But like everything else he'd said and done, she'd brushed Allison away like baby drivel.

He hadn't missed her reaction to that fleck of blue paint on his ear or the conflict in her eyes when he'd said he couldn't wait. There wasn't a doubt in Brody's mind that Louisa wanted to paint the nursery with him, so what was holding her back? He'd practically proposed once. What more could he do or say to the woman that would persuade her to give him a chance?

Not a damn thing.

He was banging his head against a wall that was never going to crumble. Another deep sigh left his lungs. This time, a decision came with it. When the wedding was over, he would call up one of those women and have himself a real date.

Why wait?

A picture of Ivy Nash came to his mind. The cute redhead from the saddle shop flirted with him every time she was in the establishment. Yesterday, she'd snatched his phone from his back pocket and added her number to his contacts.

Brody's modest salary and fixer-upper ranch were hardly luring to a woman like Ivy. As a daddy's girl and sole inheritor of the Nash Saddlery fortune, Ivy wouldn't be looking for anything other than a good time from him.

That was fine with Brody.

Hell, he might just have sex tonight. An orgasm would help his worrisome mood and exhaust some of his pent-up frustrations. Yeah, he was long overdue.

Digging into his pocket, he took out his phone and scrolled through his list of contacts until he found Ivy's number. His thumb hesitated a split second before he pressed the call button. He lifted the phone to his ear. Five rings and her voicemail picked up. "Damn."

"Something wrong?"

Louisa's voice startled Brody so that he nearly dropped his cell phone. "No," he said and quickly shoved his phone back into the inside pocket of his sport jacket.

Holding tight to the small bouquet in her hands, she took her place beside him. "You sure?"

Brody's height gave him a clear vantage of her breasts. But he wasn't going to give in to the urge to look. A man had his pride and she'd ripped his to shreds. He was done chasing Louisa Coldiron.

He knew she hated being paired to walk down the aisle with him. But there wasn't a lot either of them could do about the situation other than keep a civil tone and smile for the sake of the bride and groom.

She was a bridesmaid in dire need of an escort, and he was here to do the job. After that, they'd go their separate ways and assume their normal co-worker life until he took that job at the True Line.

"Positive." He folded his hands together, jerked his head forward, and trained his eyes on the back of Dean's head. "How's your dress?"

"Good as new," she said, her tone easy and friendly.

From the corner of his eye, Brody saw her lift her hand. In it was his handkerchief.

"You dropped it in the hallway," she said, smiling warmly. "B is for Brody. V is for Vance. What's the J for?"

Her interests threw him. Maybe he'd been wrong about her brushing Allison aside.

No, frustration was quick to cut in. *Don't do it. Don't give in. Sex. Remember how much you miss sex? Don't smile. Don't flirt. Just tell her your middle name and act like you don't give a damn.*

But he did give a damn. And though he missed having sex, it wasn't what he wanted most. He wanted something real and meaningful, something long-term and lasting. He and Riley deserved that.

He narrowed one eye and scratched his jaw. "Did…ah, you just ask me a personal question?"

Her posture stiffened and the detached confidence that was Louisa faded to expose the vulnerability he'd seen in the truck. "Yes," she said faintly, shyly holding his eyes. "I guess I did."

Louisa was saying nice things to him — a cowboy. The man she once called the lowest form of testosterone on the planet.

Don't fall for it. She's setting you up for an insult or a joke. Any minute now, there's going to be sarcastic venom spewing from that beautiful mouth of hers.

Brody errored on the side of caution. "Like a let's-get-to-know-one-another personal question? Like a casual dinner question?"

She gave him a dull look.

"I'm a cowboy." He looked around as if she had mistakenly addressed him. "Are you sure you have the right guy?"

Her hand dropped to her side and the dark sienna undertones of those cool canyon walls spilled into her eyes. "Brody, I…"

He'd been twelve the first time a horse bucked him from the saddle. Going head over heels had been an addictive dose of gut-wrenching fear and heart-stopping excitement. Seeing Louisa's gaze transform to that vulnerable shade of warm admiration while she was looking at him doused Brody with the same adrenaline rush.

He swallowed. "Yeah?"

"I'm trying to apologize."

Her words wiped away any and all doubt of foul play. This wasn't a setup. "For what?"

"For acting rude and ungrateful earlier and for being a general pain in your ass for the last two years."

Stunned by her apology, Brody was at a loss for words, but he finally managed a. "What?"

"When I saw you standing at the window, I knew something was wrong, but I ignored you like I have dozens of times before." Dropping her eyes to the bouquet in her hand, she began chewing her bottom lip. "I just wanted you to know that I'm sorry."

Louisa was apologizing to him? And not just for today. She was trying to make amends for the last two years. Was he dreaming? Had she finally come to her senses? Could this be the beginning of the relationship he wanted with her?

No. Ignore her.

"And," she continued, overriding the voice in his head. "Regardless of how I've treated you in the past, I want you to know that I'm always here if you need to talk about Allison."

"About Allison?" he repeated.

"Yes, or — or your niece or nephew," she rushed to say, her eyes so sincere and full of concern. "I assumed that's how you knew so much about Tucker's teething problem."

Louisa thought he was an uncle. Oh, brother. He guessed it was a fair assumption given the short conversation they'd had about Allison. But damn. She was so far off base. He should tell her here and now about Riley.

Brody gave his jaw a hard rub and glanced around the hallway, thinking about how that conversation would play out. The wedding was about to start, so he couldn't go into the details. He'd have to give her the condensed version, which was he'd gotten wasted in a bar, slept with a woman he hadn't known, and found out that she was pregnant two months later.

It was the truth, but it sounded seedy as hell.

"Anyway." Attempting another warm smile, she offered him the handkerchief again. "Thank you for picking me up, for agreeing to escort me down the aisle today, and for... always being there when I need you."

His resistance melted, prompting the rational part of his mind to kick in again. *Don't fall for this. Let her go, man, before it's too late. She won't understand what happened with Heather. If you tell her the truth about how Riley was conceived, you'll only reinforce her disreputable view of cowboys. Walk away, now while your heart is still whole.*

Brody had a healthy appetite when it came to women, but it had been a while since he'd dined on casual sex. Two and a half long years, to be exact. He didn't feel a thing when he looked at Ivy Nash. Not even the slightest twinge of affection. With hunger gnawing at his body, it wouldn't be hard to get past that.

But it would be damn hard to look Louisa in the eye come morning. As for the truth...his heart hadn't been whole in a long time. This lace-wrapped beauty beside him was the missing piece and the only woman who would complete him. She was the woman he wanted, in his remodeled ranch house, in his king-size bed, and his life.

Reality set in. Ivy's copper-colored hair, blue eyes, and curvy figure quickly faded into the background. He didn't want another one-night stand and that's precisely what sleeping with Ivy would be. He wasn't having sex tonight and he wasn't walking away from this conversation. But just because Louisa acted civil to him didn't mean she wanted the long-term he and Riley deserved, so he wasn't sure what to do other than return her warmness.

Reaching out, he slipped the handkerchief from her fingers. "The J is for Jameson."

"Jameson," she repeated, softly savoring the word as it rolled off her tongue.

Brody hated his middle name, so much so that he avoided saying it out loud whenever possible. But when Louisa said it, it made it seem less like a scar and more like something to be proud of.

"Mine is Marie," she offered.

Seeing those beautiful eyes stare up at him without cynicism would take some getting used to. But he would adjust, quickly. "It's pretty."

"Thanks." The side of her mouth tweaked up. "But I hate it. It's an old family name, carried down from one of my grandmothers on Dad's side."

They were having their first conversation that didn't involve work. They weren't arguing and she wasn't trying to shoot him down. It felt good and he didn't want it to end.

"I hate mine too," he admitted before he thought.

"Aw," she made a sad face by puckering her bottom lip. "Why? It's such a strong name."

Jameson Vance had been anything but strong.

He folded the handkerchief in half and shoved it into his back pocket. "It was my dad's name."

Her eyebrows shot high and her bottom jaw dropped with surprise. "Oh."

She finally wants to talk, and you kill it by letting her know you hate your dad.

Smooth.

Brody cleared his throat and gave her a wink. "Just so you know. You're my favorite pain in the ass."

If he hadn't already been in love with her, that cute, sassy smile of hers would have done him in.

She wrapped both hands around the bouquet and held

it to her heart while batting her eyes. "Cowboy, you do know how to make a woman feel special."

Yes, he did. But they were miles away from him giving her that pleasure. This was progress, though — wonderful, encouraging progress.

CHAPTER 10

As they waited for Pricilla to give them their cue, Louisa tried concentrating on what was to come, the walk, the vows, the celebration, and the joy of seeing her brother happily married. But her mind kept veering towards Brody and all the things she'd learned about him within the last hour. She unexpectedly felt excited about what else she would know now that she was trying harder to be a better friend.

But it occurred to her that her new endeavor wouldn't go unnoticed by her friends and family. Her dad, now waiting at the front of the processional with her mom, had cast several over-the-shoulder glances their way while she and Brody were discussing their middle names.

"I don't know about you, but I- ah…" Looking up, she saw Brody shift the knot in his tie. "Feel like the odd man with all these married couples around."

"Yeah," she said, suddenly relating whole-heartedly to what he'd just said. "I guess most of us have felt that way at one time or another."

"It's good to know I'm not alone."

"You're not. I feel that way a lot, more so now than ever."

A slight frown pulled at his face. "Oh?"

"After today, I'll be the only single person in my family aside from Dean." She grimaced and leaned in closer to Brody as she whispered, "So does that mean I'm destined to become a female version of that irritable workaholic?"

He chuckled. "You do work too much."

She'd referenced Dean jokingly, but deep down, she wondered if her life would be spent alone or worse, jumping from one empty relationship to another. "Look who's talking. Most of the time, you're working right beside me."

"But I take every other weekend off, remember?"

She did and now would be the perfect time to reengage their conversation about his sister. But the dull elevator music streaming through the surround-sound had changed to the wedding processional, signaling the start of the ceremony.

Brody held out his arm. "Shall we?"

"Might as well." Louisa moved closer and wrapped her arm through his. "It's the only way we'll get cake and champagne."

"My thoughts, exactly."

Holding on to his hard, masculine forearm was just the way she thought it would be. The instant the heat of his body touched hers, her legs turned to butter.

Pricilla opened the double doors of the chapel and the crowd turned to watch the procession. Jess had invited his friends from the Pro Rodeo circuit. The empty seats that were there at rehearsal last night were now filled with guests. One of those guests sitting near the back row was Cord Watts, the president of LaSorona Boots. The company had been one of Jess's biggest sponsors while he was competing.

Cord had asked her out a time or two, but she'd always said no. He had all the physical attributes she found attractive. He had jet-black hair, light green eyes, and a lean body that was stunningly packaged in a three-piece suit. But when he smiled at her, nothing happened. There were no sparks, no flushing or tingles.

Her mom and dad moved to the door and waited for their signal to walk down the aisle. Dean and Violet followed. Everything was running smoothly, but as she and Brody approached the doorway, Louisa's butter legs began to quake. With every step, his forearm grazed the side of her breast. Hoping to reduce the friction, she tightened her hold on his arm.

He mistakenly read her response as nerves. Leaning over, he whispered, "Stage fright?"

Thank God for the jacket. If his arm were bare, she would have been panting like Archie. "Something like that," she whispered back.

Brody capped his large hand over hers and squeezed it. The soft abrasion of his calloused palm on her skin made her body ignite.

This was nothing like watching him drink beer on the porch. Louisa couldn't just drop her eyes or leave the room when she got turned on.

Brody had a hold on her. Her senses were overwhelmed by him. With each breath she took, the cool but spicy fragrance of his cologne invaded her lungs: lavender, fir balsam, and juniper berries infused with the male attar that was all Brody.

"Think about something else."

He wanted her to think when the intimate rasp of his voice was blowing against her ear?

"Go. Go," Pricilla mouthed and tried waving them through the doors.

Louisa managed to make her legs move by focusing on the patterns on the hardwood floor. But her stony steps were out of sync with his.

"Lou? Are you still with me?" Brody's concerned voice drew her eyes up and straight to the broad smiling face of her dad. His brown eyes, dewy with emotion, communicated all his longings and expectations for his daughter. She was holding on to the arm of a man he loved like a son. Love. Marriage. Family.

She'd tried so hard to make her parents proud and they were. But she worried what they might think if they knew about her romance with Chris, about the price she was paying and would continue to pay. The reason she and Brody would never be the happily married couple her parents yearned for.

She swallowed, holding back the tears that burned her eyes as the emptiness that had plagued her before returned. "I—um, yeah. I'm with you."

But she wasn't, never would be. That's the way it had to be. She'd felt so guilty and been so eager to make things right with Brody that she hadn't considered the conclusions her family might draw when she smiled at him or the complications that could arise from her amity.

Everyone, including her mom and dad, though she and Brody were lovers. Now that she was home and settled into her job at the Rescue, her friends and family would expect their relationship to blossom into love and commitment, which meant that Brody conversation in the bridal suite was probably the first of many to come.

Her life was about to become a living hell and there wasn't anything she could do about it except curse and bear it.

Unless…

Her eyes whipped to Cord and an unmistakable invitation darkened his eyes as he smiled at her.

Ah-ha. Hope flickered through her, triggering a plan that might save her from this travesty. What if she could find a decoy that would make everyone, including Brody, believe her love interests were with another man?

Cord was an out-of-towner without any ties to Santa Camino. He was handsome, charismatic, and successful, appealing qualities to people pushing her towards the altar.

All she had to do was set the stage and play the part, laugh, dance, and have a couple of glasses of champagne with Cord at the reception. She'd get his number and say she'd call but wouldn't. Cord wouldn't care and no one would be the wiser. Town chit-chat would spread like wildfire with speculation and rumors to construct her and Cord's love affair. By this time tomorrow, she and Brody would be history and she and Cord would be the talk of the town.

Sure, Brody might be a little disappointed, but her plan would protect their friendship and co-worker relationship.

Again, Brody dipped his head closer to her ear. "Colorado."

"What?"

"I was in Colorado last weekend."

ONCE THEY REACHED THE END OF THE AISLE, BRODY GAVE Louisa's hand a final pat and let her arm go. He went right and she went left. They took their places and waited for the rest of the wedding procession.

With trembling hands, week knees, and a pounding heart, she tried reining in her body's response to Brody and her thoughts about who or what would make a man take a ten- to twelve-hour drive every other weekend.

Archie bounced down the aisle with his tongue flopping as he barked excitedly at guests. But he stayed on track and obediently took a seat at McCrea's feet.

The music changed to signal the bride was about to make her appearance. The guests stood. Jess straightened his shoulders and folded his hands in front of him, anxiously anticipating the entrance of his bride. The pure unadulterated happiness on his face made tears spring to Louisa's eyes.

Eleanor slipped a tissue in her hand. "I brought extras."

"Thanks," she whispered, dabbling the corners.

With a basket of rose petals and that huge toothless grin, Sophie carried her basket down the aisle. Jess gave her an affectionate wink that made her snicker and cover her mouth.

Everyone had their eyes trained on the doorway waiting for the bride. But Louisa kept her eyes on Jess. She didn't need a response of "oh's" from the guests to know the second Mallory stepped into sight. The broad smile on his face melted into a sappy, lovestruck expression.

Ed escorted Mallory down the aisle, kissed her on the cheek, and placed her hand in Jess's. Pastor Renfro began the ceremony with a prayer. The men removed their hats, and everyone bowed their heads.

The prayer ended and the guests took their seats. After the opening remarks, the pastor addressed the guests and then instructed the couple to make their vows.

Jess swiped a thumb over his eyes and took Mallory's other hand. "Mallory, I promise to protect you and shelter you. I vow to love you and only you for the rest of my life through every hardship and every sorrow. I promise to encourage you, let you shine, and never take you for granted. You are my heart, my soul, my everything, my life."

Louisa silently wept big tears.

A little teary-eyed himself, McCrea ducked his head and coughed. Then he raised a hand and gave Jess a brief pat on the back, subtly expressing his affection and support. As a husband, McCrea knew the power of those words and the responsibility they carried. To her family, marriage was more than rings and words. It was a sacred and life-long promise.

"Jess," Mallory's started her vows. "You've had my heart since the first time we met out on that dusty back-road when you gave me bad directions."

Jess chuckled and a murmur of laughter waved over the crowd.

"My long journey to you was worth every obstacle and hardship. Because of you, my life has meaning, peace, and more joy than I ever thought possible."

Again, Jess swiped his eyes.

"I promise to hold and comfort you when you're sick, help you up when you fall, and never lose faith in you. I promise to love you forever and always."

They exchanged rings and the pastor said, "You may kiss the bride." Jess did, thoroughly, breaking the kiss only when McCrea slapped him on the back a couple of times.

Breathless, frazzled, and looking like they couldn't wait for the honeymoon they turned, and the pastor introduced them as Mr. and Mrs. Jess Coldiron. Just then, the loud boom of cannon fire exploded into the air.

The Italian-style windows of the chapel rattled. Belle jumped, and from the back, Pricilla let out a resounding, "Oh, Jesus!"

Jess gave his Stetson a fling into the air with a gaudy, "Yee! Haw!" and swept Mallory into his arms.

"Classy," Louisa said, laughing.

"This escalated into a circus faster than mine did," Eleanor replied.

"That's what happens when my brothers have a hand in planning a wedding."

Loud whistles and clapping rippled through the crowd as the bridesmaids and groomsmen followed behind them less ceremonially. According to the plan, the wedding party entered the grand ballroom through the atrium while wedding guests were guided through the main entrance's double doors.

Pricilla had stopped Jess and Mallory before they could enter the ballroom. She looked frantic. Judging from Jess's annoyed expression, Louisa was betting that Pricilla was overreacting to something small.

"Lord," Belle sighed. "What's she in a tizzy about now?"

Louisa's money was on the cannon, but with Pricilla, it could be anything.

Hooking a thumb in his left jean pocket, Brody shifted his weight to one leg and leaned over to answer in a whisper only she and Belle could hear. "Pricilla's weather app started binging about thunderstorms."

"Oh, no," Belle said. "The wedding photos."

Jess and Mallory held fast to the tradition that it was bad luck for the groom to see the bride before the ceremony, so only limited photos had been taken of them and the wedding party.

"I better see what I can do to help." Belle moved to the front of the group, then disappeared into the grand ballroom.

Brody's mouth twisted regretfully. "I hope they can

work something out before the rain gets here. Mallory wanted photos of everyone on the balcony."

Teething babies and the wishes of a new bride? The man's perceptiveness and sensibilities always hit the softest part of Louisa's heart. Her eyes targeted that sexy little cleft at the bottom of his chin. It seemed to be the safest place to look at while they talked. "Ah – yeah. Me too."

But her mind had a way of corrupting even the most innocent parts of his body. And in a split second, she was thinking about how his facial hair would feel skimming across her bare thighs.

"Can I have your attention?" Belle said, walking back into the atrium. The approaching rain had changed the celebration itinerary, bumping the outside portion of the photoshoot in front of the cake cutting and the couple's first dance. Jess and Mallory had opted out of serving a sit-down dinner, choosing instead to go with a cocktail menu of assorted, high-end hors d'oeuvre, so the caterers wouldn't have to keep food warm while the shoot was going on. Guests were advised of the changes and encouraged to mingle and visit the bar until the couple returned to cut the cake.

None of them had objected.

Rhea Larky was a local photographer with a beautiful talent for capturing the picture-perfect moment. The wedding photos she'd taken of McCrea and Eleanor had been breathtaking. She was also quick and easy to work with.

Rhea jumped into action, moving people into poses and positions as she clicked away. The last one was of the groomsmen and the bridesmaids together on the balcony. She instructed them to stand facing each other and gave an example by moving Dean and Violet into place.

The position had been too close for Louisa's comfort.

Brody hadn't had a problem with it at all. He'd smiled ruefully, held out both arms in a welcoming gesture and said, "Get in here."

"Here" was miles outside Louisa's comfort zone. The last place she wanted to be was pressed against his hard chest, but she didn't see a way out of it. It wasn't like she could do an about face and walk away, so with an aloof guise, she moved into his arms. She tried keeping a few inches between them. But he wrapped one arm around her waist and pulled her snugly against him. "For the photo," he explained, though his smile said otherwise.

Her heart raced so fast she thought she might pass out. God, wouldn't that be a disaster? Her swooning over Brody Vance.

"Don't let it stray south," she warned.

He tightened his hold ever so gently. "You know I'd never let my hand go anywhere it wasn't wanted."

Brody's reputation as a gentleman preceded him. The problem was Louisa wanted his hands in places that weren't appropriate for photos or friends.

"Relax," he added, his voice falling to a low pitch. "I don't leave a mark when I bite."

She flattened her palm against his chest and pushed back a fraction so she could venture a glance up at him. "I think what you meant to say was, I don't bite."

Dropping his eyes to her mouth, Brody licked his bottom lip as if he were savoring the thought of sinking his teeth into her. "Oh, I bite, sweetheart but only in places that can be seen by a lover."

Louisa's heart stopped in mid-beat, convulsed, and fell over like a spent rabbit.

CHAPTER 11

Brody had finally gotten Louisa back into his arms. It hadn't happened under the circumstances he'd wanted, but it had happened. Her amicable actions towards him had given him a tiny shred of faith. Deep down he knew he was a fool for entertaining optimism, even if it was paper thin. If and when he walked away, he needed to know he'd done all he could to make this work.

He also knew from the way she'd gotten spooked out on the balcony that he needed to move slow and let her make the first move. That was going to be excruciating. When he'd drawn her to him for the photos, he'd heard her take in a sharp breath.

The dreamy-like way she'd looked up at him – glossy red lips with wide, desire-filled eyes. She was beautiful, sexy, and tempting. Feeling her warm, curvy body responding so easily to him had impaled him with a sharp stab of desire that hadn't faded since they'd joined the wedding party in the grand ballroom. Brody sensed a different current flowing between them, sitting next to her in their assigned seats around the large reception table. An unfamiliar flux of anxiety on her part and gut-churning anticipation on his.

Damn, he wanted a whiskey. But toasting the bride and groom with a shot of hard liquor was hardly celebratory, so he lifted his glass of champagne high and smiled through the ache inside of him.

When the toast was over, the couple moved to the center table where the wedding cake was on display. Decorated with a flourishing spray of mauve roses and peach peonies, the three-tiered white wedding cake was exquisite and beautiful. He'd tried making a two-layered birthday cake for Allison when she turned sixteen. Piping on decorative scrolls had looked easy on television. But in practice, the job called for a special touch. Ellie Daniels operated a cake decorating service out of her home and was a Picasso of pastries. After the bride and groom had had their fun by shoving pieces of bite-sized cake into each other's mouths, Ellie cut the dessert into small, individual sizes and served them to guests.

Instead of coming back to her seat at the reception table next to him, Louisa had taken her cake and walked to a vacant table near the back. She was away from the crowd but close to where a few of Jess's rodeo acquaintances were sitting. With his cake in hand, Hardin had stopped on his way back to the table to talk with one of the men. Brody thought the man's name was Cord. He'd met him last year at a fundraiser for the Rescue. Tall, with dark hair and manicured hands, he was some sort of high-ranking executive for a boot company in West Texas.

While Hardin and Cord were deep in conversation, Brody turned his attention back to Louisa. She'd changed from her bridesmaid dress back into the jeans and pretty, pink top she'd had on when he'd picked her up for the wedding.

He debated on joining her because he didn't want to scare her away by pushing too hard, but he didn't want to give her too much time alone to overthink what had happened out on the balcony.

Gentle, persuading pressure was what she needed.

Brody scooted his chair back from the table and walked to the bar to get that whiskey he wanted. He wasn't a heavy drinker and when he did drink, it was usually a beer. Years of watching his dad drink through his mom's hard-earned money had kept him away from the hard stuff. But he needed something to help loosen the tension in his body.

With the drink in his hand, he leaned an elbow against the bar and sipped until the soothing started. Jess and Mallory went to the center of the room for their first dance when the music started. Locked in a tender embrace and with Rhea's camera flashing, they floated around the room to a song titled "Thinking Out Loud." There wasn't a dry eye in the room when it ended, and the couple kissed.

Brody set his glass down and joined in the hearty applause. The DJ picked another slow, romantic ballad that drew other couples to the dance floor. A waiter stopped to offer him an hors d'oeuvres. The bite-sized food was just enough to whet a man's appetite without bedding it down. He passed, knowing his taste buds were craving something that wasn't on the serving tray.

Drink in hand, he turned back to the bar and cut a glance in Louisa's direction. His body went cold. Hardin had gone back to his seat next to Belle, and Cord had vacated his table to sit with Louisa during the first dance. Brody watched as a smile hit her face. Not one of the forced, placid ones or even one of those friendly smiles she'd given him while they were talking in the hall. This was a genuine smile, warm, flirty, and…leading.

Bile rose in his throat. He washed it down with the rest of his whiskey and set the glass on the bar.

That goddamn, soft-handed, boot-selling, son of a —

"Hi!"

Ivy's chipper greeting brought his head around. He knew the second he looked at those bright blue eyes of hers that he was going to have to lie like hell to get out of that phone call he'd made. "Oh — ah, hi, Ivy," he mumbled.

Holding up her phone, she teetered it back and forth while wiggling her eyebrows. "I have a missed call from you."

He tried to look surprised. "From me?"

"Uh-huh," she said, smiling in a sexy kitten way.

Brody looked over to the corner table. When he saw it was empty, his eyes began jumping from guest to guest. He found Cord and Louisa walking to the dance floor.

"Hmmm," he said, motioning the bartender for another drink. "Tucker had my phone earlier. He must have accidentally hit your number. Sorry."

"Oh." Her smile melted, making Brody feel like an asshole.

Killing the drink in one gulp, he watched Cord and Louisa sway hip to hip to some slow country song. He had to get on that dance floor and Boot Boy on the trail of a different woman.

His eyes swung back to Ivy. "But there's no sense letting a good song go to waste. How about a dance?"

Her smile bounced back. "Thought you'd never ask."

Brody felt like a dick for misleading Ivy. But if his plan worked, she'd have a willing man in her bed tonight. And he'd have a chance to dance with Louisa.

The music playlist covered a wide variety of genres, everything from rock to country to pop. The next song up was a classic from George Strait. Brody could two-step in his sleep. Ivy was a good dancer, keeping up with his quick steps and sometimes out dancing his moves.

He made sure he and Ivy kept up with Louisa and Cord, so when the song was over, the four of them would be close enough for a casual introduction. He'd caught Louisa looking at him and Ivy a few times since the dance started. That glint of jealousy he saw flashing through her eyes caused him to play up the excitement.

He spun Ivy around one last time and ended the dance with a dip. Laughing, she wrapped both arms around his neck and went in for a kiss. He saw the lip-lock coming, yanked her upright, and enveloped her in a big hug to avoid it. Then he guided her over to where Cord and Louisa were.

Wrangling his hold on a friendly smile, he held out his hand to Cord. "Cord, right?"

The man took his hand. "Have we met?"

"Yeah," Brody answered. "Jess introduced us last year at the spring fundraiser."

Louisa let her tight lips relax long enough to say, "He's the horse trainer for Promise Point."

That registered with Cord. He pointed his finger at Brody as if it would help nail down his name. "Vance."

"Brody," Ivy added, sliding her arms around Brody's waist.

Louisa cocked her jaw sideways and eyed poor Ivy as if she were a steaming pile of fresh, hot horse manure.

Brody subtly slipped Ivy's arms to the side. "Cord, this is Ivy Nash."

"As in Nash Saddlery?" The name, attached to eight retail stores across Texas, caught Cord's interest. Each store carried a wide variety of LaSorona Boots.

"That's us," Ivy said, with little enthusiasm for Cord or the conversation about her daddy's company.

"Cord works for LaSorona Boot Company," Brody went on to say, hoping to tease Ivy's money interests.

"Actually, I'm the president." Cord's eyes gave Ivy's curvy figure a long rake-over and he held out his hand. "Nice to meet you, ma'am."

Ivey's kitten smile returned. "Call me Ivy."

A slow country ballad with a sexy beat began oozing through the sound system.

Brody waited. Come on, Boot Boy. Ask her to dance.

"Ivy, would you like to dance?" Cord asked, ignoring Louisa and her open mouth.

Ivy giggled and took his arm. "I'd love to."

As Cord and Ivy disappeared among the dancing couples, Brody grinned. His plan had worked, and he had no doubts about Ivy keeping Boot Boy occupied for the rest of the celebration.

But before he could truly bask in the success of his plan, he felt a sharp stab in his ribs.

"Ouch," he said, turning around while rubbing his side.

Louisa narrowed her eyes speculatively. "You did that on purpose."

"Would you have danced with me if I'd cut in?"

Surprise arched eyebrows. "You did all that for a dance?"

"Maybe," he said, holding out his hand with a silent invitation.

This wasn't like the photoshoot. She didn't have to dance with him, and he wouldn't have been surprised if she'd twirled around on her boot heel and left him standing on the dance floor alone.

People would laugh and make puns at his expense. But he didn't care. He was used to the back-fence jokes about how he was sleeping with a woman who had piss and vinegar running through her veins.

What mattered to Brody was that he made some progress in his relationship with Louisa. She'd shared her middle name with him, smiled at him without contempt, held his arm, and walked down the aisle with him, and they'd talked without arguing. Dancing would be another step forward. He wanted to kiss her and hold her, make slow love to her and show her how special she was to him. But right now, there was nothing he wanted more than this dance.

He kept his outstretched hand steady as he waited for her to make up her mind. But his legs were quaking in his boots. His mouth was so dry that he thought he might choke on his own tongue. When she dropped her head and crossed one boot over the other, his heart tumbled to the floor. He knew that spin and walk-away was coming. But then her head lifted. Holding up that forefinger she'd used to gouge him in the ribs, she smiled shyly. "One dance, Brody."

As she placed her small hand in his and stepped into his arms, Brody's heart started to race. He placed his hand on her lower back and guided her closer. She leaned into him and surrendered to his lead. Slow dancing was about as close as two people could get without having sex. The motion of her body swaying back and forth with his was arousing. But the way her head tilted towards his chest was more satisfying than any orgasm he'd ever had. It was a subtle gesture that communicated trust and affection.

He rested his jaw against her head. Her hair was silky smooth against his face and held a trace of cherry blossoms and vanilla, a signature smell he only associated with

Louisa. Her breath was warm against his neck and Brody was in heaven. The suppleness of her feminine curves pressing against his body and the gentle sway of her hips were spellbinding.

Her hand had slowly made its way to the back of his collar. The way her fingers fidgeted with his hair gave him goosebumps.

"You totally blew my plans with Cord," she said, looking less perturbed than before.

Brody didn't want to talk, especially about Boot Boy. He wanted to enjoy the moment and her body against his. But he couldn't ignore that she did, so he tried focusing on what he should say.

Louisa was an energetic, unattached female in her late twenties. Sex was a driving force in her life, but was sex the only thing she wanted from a man? Cord was an executive, drove a fancy car, probably had a ritzy house or apartment somewhere in the city, and a bank account with lots of commas. "Plans for what? Sex?"

She scrunched her face. "I am not going to discuss my sex life with you."

"Please, don't," he answered, wishing he'd gone a different direction with the small talk. "I'm just asking if that's all you wanted from Boot Boy."

"Boot Boy?" she asked her expression, moving towards amusement.

He shrugged. "The name fits."

"But Cord isn't a boy," she pointed out.

The scowl he replied with made soft laughter spew from her throat. "You could do so much better, Louisa."

Her smile dwindled with a shake of her head and a somewhat exhausted sigh. "Not in this town."

Brody wanted to say that better was standing right in

front of her, holding her and waiting for her. But he stayed silent, keeping his thoughts to himself and his pride intact.

"Mom had to practically beg you to be my escort."

"She didn't beg me," he said, casually placing her hand on his jacket so he could rest both hands on her hips. "I was just waiting for the right time to offer my services."

"I bet you were." She rolled her eyes towards the ceiling. "Truth is, most of the men in Santa Camino are cowboys, and the ones who aren't, aren't exactly knocking down my door."

He was relieved to know that her door wasn't seeing any action from local men. But how many times had out of town men like Cord turned her knob? "Why do you think that is?"

His question flatlined the curve of her lips in such a dramatic way that he felt guilty. Dropping her eyes to his jacket, she started fidgeting with his lapel. "You tell me, Brody. You seem to have all the answers."

"Hardly. I just know that people think we're lovers, which is probably why men in this town don't approach you." He provocatively wiggled his eyebrows. "They think you're mine and vice versa."

"I know what they think about us. I've heard the gossip, but," she threw a nod in Ivy's direction, "Little Miss Saddle Shop didn't seem to care about the vice versa."

That was true enough and Brody suspected that not even a wedding band would detour Ivy's pursuits if she wanted a man badly enough. But he wasn't going to plant a thought like that in Louisa's mind, just in case their new friendship did lead to matrimony. So he offered another reason. "Ivy doesn't live in Santa Camino, so she probably doesn't know that we're lovers."

CHAPTER 12

Louisa had heard those wild claims about her and Brody being lovers a thousand times before. And for the most part, she was immune to them because until now, she'd only allowed her mind to tiptoe over the surface of that untruth. But locked in the very intimate embrace of a man who desired her opened the floodgate of her imagination.

The slow, arousing sway of their bodies brushing against one another in beat to the country song transported her to another place and time where she could have the man holding her, to an alternative universe where her mistakes didn't matter. Her mind drifted to his cabin. The sunset's golden light splayed across his nude chest, her legs locked around his narrow hips, her body absorbing his long, hard thrusts…

Do not go there.

Why hadn't she waited until after the wedding to try and build their friendship? Closing her eyes, she pulled in a shaky breath. The when and where of their new alliance didn't matter. When two people were attracted to each other, there was going to be friction. Delicious, enticing resistance. Her body tightened as the phantom impression of Brody's hard and naked physique slid over hers.

In a panic to separate her thoughts from the moment, she closed her eyes as her mind tossed out Cord. *Think about Cord. His face. His body.*

There could be so many pleasurable possibilities with the man if she wanted to take things further. But the thought of being skin to skin with Cord was like wrapping a cold, wet cloth around her body. She wanted to shrug out of it and run back to the warmth, back to the arms of the cowboy holding her.

Louisa wanted to grab hold of Brody's hand, cup it to her face, and savor the warmth of his touch while he soothed away her inhibitions with a kiss. How wonderful would it be to lay her head against his chest and let his heartbeat drown out the battle inside her head? She craved Brody with an unfamiliar hunger.

Dear God, what was happening to her?

You're falling in love, her heart explained sympathetically. *You've been falling for quite some time now.*

No, her stubbornness answered back. It was in charge and wouldn't let this attraction go any farther than friendship.

Right, her heart laughed. *Honey, you're foolin' yourself.*

Was she?

Had she somehow let herself fall for this cowboy?

Homing in on the words of the song, Louisa determined that the tune they'd started dancing to had ended and they were now slow dancing to a second song.

Blinking, she tried to make sense of the confusion buzzing around in her head and her body's position next to his. She moved her fingers and was surprised to feel the warm, sculpted muscles of Brody's back beneath their tips.

At what point during their slow dance had her hands found their way under his jacket? How had she let herself get so close to him?

Because this feels right. Wanting Brody feels right. Let this happen. Don't pull away. Don't mess this up. Tell him what happened with Chris. Tell him everything. If he really cares for you, he'll understand.

And if he doesn't?

"Hey, you." The softness of Brody's voice cut through her thoughts and floated over her with the sensuality of a lover, drawing her closer to the temptation of what could be.

She looked up at him.

Filled with longing and a tenderness she'd grown accustomed to, his eyes crinkled at the corners as he considered her. He raised a hand to her face and gently brushed a thumb along her jawbone. "Sweetheart, are you alright?"

There was nothing clever or fancy about the word sweetheart. But when Brody called her that... Emotion fisted tight around her vocal cords, choking a verbal response to his question. No, she was not okay. Nothing about the way this man made her feel was okay. She was falling hard for a man she could never have.

"W— we," she stammered and swallowed. "Aren't lovers, Brody."

Placing a hand on the back of her head, he kissed her forehead. "No one knows that better than me."

So why hadn't he gotten it through his thick skull that they never would be? *Maybe because he's falling in love with you too...*

No.

That was absurd and she was overreacting. They were co-workers. Friends. That's all. She just needed to get her mind off Brody and back on her plan. A plan that seemed fruitless now because Cord was dancing with Ivy.

And what about your feelings for him? Louisa ignored her heart's question. She could strut down the runway, wearing denial like it was the newest fashion trend and look damn good doing it.

Brody debated on whether or not he should shut up and enjoy what was left of their dance or try to lay everything out to Louisa like had Jess suggested. He prided himself on having patience, but he was damn tired of holding on. "About this cowboy rule of yours…"

"Don't, Brody," she whispered, looking a half a shade paler than when they'd started around the dance floor the first time. "I'm really not up for this."

Neither was he but having waited almost two years for a dance made him wonder how much longer he'd have to wait for a kiss and that love he wanted to make, so he continued. "You say all cowboys are womanizers and can't be trusted. But how can you think that when your dad and brothers are cowboys and are in faithful relationships with women they love? Your parents have been married for over thirty years. Do you think your dad has ever stepped out on your mom?"

She scowled at him. "Of course not. Dad would never cheat on Mom."

Having made his point, Brody felt like he'd earned the right to look smug. But they were in the middle of a crowded dance floor, having a heated discussion about a topic that could easily ignite and blow up in his face. "There you go," he said without haughtiness. "Proof that not all cowboys are philanderers."

"Okay, so," she answered with a slight roll of her jaw. "Maybe not all cowboys are womanizers. Some can be tamed and their tendency to roam cured. But…"

"But what?"

The song ended and soon there was noisy conversation chatter and laughter from the guests seated at the table filling the ballroom. The space around them quickly became a whirl of laughter and excitement as couples prepared for the next two-step.

"I agreed to one dance and you've had two," she said.

Brody wanted to lead her away from the crowd so they could talk without an audience. But he knew the moment he let go of her, she'd bolt the other way. So it was all or nothing. "I know a bruised heart when I see one, Louisa. You're afraid of what might happen if you give in to me, a cowboy you've labeled wild and undomesticated."

"I'm not afraid of anything," she said, through clenched teeth. "I'm just not interested in trying to tame another cowboy!"

And there it was. The first vague reference towards the cowboy who'd caused the damage. "Another one?"

She glared at him, that stubborn chin of hers welding her mouth shut.

"Who was he? What's his name?" he asked, though he already knew. "Tell me about the cowboy whose sins I'm paying for."

Her anger gave way to remorse and hurt. Wedging a hand between them, she shoved at his chest. "I'm not having this conversation with you. Not here. Not now. Not ever."

Why couldn't he find true north with this woman? She always kept his compass spinning and his course changing. One minute he was walking in a straight line with possibility and optimism lighting his path. Then in the blink of an eye, he was in complete darkness with the heaviness of rejection riding his back.

He'd hit a wall again and like every other time, her rejection made him want to drop to his knees and give up. Friendly conversation and dancing weren't going to change two years of denial or calm her fearful heart. Passive patience wasn't getting him anywhere. He needed to do something drastic.

Brody let his arms fall. "Then let's have another conversation."

"No." Louisa kicked her heel down, preparing for a spin and stomp from the dance floor.

But Brody halted her retreat by grabbing her arm. "Damn it, woman. Hear me out. I've been offered a job in Colorado."

He felt the fight leave her body. "What?"

Brody didn't have time to go into the details about Heather or Riley, so he said the first thing that popped into his mind. "Allison has offered me a full position at her ranch."

She searched his eyes. "So, you're leaving Texas?"

More guests had filtered into the ballroom. Tom McCallister, the local postmaster and his wife, Ruth, were standing close by. Several other couples also had their eyes and ears trained on him and Louisa. Did he want to do drastic now, in front of all these people?

Hell, yes. If this was their dreaded goodbye, Brody wasn't going to leave anything unsaid. Gawking eyes and gossiping whispers be damned. He answered as truthfully as he knew how. "That depends on you, Lou."

"Brody – I..." The smooth lines of her neck contracted with a quick swallow. "I don't know where you're going with this. But now isn't the time —"

"Yes, it is." Sliding his hand down to her wrist, he

gently pulled her to him. "You have to know how I feel about you. I'm in —"

"Don't do this," she interjected, softly. Holding back tears, her eyes pleaded with him to stop. "Please, Brody. Walk away and let me go."

Her stark request shook him. Couldn't she see that he couldn't do that? He could walk away from his friends, his job at the Rescue, and his ranch for a life in Colorado with his son, but he'd never to be able to let her go. Not like this. Not without her knowing how he felt about her.

"That's the bitch of it, sweetheart." He stroked her jaw with his thumb and felt her shudder beneath his touch. "I'm in too deep to just walk away because of some half-ass cowboy rule. I need a good reason to leave."

Licking her lips, she nodded. "Okay, then. I…"

He waited. "You what?"

"I, ah…" The frantic movements of her eyes mimicked a caged cat. "I'm… in love with another man."

Louisa's confession was Brody's greatest fear. "With Chris."

The mention of Chris's name whipped her eyes to a sharp focus. "What? No!"

He hadn't expected that harsh reaction, but her denial didn't help quell his need to know. "If it's not Chris, then who is it?"

As if cued by the question, Cord let out a laugh from across the room. Louisa glanced his way then quickly pulled her focus back to Brody.

Brody let out a scoffing laugh. "Don't tell me you're in love with Boot Boy."

She neither acknowledged nor denied her interest in Cord. Instead, red blotches had colored her cheeks as tears pooled and threatened to spill over her bottom lids. "Who told you about Chris?"

Realizing he hadn't accomplished a damn thing except make her cry, Brody knew he should have dropped the subject and walked away. But the cold determination in her eyes told him that Louisa wouldn't let him off that easily. She'd be hot on his heels, demanding he name his source. "Ah, hell," he sighed. "This town is too small for secrets, Lou."

"That's not an answer."

He didn't want to lie, but he also wasn't going to give her a reason to tear into the groom, so he went out on a logical limb. "Shorty dropped his name before I threatened to kick his ass."

Her willpower succumbed to tears and with a trembling bottom lip she let out a shallow curse.

Brody had never dug a grave, but right now, he felt like he was shoveling his way farther and farther into a hole he might never be able to climb out of. "Sweetheart," he whispered. "I didn't mean to hurt"

"Don't," she bit out, glaring as more tears flowed, "mistake these tears for hurt. Just say what you have to say and let's get this over with."

Brody had never been good with words and bringing Chris's name into the conversation had made matters worse. Pushing up the brim of his Stetson, he rubbed his forehead and tried a new approach. "I can throw a saddle on the meanest, most stubborn horses on the planet and ride them until they break. I just dig my spurs in and hang on. I'm that damn persistent when I want something."

She promptly skimmed a forefinger under her eyes and swiped her face with the back of her hand. "And just what is it you want, Brody?"

That was a complicated question and to answer it properly, he'd need more than a few seconds on a crowded dance floor. But the music had started, and more people were gathering around. Time wasn't on his side, so he had to muster the testicular fortitude to answer her right here in front of the whole damn town.

Any fool could see that this conversation was going to end badly. But he'd started it. And it didn't matter if it was now, when half the town was watching, tomorrow at church or Monday morning at work, the question of what it was he wanted had to be answered. "I want a beginning or an ending."

"To what?"

"To us, Louisa. Let's fuel the fire under those rumors about us being lovers and commit to pursuing that endeavor or…" He paused. "Or douse 'em out cold."

She struggled to swallow. "And just how do we do that?"

His heart did a nosedive. He'd been digging a hole, alright, and he'd just hit the bottom. This was it. The beginning of the end. There was nothing but rocky ground beneath his feet and there was no going back. No climbing out, walking away, or waiting.

He took her small hand and fashioned her fingers and thumb into a fist. "Hit me."

Aghast, her bottom jaw dropped.

"Rattle my teeth so hard there's not a doubt in any man's mind that we're over and done with."

"You want me to hit you?" she asked, incredulously.

"No," he said, praying this didn't go the way his gut was telling him it would go. "But if you do, men will start knocking on your door and you'll be rid of me."

Her eyes went wide. "You've gone loco."

He thought maybe he had lost his mind. What sane man would ask a woman to hit him?

A desperate one.

"One punch right in the kisser and I'm out of the

picture. Forever. I'll take the job in Colorado and you never have to see me again or," he said, knowing the words he was about to say could end it all, "give us that beginning. Give me a chance. Kiss me, here in front of the whole town, and let's really give them something to talk about."

CHAPTER 13

Louisa flung her bags into the cab of Violet's little 4x4 truck, climbed into the passenger's seat, and slammed the door.

"I can't believe you hit him," Violet said, piling into the driver's seat before starting the engine.

The adrenaline that had been racing through Louisa's body for the last half hour was wearing off, leaving her with a numb shock that made her nauseous. "Neither can I!"

Violet shifted the truck into reverse and backed out of the parking space. "What happened?"

Their dance had been so perfect until he'd blindsided her with Chris and the comment about bruised hearts. She dropped her head into her hands and covered her eyes. Was she that easy to read? "He's leaving, Vi."

"Oh, honey," Violet shifted gears. "He's already gone. I think he left right after you threw that punch."

"No," she cried, raising her head to stare out the bug-splattered windshield. "He's leaving Texas."

"What?"

Shaking her head frantically, Louisa searched the truck for something to blow her nose on. She found a small stash of Pixies napkins in the glovebox. "He's been offered a job in Colorado."

"No."

"Yes," Louisa said as a new wave of tears hit her. The disappointment and finality in Brody's eyes as he dropped his hands and walked out of the ballroom…God, she wanted to cry. Hard, loud, and without shame.

Violet guided the truck down Winery Road and stopped at the stop sign before turning left towards Louisa's place. "Is that why you hit him? Because he told you he was leaving?"

Brody had unraveled her. He'd taken her by the arms, looked into her eyes and seen the pieces Chris had left behind. Then he'd looked farther, past the hurt and fear and into the softest part of her heart. He'd saw that trusting and vulnerable part that was, in some ways, still nineteen, full of hope and steadfastly guarding the belief that love was worth all the chaos and pain it sometimes caused. And that no matter what happened, two people who were truly in love could overcome any obstacle.

"No," she hiccupped and blew her nose. "I mean, well, yes. But technically, no."

Violet looked confused. "Um, okay."

Brody hadn't sugarcoated a thing. He'd laid it all out on the line and been straightforward about his perceptions of her and her bruised heart. And he'd been right about all of them except one. "He said that…that, he," she rubbed the napkin over her nose again.

Through the rumble of the road and the vibration of the truck's motor, Louisa heard the softness of Brody's voice brush against her ear. *You know how I feel about you.*

The glimmer of warmth in his eyes as he'd said that

had taken her completely by surprise because, until that moment, Brody's feeling towards her had all been speculation by her mom and friends.

"Don't leave me hanging, Lou," Violet demanded. "What did Brody say?"

"I think he said," Louisa swallowed. "That he's, he's in..."

"In love with me," Violet filled in the rest of the sentence and made a motion with her hand to Louisa to continue. "Go on. You can say it."

"No!" she yelled. "Brody Vance is a – a womanizing, undomesticated, tomcat!"

Violet wrinkled her face in disagreement. "No, he's not and whether you choose to accept it or not, the man is in love with you."

Louisa could shoot holes in Brody's character and dust him off as just another cowboy, a roamer, and a player. But at some point, she had to be honest with herself and him about the man she knew he truly was, about why she'd shoved him into that general category of men she didn't date. It wasn't because he was a cowboy. As he'd said at the reception, her dad and brothers were cowboys and faithful to the women they loved.

The reality of why she wouldn't let Brody close was all too clear to her now. The possibility of a man genuinely caring for her, instead of using her and then dumping her after he had what he wanted, scared her. It also explained why that empty acreage inside her chest felt smaller when Brody was around.

"How?" she cried. "How is it possible that he's in love with me?"

"When you've gone out of your way to make him hate you?" Violet let out a laugh. "Beats the hell out of me, Lou, but he does. And there isn't a soul in this town or county that doesn't know it."

That unleashed more tears, prompting Louisa to grab another stack of napkins.

"Don't worry." Violet raised a hand to Louisa's shoulder and gave it a pat. "Everything will be fine after you've had a few glasses of wine."

No, it wouldn't. Alcohol wouldn't calm the chaos in her head, and it wouldn't lighten the heavy load of guilt riding her shoulders.

Sniffing, Louisa looked down at the gorgeous peony arrangement in her lap. She'd caught the bridal bouquet just before she and Violet slipped out the door. It had sailed over the heads of at least fifteen eligible women and straight into her hands.

Snagging it meant she was next in line to be married. Her? Married? That silly superstition was laughably ironic, especially now that she'd punched a man who might be in love with her. "What am I supposed to do with this damn thing?"

Violet gave the pink and white spray a leery once over. "I don't know but keep it away from me. We Gateses have a horrible track record with marriage."

There wasn't much Louisa could say to that. They all trod softly around the subject of Violet's parents. Thea and Emmett Gates's marriage and turbulent love story had all the elements of a riveting drama without a happy ending.

After they arrived at her trailer, Louisa changed into her favorite shorts and a short-sleeve t-shirt and opened a bottle of wine. The sun was dipping closer to the horizon and a breeze was now blowing through the trees.

As spring turned into summer and the weather warmed, the small gravel parking spot in front of her trailer doubled for a late evening dining space. Louisa had been so eager to enjoy her meal with the view that she'd purchased a propane heater to go along with her humble outdoor furnishings of a charcoal grill, two wooden Adirondack chairs and a matching table. A cozy fire pit was next on her list.

Violet helped herself to a beer and went outside. Lounging comfortably in one of the chairs, she held up the frosty bottle and explained it. "I'm driving. One beer is my limit."

Louisa wasn't driving anywhere, at least not until her truck was fixed, and she was off duty at the Rescue until Monday, so she snagged a finger around the neck of the wine bottle and grabbed a glass before she went out the door. Letting go of a long sigh, she plopped down in the chair beside Violet and drew her legs up.

"You've added a flower trellis," she observed.

The square metal frame she'd purchased at the local thrift store could be hardly be classified as a trellis, but she'd big aspirations of it sprucing the place up. Those aspirations were now lying in a scattered mess of dead rose petals around its base.

Violet squinted. "What's that scrawny green thing coming up out of the ground?"

"That's a rose, Vi."

"Oh," Violet kicked her boots off and hiked the hem of her bridesmaid dress to mid-hip. "Weddings are exhausting," she said, wincing at the bandage Louisa had applied to her knee. "Weeks of preparation and planning and hours of makeup and hair stylin' for thirty minutes of show." Gulping a long swig of beer, she draped one leg over the arm of the chair and relaxed.

"But they give us a chance to show off our pretty side," Louisa said, pouring herself half a glass of wine.

Violet snorted disagreeably before taking another gulp.

After Rhea finished taking the photos, Violet had shoved on her everyday dark-rimmed glasses and wigged her long hair into a ponytail. The combination made her look like a nerdy teenager, not a woman in her mid-twenties. She only wore her contacts on special occasions, sighting that they irritated her eyes and that vanity wasn't worth the trouble.

Her friend was beautiful, with striking features that intensified when she took the time to dust on a little makeup and unbraid her hair.

"You should wear contacts more often," Louisa told her. "They make you look sophisticated."

Violet made a snorting sound. "That'll come in handy next weekend."

On top of her guilt over punching Brody in the mouth, Louisa felt a sense of dread creep into her chest.

Violet hadn't had a wild bone in her body until a few years ago, when her older brothers, Logan and Tyler, started meddling in her newfound love life. Because they refused to see her as anything but an adolescent they needed to protect, she'd launched a full-blown rebellion.

Last month, she'd gone on an overnight getaway to a music concert in El Paso. When Logan heard she was sharing a room with Cody Peters — a hotheaded cowboy who turned rowdy when he drank — he'd driven to El Paso in the middle of the night and made a scene at the hotel where Violet was staying.

Things had been snowballing downhill ever since. Louisa worried that whatever was happening this weekend might be part of another insurrection. "Please tell me it doesn't involve Cody."

Violet made a grotesque gesture with her mouth. "God, no. Me and Cody were never a thing. Can you see me with a guy like that?"

No, she couldn't, but Violet wasn't acting like her normal self. "Well, whoever the guy is, please promise me that you'll use protection."

"Jesus," Violet swore under her breath. "You sound just like Logan."

Louisa knew how smothering and stubborn older brothers could be about protecting their baby sister. But she also knew how easy it was to trust a man with your heart and your body and then have him betray you. So she felt obligated to warn her friend. "I'm just worried about you doing something that might ruin your life."

"Like my mother?" Violet snapped.

Louisa felt like backtracking but couldn't. "You know I didn't mean —."

"I know," Violet cut in with a wearisome sigh. "Forget I said that. It's just, lately, that's all I've heard from Logan. How I'm going to ruin my life like she did." The affair between Clayton Durant and Thea Gates over twenty years ago had produced a son out of wedlock and caused a deep rift between the families. A fissure Logan sought to widen. "She's why he's so hard on Ty and me."

Being the oldest sibling, Logan had carried some tough responsibilities during his parents' marital problems and divorce. He'd sacrificed most of his teenage years and given up a football scholarship to stay at home and help Emmett keep the ranch running. He'd also handled most of Tyler and Violet's parental responsibilities after Thea left, which had made him resentful towards his mother and more like an overbearing father to Violet than an older brother.

The affair had been a weighty burden for Tyler, who'd spent most of his life having to choose between loyalty to the people he loved and the blood running through his veins.

"Clayton," Violet continued, staring down at the bottle in her hand, "has invited us to his house Saturday night. It's his birthday and he's having some sort of big bash to celebrate. The invitation was to the three of us, but Logan said he'd rather burn in hell than go. And he's forbidden Tyler and me from setting foot in the Durant house."

"So, the two of you are going to spite him." Louisa chuckled, feeling the wine slowly ink its way through her system.

"Damn straight," she answered while angrily fishing bobby pins from her hair. "I might even seduce the sheriff while I'm there. That'll really piss Logan off."

It wasn't the first time Louisa had heard Violet make a pun about seducing the sheriff. Finn Durant was a handsome bachelor and though most of the time he chose to wear jeans and a button-up shirt, he did look damn fine in a uniform. Half the women in Santa Camino had probably fantasied about handcuffing the man to their beds.

But the devious intent brewing in Violet's eyes as she hurled those pins across the drive made her comment seem less like a joke and more like a well-thought-out plan.

"Sleeping with Finn would only make things worse," Louisa said. Not that Finn would ever allow that to happen. He and Logan had belted it out more than once in high school and twice before Finn was elected sheriff. "Ty and Finn are at least civil to each other now, but Ty would feel obligated to take Logan's side if things escalated. He always does."

"I know." Groaning, Violet covered her eyes with a hand. "What am I going to do? My brothers are killing me!"

Violet was a financially independent woman who'd built a business from nothing. Before Pixies opened, no one in the small cattle town knew or cared about the difference between a Frappe and a Latte. Coffee was simply a staple, brewed strong and consumed black. But Violet, using her sweet personality and innocent smile, had pulled in customers and tempted the palate of some of the most diehard cowboy coffee drinkers into trying something new.

The shop itself had done more than introduce towns-folk to a diverse coffee selection. Pixies had brought people together in a daily routine and revitalized the downtown section of Santa Camino. That was quite an accomplishment not many people, including Logan, recognized.

"Just take a breath and try to think of something that won't make Logan want to strangle Finn." Louisa emptied her glass. "Speaking of brothers, I should probably text mine and apologize for making a scene at his wedding."

"Probably."

She started to reach for her phone but then stopped. "But if I do, he'll want details." Details she couldn't explain. At least, not yet.

Violet pointed her finger at her chest. "I want details."

Louisa needed time to process what had happened before she tried explaining to Jess why she'd hit Brody. But her thoughts were so scattered. Her mind was whirling with bits and pieces of the dance while her heart was teeming with pain.

"Everything was going good." She refilled her glass and settled back into her chair. "And then Brody started hounding me with questions about why I don't date cowboys —"

"None of us are clear on that one," Violet murmured under her breath.

"He gave me a choice, Vi, and I honestly don't know if I made the right one. It all happened so fast. I—I panicked and took the safest choice."

"Which was?"

She took a couple of fortifying sips before she spoke. "He said I could punch him, he'd take the job, and I'd never have to see him again or," another sip followed, "I could give us a beginning and kiss him."

Violet's face showed her shock. "And you chose the right hook?"

Louisa let her head fall against the back of the seat. "Punching him was the only thing I could do. Right?"

Lifting an eyebrow, Violet shrugged a shoulder. "You're the only one who can answer that, Lou."

"If I'd kissed him, he would have expected more."

"Yeah." Violet paused to let out a deep belch and set her empty bottle on the ground. "But are you sure you don't want more?"

In a little over a year, Brody had bought a ranch and remodeled a house and was preparing for a future Louisa couldn't possibly be a part of. "The man is picking out nursery colors and – and talking about teething babies," she said, forcing down more wine. "I— I'm not ready for that."

"Me neither, but that doesn't mean I wouldn't mind having a hard body like Brody Vance to roll over to every morning. Have you seen the size of his feet?"

Louisa rubbed her eyes, annoyed her friend was straying off target. "That's a myth. There is no scientific proof that there is a correlation between a man's shoe size and the size of his penis and, yes. Waking up to Brody would be... nice, but having that hard body next to you always comes with a price, Vi. Remember that."

"Is that your way of telling me I shouldn't elope with Finn?" Violet mocked, dully.

It was going to be a long time before her friend settled down. That was unless she found a man who loved her more than he feared her brothers. "No, that was my way of telling you to be cautious."

"Your concern is duly noted and now that I've had time to think about it," Violet pulled herself to her feet and grabbed her boots, her face assuming a studious expression, "you did the right thing. Punching Brody in the mouth was more humane than leading him along. You've been playing with that cowboy's heart long enough."

Louisa knew Violet was teasing her, but it wasn't the first time she'd been told that she should either cut Brody free or claim him. "Now you sound like my brothers."

Violet gave her a wiry smile over her shoulder as she walked to her truck. "Ty's home for a few days. I'll send him over in the morning to look at your truck."

Tyler worked as a mechanic on offshore oil rigs in the Gulf. When he wasn't at work, he was under the hood of one of the ranch trucks or repairing equipment. "Thank him in advance for me."

Violet opened her door and climbed inside the cab. "You want a ride to church in the morning?"

After what she'd done at the reception, she needed a good sermon, but like Jess, her parents would want details about what had happened between her and Brody. "Doc's on duty at the Rescue tomorrow, so I think I'll spend a quiet day at home."

"I see." Violet laughed. "You want to get your story straight before you face your folks."

She covered her eyes with her hand, dreading that conversation. "Yeah."

CHAPTER 14

BY NOON THE NEXT DAY, TYLER HAD RAISED THE HOOD OF Louisa's truck and was inspecting the motor with a mechanic's eye. "Try cranking it."

She slid the key and turned the ignition. The truck's headlights beamed to life, reflecting off the camper's shiny exterior, but the engine didn't crank. "The battery is only a couple of months old and it can't be dead if the headlights come on so, what's the problem?"

"Not sure," Tyler replied, disappearing to the bed of his truck.

She jumped out of the cab and crammed her hands into the back pockets of her jeans as he came back carrying a heavy-duty toolbox. Dents and scrapes covered the sides and top of its faded red surface, a clear indication to her that the old steel container had probably belonged to Emmett.

He planted the toolbox on the ground near her feet, opened the lid, and removed a small black computerized device with two cables extending from the bottom. Attached to the ends were a set of black and red clamps.

After attaching the clamps to the positive and negative battery terminals, he watched the digital gage.

"Sometimes a battery can have a bad cell." He unhooked the cables and returned the gadget to its place in the toolbox. "But the voltage is good."

"Told you," she murmured.

Tyler's mouth pulled to one side as he thought about the problem. "You say it was fine when you went into town yesterday morning?"

"Yeah. It just doesn't make any sense."

He agreed with a grunting, then twisted the dingy blue bill of his Durant Resources ball cap around before he sat on the ground and rolled under her truck.

Hunching down beside him, Louisa ducked her head so she could see him. The longer she waited, the more uneasy she became. Why couldn't she shake the feeling this was more than just a faulty part? "Find anything?"

"No. Everything looks — ah, wait a second."

Uneasiness tightened its hold. "What?"

Rolling out, he stood to his feet and dusted the dirt from his shoulders. "Your starter wire has been cut."

Alarm triggered inside her. First her tires, now her starter. No, no, no, she told herself, unwilling to panic without cause. *You just heard him wrong.* "You mean the wire rubbed against something and is worn in half?"

"No." Digging into his back pocket, he pulled out a rag and began wiping his hands. "I mean, it's sliced clean in half and if the truck was running when you drove it into town, then the only logical scenario is that someone crawled under the truck while it was sitting here."

A lump lodged itself in her throat. "You mean while I was inside my trailer?"

Tyler nodded grimly.

"No," she scoffed, trying to dismiss his explanation. "That's absurd. I would have seen them."

"Not necessarily. There are coyote tracks all over the ground." He pointed out different places on the ground, indicating the presence of coyotes. "Have you seen them?"

He did have a point, but this wasn't Shorty's style. Why go through the trouble of crawling under her truck to cut a wire when he could just as easily annoy her by slashing her tires as he had in the past?

Tyler tossed the greasy rag on top of the toolbox and pulled out his cell phone.

"What are you doing?"

He started punching in numbers. "Calling the sheriff's depart —"

"Don't you dare," she said, snatching the phone from his hand. "And under no circumstance are you allowed to say anything to my brothers or my dad about what you found."

He gave her a bemused frown. "Lou, your truck was intentionally disabled."

"So?"

He rested a hand on his hip and swung the other one towards the stretch of isolated pastureland. "You are miles away from help out here."

Fear ripped through her. "I have my phone."

"And what if this guy gets to you before you get to your phone?"

"He won't," she rushed to say.

Tyler rubbed his face with a groan. "You don't know that."

"Yes, I do." She laughed, trying to downplay the seriousness of the situation. "I know him and trust me, he's —"

"Don't," Tyler interjected while pointing a grease-stained finger at her, "underestimate Shorty Turner."

It shouldn't surprise her that Tyler knew about what had happened with Shorty. Like Brody had said, this town was too small for secrets. "We don't know Shorty did this."

"Do you have someone else in mind?" he asked, his eyes narrowing.

"No."

"Then you need to assume it was him. You cost him his job, shredded his pride, and nothing is off-limits for a lowlife like him if he wants revenge."

"I know." She gave in with a sigh as she handed him his phone. "But don't call Finn. I'll stop by his office in the morning before I go to work."

"And just how are you going to do that without a vehicle?"

She could call McCrea or her dad and ask to borrow one of the ranch trucks, but then they'd offer to fix her truck, so that wouldn't work. She could ask Violet for a ride, but then she'd want to know why she needed to stop by the sheriff's office. Groaning, Louisa rubbed her forehead. "I'll figure it out."

Tyler picked up the toolbox and headed towards his truck, motioning her to follow. "I'm not leaving you without a ride. If that asshole shows up, at least you'll have a way out of here. Get in. You can drop me off at the ranch."

"That's not necessary."

He ignored her answer. "Logan's going to Austin in the morning. He can drop me off here. I'll fix your truck, drive it to the Rescue, and pick mine up. It's a simple swap and no one has to know. But, damn it, you have to swear you'll let Finn know what's going on."

"I will."

~

Louisa had intended on keeping her promise to Tyler, but an emergency had happened at the clinic.

"It wasn't like I had a choice," she said, looking up from her desk as McCrea sat in the chair across from her.

"I know." He pressed four fingers against one eye and rubbed the socket, his face reflecting the loss they both felt. "I just wish there had been something else we could have done."

She'd wished that all morning. But some things were out of her control. "The horse was suffering. There wasn't anything anyone, including Doc Tolbert, could have done to save her."

McCrea's head came up. "I do not doubt your skills, Lou, nor am I blaming you. I know you did everything you could to save Blue Bayou."

Growing up, her brothers had been pains in her backside and her rivals at everything. Riding and racing horses, fixing fences, swimming, fishing…Whatever they could do, she'd wanted to do better and often had. As the three of them grew older, her competitiveness towards them waned and then vanished completely. She no longer felt like she needed to earn her place with them.

But when she lost a patient, she took it personally.

Knowing McCrea was grieving for an animal he'd nicknamed and grown to love had Louisa near tears. She'd already cried buckets of them this morning after she'd administered the lethal injection.

The roan mare had tangled in a roll of rusty barbed wire and suffered a severe laceration to her left foreleg before McCrea and Brody had rescued her. Louisa had disinfected and stitched the wound and given her antibiotics, but the horse had been slowly going downhill since her rescue two weeks ago.

"Go home," she told him. "Have a good cry and let El hold you."

McCrea lifted his bloodshot eyes to hers. "Who's going to hold you?"

She grabbed a pile of reports and started stacking them into neat piles. "I don't need holding. This is a part of my job and I have plenty of other patients who need me."

"Have you seen him?"

Louisa knew without asking that her brother referred to Brody. But she decided to play dumb. Maybe McCrea would take the hint and change the subject.

She reached for another stack. "Who?"

"You damn well know who," he said, giving his eyes another hard scrub. "The man you punched in the mouth at our brother's wedding reception. Remember him? The big guy who has a soft spot for children, horses, and stubborn women?"

McCrea didn't need to remind her of what had happened at the reception. She hadn't been able to eat or sleep because of what she'd done to Brody and his soft spot.

Yesterday, he'd made an excuse not to go fishing with her dad and this morning, thanks to the emergency with Blue Bayou, she'd gotten here hours before anyone usually arrived for work. "No, I haven't seen him. But I'm sure he's around somewhere."

Physically, she hadn't hurt him at all. Under different circumstances, he would have thrown back his head with a big laugh and dismissed her little jab like it was a bothersome gust of wind. But emotionally, she'd made him bleed. She'd never struck another human being in her life. And the fact that her first blow had been to a man who sincerely cared about her made her want to throw up.

She spun her office chair around and stood, needing to do something other than sit in her office and do paperwork until it was time to make rounds when a movement through the window caught her eye.

It was Brody slowly making his way down the porch steps of the cabin. With a gray travel mug in his hand and his head hung low, he headed towards the clinic.

Rattle my teeth so hard there's not a doubt in any man's mind that we're over and done with…They'll start knocking your door down…

Louisa didn't want men knocking down her door. She wanted things to be the way they used to be between her and Brody. Cautious, limited, predictable…Friendly.

I'm out of the picture. Forever. I'll take the job in Colorado and you never have to see me again…

That was the part that haunted her the most. Now that she'd rattled Brody's teeth, was he going to leave the Rescue?

"You're not going to tell me what happened, are you?"

Telling McCrea that she'd hit Brody so she wouldn't have to kiss him would only deepen the plot and spur more questions. Her brother was an intelligent, well-educated man with plenty of common sense. But he wasn't exactly emotionally sensitive.

"Did you know about Colorado?" she asked.

"Colorado?" McCrea coughed and sat up straighter in the chair. "Ah—yeah. I know about Colorado."

"And…?"

His mouth opened and closed like the words were being pumped up his throat. "And what?"

"How do you feel about it?"

"I...don't...know," he said, cautiously narrowing his eyes at her. "How do you feel about it?"

Her feelings had nothing to do with this. This was a business decision. He could use money to sweeten the deal and encourage Brody to stay. That was, assuming an increased income was the reason he was taking the job. "You're the boss. Offer him more money."

A crease fashioned between her brother's dark eyes. "More money?"

She heard the electric chime on the front door ping from Brody's entrance into the clinic.

"Morning, Brody," Kara greeted him.

"Morning." His return was friendly and easy.

Usually, after he collected his mail, he headed towards the stables to check on the horses. But Louisa knew once Kara told him about Blue Bayou, he'd be knocking on her door. What had happened at the reception wouldn't affect Brody's professionalism.

"He's a vital member of the rescue team," she pointed out, lowering her voice to a whisper. "And the best horse trainer this side of the Mississippi. If he takes this job in Colorado, we'll never be able to replace him."

"Job?" McCrea blinked and scrubbed a hand over his forehead, smoothing away the shallow lines of confusion. "Oh, right. The job. No, *we* can't afford to lose him."

Brody's footsteps grew closer, stirring anxiety in Louisa's chest. When he appeared in the doorway, her heart did that same old trip and fall. From the looks of it, he hadn't shaved since the morning of the wedding. His five o'clock shadow had thickened, covering his jaw with a full beard. It was a new look for Brody that fit him well. It enhanced the strong, masculine structure of his handsome face.

Louisa had been so absorbed by the change in Brody

that she'd lost all sense of time and space until she met his stormy blue gaze. "What happened to her?"

She laid the stack of papers back on the desk and planted her butt in her office chair. "Patty called me at three this morning and said she'd taken a turn for the worst. When I got here, the infection in Blue's leg had spread. She was struggling for every breath and in pain. I did the only humane thing I could."

Propping a forearm against the door frame, he shifted his weight to one hip and bit out a shallow curse.

McCrea removed his hat and tossed it onto her desk. "I don't like finding a ghost horse, and three in less than a month ain't a coincidence."

Ghost horses were what they called horses that appeared out of nowhere with no traceable owner. They were usually stolen animals that had escaped transport while on their way to a slaughterhouse.

They'd found Blue Bayou out by Darby Center's ranch. The other two horses had been found a few miles down the road. No one suspected Darby of foul play. But horses didn't just show up in the middle of nowhere.

CHAPTER 15

Thanks to the combined efforts of the Rescue, local law enforcement, and the county humane society, the number of equine abuse cases in Gilmore County had dropped considerably over the last four years.

Louisa picked up an ink pen from her desk and ran her fingers along the smooth contours of the cylinder shape, her thoughts going back to the year Brody had come on board the Rescue team.

It had been a rough time for McCrea. He'd gone through a difficult divorce and suspected that one of his ex-wife's lovers, a man named Tony Chaves, was stealing antiquities from an archeological dig at the old Vera la Luz Mission.

While rescuing a pregnant mare from the Twisted J, he'd found pottery artifacts that connected Tony to an illegal horse operation. The ranch was secluded and had been abandoned for years before Brody bought it, making it the ideal place for illegal activity.

"So, what do you think is going on out there at Darby's

place? Another slaughterhouse operation?" she asked McCrea. "Finn never apprehended the people responsible for what happened at the Twisted J. It could be the same people transporting horses across Darby's land."

"I don't know. Maybe," McCrea said, looking skeptical as he massaged the back of his neck. "The Twisted J is closer to the main highway. Darby's place is on the other side of the county, and it's a good five miles away from a blacktop road."

"It was before the county built the bypass," Louisa said.

McCrea frowned. "True."

"There's nothing out there," Brody said, supporting McCrea's point. "No barns or buildings."

"But there is." She pointed the pen at her brother. "Remember that old abandoned homeplace on the other side of Pinyon Ridge? We went out there once when we were kids."

McCrea thought back, his eyes shifting from the floor to her. "You're right. Granddad took us with him to look at some antique ranching equipment. I'd forgotten about that."

"It's isolated just like the Twisted J was," she added. "It'd be the perfect place to hide horses."

Kara joined Brody in the doorway with a piece of paper in her hand. "Darby just called. He's seen the bay again. I don't know why he felt coordinates were necessary."

"Darby's retired military," McCrea answered.

Her hands went palm up. "Anyway, he said he saw it out towards the west ridge early this morning."

Brody took the paper, hard lines of determination settling into his face. "I'm going out there and this time, I'm not coming back without that horse."

The first time they'd visited Darby's place, the old rancher had spotted the horse near one of the barns, so they'd kept their search close to the house and a nearby field. But by the time they'd arrived, the horse had vanished. The ranch covered thousands of acres, and they hadn't had a clue which way it had gone until now.

McCrea came to his feet. "I'll pack my gear."

"No," Brody objected, easing his body into a full stance as he prepared to leave. "With Jess gone, one of us needs to be here."

Fear enveloped Louisa. "You can't go out there alone. If this is what we think it is, you could be walking into a dangerous situation."

"I'll park the trailer at Darby's and leave a copy of the coordinates with Kara." Again, Brody ignored her and spoke directly to McCrea. "I won't be gone longer than a couple of days. If I don't come back, you'll know where to look."

Panic brought Louisa up from her seat. "Know where to look? For what? Your body?"

Brody turned without answering and headed back to Kara's desk.

Louisa fully acknowledged that after that punch at the reception, she deserved to be ignored. But she had to make him see that this was too dangerous for one man to go at alone. It didn't take her long to catch up with him. "What if there's nothing left of you to find?"

He handed Kara the coordinates and waited for her to write them down. "I know how to take care of myself."

"No heroics," McCrea ordered. "If you find the horse running loose, rope it and bring it back. Do not try to free it if you find it penned."

Kara handed the paper back to him, her eyes apprehensive. "Let me call the sheriff. I'm sure he'd be more than happy to send one of his deputies out with you."

"Finn's shorthanded as it is," McCrea said, looking a little worried himself.

Brody scissored the paper between two fingers and twisted the corner of his mouth up. "I'll be fine, Kara."

That half-smile revealed a tiny cut on his bottom lip. Louisa's heart sank. Had her punch done that?

"Cell phone service is hit and miss out there, so take the satellite phone." McCrea held up two fingers. "You have two days. If I haven't heard from you by noon on Wednesday, the whole town will be out at Darby's place looking for you. Understand?"

Nodding, Brody pushed his back against the glass door and exited the offices.

Louisa hurried down the hall and back to hers for her portable vet pack. She switched off the light and shut the door behind her.

McCrea blocked her way up the hall. "Where are you going?"

He was bigger and stronger than she. All he had to do was wrap his arms around her and she'd be trapped. But eventually, her brother would have to let go and when he did, there'd be hell to pay.

"You can't stop me from walking out that door." She dodged right, then left, but he blocked her every move. "Don't make me call El."

"My wife will agree with me," he said, unmoved by her threat. "This isn't an average rescue, Lou."

"Which is why he can't go out there alone," she said, stepping around him.

"Pinto," he said softly, reaching out to gently catch her arm. "Stop."

The endearing way he spoke her childhood nickname made her pause. "What?"

"I don't know what's going on between the two of you, but now isn't the time to hash out differences."

Differences? This wasn't about what had happened on that dance floor. This was about life and death. Seeing Brody walk out that door, knowing there was a possibility that he might be injured or worse, not come back at all, was tearing her heart in two.

"I'm a veterinarian. I have medical training that can save lives, his life if necessary." She looped her arms around his neck because she knew her brother was only trying to keep her safe. "Don't worry about me."

He hugged her tight, making her feel safe and loved like he had when they were kids. "Be careful, Pinto. Don't do anything stupid."

She was riding into the backcountry to spend two nights alone with Brody. She was miles past stupid.

≈

BRODY PACKED HIS SUPPLIES, LOADED HIS HORSES AND PACK mule into the horse trailer, and was on his way to Darby's by lunch.

He'd had every intention of walking into the clinic this morning like it was an ordinary workday and take whatever backlash Louisa threw at him. But he knew the second his eyes met hers that she regretted what had happened at the reception just as much as he did. What he didn't know was what to do about it. Or which part she regretted. The punch or the choice?

His mind was running in a hundred different directions. Riley, Allison, her job offer at the True Line… Louisa. He wasn't happy about going into the backcountry by himself to hunt for a horse that might be running from thieves. But he needed to put some distance between himself and all the chaos in his mind. And he needed to find that bay before it was too late.

Because of the wedding, he'd missed his weekend with Riley. He called every day to check on him, but yesterday Flint Early, one of the True Line's ranch hands, had answered the house phone. He informed Brody that Allison had taken Riley on a church outing and Flint hadn't expected them home until later in the evening.

As McCrea said, he probably wouldn't have cell service out at Darby's, and Allison wouldn't recognize the satellite phone's number. If she didn't hear from him, she'd be calling the Rescue. He didn't want Louisa answering that call and he didn't want to worry his sister by not checking in.

There was also a slim possibility that something might happen to him, and he would never see his son again. That thought was enough to make him pull his truck over to the side of the road and take out his phone. He hit Allison's number, put the phone on speaker, and opened his photos.

Three rings and she answered. "Hey! How was the wedding?"

"It was – ah, good."

Allison knew him too well to let that slight hesitation in his reply pass. "What did Louisa do?"

Brody winced. He should have never told his sister about Louisa. "Nothing, she was…nice."

"Oh," she said, sounding surprised. "Then why do you seem so down?"

Scrolling through the photos he'd taken of Riley when he was a newborn made tears burn his eyes. Now nearly two years old, his son was full of words and curiosity. Some words were clear while others were a jumble of sounds that had to be deciphered. Last month, he'd surprised Brody by popping out the word Daddy.

Brody's chest tightened. Hearing that sweet little voice could brighten the darkest day and right now, he needed a little sunshine. "I'm going on a rescue and probably won't have cell reception for a few days. I wanted to talk to Riley before I left."

"He's taking a nap, but I'll wake him."

"No, don't," he tried laughing to soften the disappointment. "Don't do that. He's cranky when he doesn't get his nap in."

"Are you sure?"

"Yeah, let him sleep." He closed the photos and wiped his eyes. "Tell him his daddy loves him."

"I always do." Allison's voice was full of concern. "Brody, is everything alright?"

"Everything is fine, Allie. I'll call you when I get back."

Brody hung up, shifted the truck into drive, and after checking his side mirror, guided the truck back onto the road.

When he'd gotten the call from Heather saying that she'd gotten pregnant during their one-night stand, Brody's world had flipped upside-down. Those long months when she didn't call, he'd nearly worried himself to death thinking about her and his unborn son's welfare.

After Riley arrived, he'd learn how to work while worrying, and he'd learned how to deal with missing his son. He pushed through the heartache and focused on the job he had to do. Brody was pushing now, but he wasn't making much headway.

He turned off the main road and followed the five-mile gravel road to Darby's place. He parked in the shade of a juniper tree and slid out, making sure he had the satellite phone and his slicker before reaching to the back for his rifle.

As he headed towards the horse trailer, he saw a gnarled finger hook around one of the yellow, sunbaked curtains hanging over a dingy window. A second or two later, the front door opened, and Darby's unmistakable form filled the shadow. A dingy gray pinch-front hat, a bushy ocher- colored beard, thin ribs, and bowlegs that resembled a wishbone clad in dirty jeans.

By Brody's estimation, the man was near seventy. He'd never married and the only children he had were the bedraggled Australian cattle dog he called Fred and a horse that looked to be as old as Darby.

Darby let the screen door slam shut, nearly clipping Fred's tail as he trotted out the door behind him. He stopped at the edge of the porch and bit into the half of a sliced sandwich, chewing slowly like a cow enjoying the first taste of spring grass. "You alone?"

Brody opened the trailer door. "Yeah, I'm alone."

Now was not the time for brooding reflection or an in-depth analysis of how accurate the old man's words were. His impatience had destroyed one of the best chances he'd had at building intimacy with a woman he was in love with, and his son was in another state.

"You say you saw the bay on the west ridge this morn-ing?" he asked Darby.

"That's right." He pointed to the camera with a high-powered lens and an aged topical map sitting on a three-legged table by a foldout camping chair. "I saw it clear as day."

"I'm guessing there's a water source out that way."

"A creek that runs about twenty feet away from the base of the ridge. You can't miss it." Darby peeled back the brim of his hat and squinted as he looked up at the sun. "It rained last night, so there should be plenty of tracks baked into the ground."

"Have you noticed anything suspicious going on out towards Pinyon Ridge?"

Darby shook his head. "I don't ride out that far anymore. Shrapnel in my hip won't let me sit long in the saddle."

From the looks of the land, house, barns, and fences, the shrapnel stopped old Darby from doing more than just sitting in a saddle. It had been years since cattle and cowhands had roamed the countryside of the old rancher's land.

"It's just as well," Brody said, backing Stella out of the trailer. "It could be dangerous. Those horses didn't get out there by themselves."

Darby gave a thought-filled scratch to his left sideburn. "Never thought I'd be thankful for shrapnel."

Grinning, Brody turned his attention back to the horses. Stella was a beautiful seven-year-old black Quarter Horse born for riding. He'd brought her from the True Line after he'd decided to settle in Santa Camino.

Milkshake was a buckskin Quarter Horse. The gelding had been turned over to the Rescue by his owners a few years ago. Because of his resigned and tolerant temperament, the horse had been placed into the equine therapy program. His sensible behavior and quiet reserve made him easy to load and loyal to the road horse which is why Brody sometimes brought him along for rescues such as this.

Darby shoved the last bite of his sandwich into his mouth and dusted the crumbs from his beard. "Where's that sassy vet you had with you the other day?"

"She doesn't like my company," he said, going back into the trailer to get his saddle from the rack.

Darby walked closer, frowning curiously at Brody's mouth. "She the one who split your lip?"

"Yep."

"What'd you do?" The old man's face crinkled mischievously. "Try stealing a kiss?"

"Something like that," he returned, dryly.

CHAPTER 16

B<small>RODY HAD THE SADDLE ON</small> S<small>TELLA AND WAS ABOUT TO</small> cinch it up when he heard spinning tires and flying gravel. Looking over the horse's back, he saw Louisa's truck and horse trailer barreling up Darby's driveway. "Shit."

When she rolled to a stop in front of them, Darby coughed and swatted a hand through the air to clear the dust. "Looks like she's changed her mind."

Brody intended to stop her before her feet could touch the ground. But she was already at the back of the trailer by the time he made it to her truck.

She'd traded the teal-colored scrubs she'd had on this morning for her everyday ranch wear and was clothed in a pair of comfortable jeans that were faded thin at the knees, well-worn boots, and a breathable, light yellow top with a long-sleeved overshirt. It took every ounce of Brody's willpower not to stare. The practical riding attire was just as flattering to her figure as that form-hugging dress she'd worn at the wedding.

She'd braided her hair, secured it with a plain brown band, and shaded her head with a cream-colored straw

Stetson. Dusty from the last time she'd worn it and bent in places along the brim, it wasn't anything fancy. But damn, it was sexy on her. "What the hell do you think you're doing?"

"My job," she answered, lifting the latch.

He planted a hand against the door. "Get back in your truck and go home, Lou."

Sensing the tension, Clyde, her Palomino gelding, let out a high-pitched whinny inside the trailer.

She lifted her chin and shot Brody a determined glare. "No." After shoving his hand to the side, she lifted the latch and swung the door open.

Clyde backed out of the trailer without any help from her, veered around, and let out a big snort in Brody's direction.

Brody wasn't in the mood to entertain Louisa's stubbornness or be bullied by her horse. He took a firm hold on Clyde's halter. "This rescue is too dangerous."

She held her ground. "It's been over a week since Darby first called in the report about the bay. If the horse is out there, it could be gravely injured. The sooner I can get to it, the better its chances are at survival. Please, Brody."

He'd never heard Louisa plead for anything and until this moment, he hadn't been sure that the word please was even in the woman's vocabulary.

Over the last few days, Brody had spent a lot of time trying to figure out what to do next. Turn in his resignation and leave Texas or tell her he was sorry and ask to start over. Having her riding beside him for the next two days would help him make up his mind, but at what cost?

Right now, they were talking to each other. If he left town, he wanted it to be on amicable terms. But he was already sexually frustrated to the point of chewing nails.

Louisa bathing in streams and sleeping alongside would make him an irritable bastard. She'd think he was angry at her and retaliate. He didn't want to spend what time he had left in Texas arguing with her.

End of story. Tell her no.

But…what if he didn't leave town? What if he apologized and she wanted to start over?

She doesn't and you're a fool for thinking she will.

Louisa had made her choice with that punch. He should stick to his word and walk away. But he couldn't stop thinking about the remorse in her eyes this morning. What if there was a slim chance that she didn't want him to leave. What if she wanted to start over? What if she wanted that kiss? That beginning?

She'll be bathing in streams and sleeping beside you.

The lower half of his body responded, hardening with a painful erection. Frustration stepped back and in walked desire. Big, bold, and vivid in his imagination. In his mind, he saw gorgeous, cream-colored breasts floating in pools of cool, clear water. Damp hair, firelight, cries of pleasure. Her soft body climaxing tightly around his…

Clyde jerked his head up and whinnied as if to say, *Snap out of it, cowboy.*

Brody scrubbed a hand over his face, knowing he couldn't base his decision to let her go on desire. This was a serious situation.

"Brody," Louisa cut in, her voice soft as a caress. "I don't want to euthanize another horse. Please, let me ride with you."

Louisa didn't need to tag along with him. She wasn't a tenderfoot when it came to surviving in backcountry. She'd grown up camping and horseback riding with her dad and brothers through some of the toughest terrains in Texas. If he told her no, she'd ride out on her own. And she wouldn't stop with finding that bay. She'd do whatever it took to rescue it even if it meant laying her life on the line to do so.

"Goddamn it," he growled, thinking he'd done more cursing over the last few days than he had in a year. "What I say goes. No debates. No arguments. The first time you refuse to do what I tell you to do, your ass will go home. Got it?"

She nodded, then eased his grip from Clyde's halter. "I got it."

After Stella was saddled and ready, Brody secured the canvas panniers to Milkshake and began loading provisions. He planned on packing light, taking only the basic supplies he needed for the two-day trail ride.

From the looks of her bags, Louisa had done the same. But she hadn't bothered with a pack animal. He found it hard to believe that everything she needed was in those light-weight bags strapped to the back of her saddle and across the horn.

If she was counting on him for shelter and a hot meal, she was out of luck. Bringing along luxuries like a tent and stove would only slow him down and add extra weight to the horses. Cooking would have to be done over the campfire, which most of the time required a skillet or pan unless she caught herself a varmint and skewered it on a stick.

"Let's get going." Brody hooked his boot in the stirrup and swung his leg over Stella's back. "I want to make it to the west ridge before we lose the light."

She mounted Clyde with polished smoothness and situated her hat so that it shaded her eyes. She wasn't a dolled-up model sitting on the back of a horse. Skillful and in control, Louisa was the real deal. A true horsewoman if he'd ever seen one. A down-home, fresh-faced, original beauty with grit and intelligence.

His body grew harder.

Damn, it was going to be a long trip.

Nudging Stella, Brody set a course westward.

Fred jumped from the porch and ran to catch up with them.

"Don't worry," Darby yelled, throwing up a hand. "He knows his way home."

~

LOUISA AND BRODY STOPPED A COUPLE OF TIMES TO LET the horses rest, but they hadn't dragged their feet. They'd planned to make camp tonight near the west ridge and head towards Pinyon Ridge at sunrise to look for the bay.

As the crow flew, the ridge wasn't more than a mile or two away. But on horseback, it was a day's ride. Navigating through dense thickets and around rusty barbed wire fences so the animals wouldn't be injured was tedious and time-consuming.

The morning had been chilly, so she'd welcomed the warmth of its rays as the sun rose higher in the sky. But after a few hours riding, she'd shed her overshirt.

The forecast was calling for clear skies through tonight, but tomorrow, more storms were expected to roll into the area. She'd been in such a hurry to catch up with Brody, she hadn't remembered to pack her slicker, so if it did rain, she'd have to find shelter. Maybe she'd get lucky and they'd find the bay before then.

As they led their horses down a small incline, Louisa saw a clump of bright yellow buttercups growing near a decaying cedar stump. Nitrogen-rich showers had boosted buds, loosened soil, and brought an array of vibrant colors to the countryside. Spring had been a showy season this year, announcing its arrival with a radiantly painted landscape.

Bluebonnets had dotted the roadside and the redbud trees outside her parents' house had burgeoned with dark magenta blooms.

Pulling her gaze away from the countryside, Louisa turned her attention to Brody. His body moved in an easy rhythm with the horse. Tall, broad, and self-confident, the man set a horse like a sovereign king. The thin cotton material of his pale blue t-shirt had become translucent from perspiration, clinging to every ripple and muscle along his broad shoulders.

In her freshman year of college, she'd gone with a group of friends to see a male strip show. That hadn't been nearly as satisfying or stimulating as watching Brody's hips rock back and forth in that saddle. And not one of those oily, bronze beefcakes had shoulders that made her fingertips tingle with temptation.

She couldn't believe he'd given in so easily about letting her come along. Holding tight to Clyde's halter, he'd been deep in thought, scowling and looking like he wanted to gnaw through leather, then suddenly, his eyes had changed to that seducing metallic blue.

He hadn't said more than a handful of words to her the whole trip, and she didn't expect that would change when they made camp. It would be a lonely night. But at some point, she had to tell him she was sorry. She dreaded that conversation and the outcome.

Shifting for a more comfortable spot in the saddle, she let out a frustrated sigh and swatted at one of the bothersome insects that had kept her company for most of the ride.

They rode through a clearing and followed the trail to what had once been a dense grove of pines. Many of the trees had been uprooted by past storms and lay scattered on the ground like a box of spilled matches.

Brody stopped his horse near one of the fallen trees and folded his arms over the saddle horn as he surveyed the haphazard obstacle course. Panting from the trip and heat, Fred planted his bushy behind on the ground and waited for instructions.

Louisa brought Clyde to a halt beside Brody. "If the rest of the trail is like this, we're going to need more than two days to make it to Pinyon Ridge."

"Maybe," he said, his tone flat and his eyes fixed on the trail in front of them.

He'd dismissed her previous attempts at conversation by answering her with a grunt, shrug, or nod, and then he'd nudged his horse to a gallop and ridden a few hundred feet ahead of her to form a distance between them. She'd given up and accepted that most of their trip would be spent with the catastrophe of her right hook and her decision to end it all wedged between them. "Brody, we need to talk about what happened."

He turned his head and looked at her. His eyes were shaded by a pair of polarized sunglasses he wore when fishing, making it hard for her to read them. But if the hard grind of his jaw was any indication of his mood, she was better off enduring the silence.

He raised, shifted in the saddle, and turned his attention back to the trail. "Pay attention. Those broken branches are sharp. If your horse goes down, you could sustain serious injuries." He ordered his horse forward with a soft click of his tongue and waded into the tangled mess of fallen pines.

Fred leaped to life. Hopping over and sometimes crawling under the debris, the dog quickly and efficiently navigated the trail. They made it through without incident and picked up the pace when the trail cleared. It would be dark soon and they needed to set up camp before sunset.

Louisa longed to stretch her legs and find a place to wash away some of the sweat and dirt she'd collected from the trail. But she wasn't going to make a big deal out of needing a bath. She'd go exploring and find a stream after they made camp.

It was nearing five when they rounded the last bend, and the west ridge slowly appeared a few hundred yards in front of them. They guided the horses to a clearing and the sound of flowing water caught Louisa's attention. "Is that a stream?"

Brody shifted his weight back and stopped Stella with a "Whoa," then dismounted. "Darby said there was one nearby."

"Hallelujah," she mumbled under her breath.

Leading the horses to a grove of oaks near the ridge's base, he nodded towards the stream. "The sun will be behind the ridge soon. If you want to wash up, do it now. You don't need to be roaming after dark, especially by the creek."

Biting her tongue to keep from saying this wasn't her first rodeo, she swung her leg over Clyde's back and dismounted.

"Put your bags on those rocks," he said, unpacking the panniers attached to Milkshake. "I'll tend to the horses before I set up camp."

"I can take care of my horse and pull my weight in camp." She unfastened her saddlebags and hauled them to the rocks. "We'll need firewood."

He removed the sunglasses and hooked them in the neck of his shirt. "If you want to gather firewood, do it on your way back from the creek."

"But I —"

"I said, no arguing."

She wanted to tell him to go straight to hell and find her own campsite. There was plenty of room out here and it wouldn't be the first time she'd camped alone.

But something about the way he was standing with his arms crossed, daring her to say another word about that firewood, made her extremely happy. Because this standoff reminded her of how things used to be before she'd punched him, before she'd known he had feelings for her. Fun and flirty and teeming with possibilities of what might be if she'd just let Brody closer.

Those days were over and there was no going back. There were only the present and the future. The now was this standoff — Brody guarding the wounds she'd inflicted with hooded eyes and a solemn and indifferent stare.

If she went off to find another campsite, she might not get another chance to say she was sorry. He might take that job in Colorado and she might never see him again.

Her mind jumped to the future, one without Brody in it. There'd be no more watching him from her office window, no more homemade chili for lunch, no more corny jokes or pick-up lines, and a missing plate around her parent's dinner table.

She couldn't let that happen. "Fine, if you want to do all the work," she forced a nonchalant smile. "Have at it."

Over the years, she'd accumulated all sorts of nifty gadgets and lightweight camping gear. She'd also learned how to organize her things so that they fit compactly into a backpack.

Looping a hand through her water-resistant bag containing her clothes and travel-sized soap and shampoo, she unrolled her sleeping bag and snatched her towel from the middle.

She tossed the towel over her shoulder and set a path for the stream.

"Take Fred with you," he said, his voice usually coarse and low. "He'll help keep the snakes away and alert you if there's trouble."

At the mention of his name, the dog's ears perked to attention. She reached down and gave his head a scratch as she passed. "Come on, boy."

The west ridge was one of the highest elevations on the property. From a distance, it appeared to be nothing more than a small rise along the horizon. But up close, its mammoth rock layers towered above the tall oaks and junipers at its base. Strata of solid limestone and soft clay, along with time and erosion, had fashioned jutting cliff faces and a stairstep design.

When she camped by herself and knew it was safe and there wasn't a chance that someone might see her, she sometimes indulged in skinny-dipping. But the distance from the stream to the campsite was probably less than a hundred feet. Taking a glance over her shoulder, Louisa could see Brody well enough to know that the scowl he'd had on his face for most of the day was still there. And if she could see him, he could see her.

There'd be no skinny dipping on this outing.

Shin oaks were scattered along the rocky floor's hard surface and a large one grew near the creek. Multitrunked and hearty, the trees formed thickets and gave Louisa privacy to change into the bikini she'd brought along for bathing.

Leaving her clothes on a branch, she ventured towards the creek. The stream flowed steadily, gliding over rocks and roots of the trees that grew along its banks. Water trickled over the cliffs, carving a fretwork of fissures into the limestone. It dripped from the overhang and pooled in a shallow dip near the base of the rock.

Like the cliffs above, water and time had carved a path into the rocky creek bed, leaving behind small ledges and a deeper pool that was perfect for bathing. There was a complex system of underwater aquifers beneath Hill Country's surface that sometimes supplied rivers and streams. This stream was probably being fed by one of those sources.

A low growl from Fred brought her attention around and to the shin oaks from where they'd just come. He growled again, backing it up with a couple of sharp barks that spooked a rabbit out of the brush.

She saw Brody raise his head and take a step towards them. "It's a rabbit," she yelled. "Nothing to worry about."

He threw up a hand, indicating he'd heard her, and went back to unpacking supplies. She set her shampoo and soap on the bank and dipped her toes beneath the water. After being filtered through rock, the water was crystal clear, inviting, and ice cold.

Her eyes followed the stream to where it curved around the ridge and sunlight warmed the water. It was nearly fifty yards away, give or take a yard or two. Navigating there in the dusky dark would be tricky, but the water would be warmer. She hesitated, then decided to endure the frigid water. Going downstream was a direct violation of the orders Brody had given her.

Biting her bottom lip, she stepped one foot into the water and then the other. She ventured further in, stepping down a few inches at a time until she was waist-deep in the pool. The secluded bath spot was a treat. But she wouldn't indulge herself by soaking. The sun was slipping closer to the horizon, and she needed to gather firewood on her way back to camp.

Brody probably wanted a bath too, and she would bet her entire savings account that he hadn't brought swimming trunks.

She grabbed her shampoo and began lathering her head, trying to block out the mental picture of Brody bathing naked in the cool, dark pools of the west ridge.

CHAPTER 17

AFTER THE FIRE CAUGHT, BRODY TOOK A SEAT ON THE rock next to their supplies, dropped his hat onto his bag, and lay back to look up at the stars. They were just faint specs of light in the phase of twilight, glittering across a blue-gray backdrop. Only when the sun was fully hidden beneath the horizon would they burst forth and twinkle.

That pulled a smile to his lips. "Twinkle, Twinkle, Little Star" was one of Riley's favorite lullabies. Last summer, the two of them had spent a lot of time on Allison's back deck, looking up at the stars as Brody sang him to sleep.

He folded his hands under his head and shifted his boots into a more comfortable position. He could be in Colorado right now, rocking his son to sleep. But instead, he was here, in Texas, under a sky that seemed as empty as he did, chasing horses and dreams of a future that that was slipping farther and farther from his grasp.

What the hell was wrong with him?

"Your turn."

Louisa's voice pierced through the heaviness of Brody's thoughts, tempting him to move his eyes from the sky to her. But he remained steadfast in the promise he'd made to himself when she disappeared behind that cluster of shin oaks.

He wouldn't look at her. He'd keep his eyes to himself and not let impatience or desire get the best of him. Sitting up, he shifted lower on the rock and planted his boots on the ground.

Fred barked and launched his body into a shake to rid his fur of creek water. The dog was at least two shades lighter, so he'd either fallen in or Louisa had bathed him. Fred happily trotted over to where Brody sat and shook again, pelting him with droplets of water that carried the smell of Louisa's cherry blossom shampoo.

Yeah. She'd bathed the damn dog.

She dumped an armload of small branches near the fire pit he'd constructed and hunched down to warm her hands. "I swear that stream has ice cubes floating in it. But it feels good to wash away all that trail dirt."

It was probably best if he skipped the stream and went straight to bed. But he wasn't sleepy. Tired to the bone, but not sleepy. And even if he did go to bed, he couldn't sleep, not when she was wide awake and rattling around camp freshly washed from her bath.

Fighting thirst and desire, Brody dug a bottle of water from the cooler he'd packed and twisted the cap free. He lifted it to his lips, ready to chug down half as Louisa rose from the fire and walked over to the rock where he was.

He kept his eyes locked on the fire but knew she'd placed something on the rock next to him. "You can use my soap and shampoo. They're both all-natural and safe for the environment."

Her voice was softer now and lacked its usual take-charge tone. Maybe she was tired from the ride, or maybe she was just as aroused as he was.

Brody had been born with an acute sense of smell. Like a man sampling fine wine, he turned his head towards Louisa and drew in a deep breath through his nostrils. Through the mask of cherry blossoms and fresh creek water, he smelled the uniqueness and essence of desire.

Lust clawed at him and tightened the ache in his body. Staring at that flame was getting him nowhere because, in his mind, he was already making love to her.

He couldn't resist looking at her any longer. His eyes moved from the fire to her feet. Delicate, small, and protected by flip-flops. Beautifully shaped ankles, elongated calves, flawlessly sculpted knees, and thighs.

"Brody?" The sound of his name echoed through the air, faintly penetrating his ears. His gaze jumped from her thighs to her shoulders. Bare and with a hint of dampness clinging to them, they tempted his thirsty tongue.

Strings from a bikini he knew was skimpy disappeared beneath the large beach towel she had wrapped around her. The wet cloth molded to the curve of her breasts like a second skin. Gorgeous, palm-filling breasts with pert nipples perfect for teasing, sucking, and nibbling.

The desire pounding through his body intensified. The sound of his heart hammering away in his ears was nearly deafening.

"Brody?"

His brain finally kicked in, prompting his stare to her flushed face. He didn't care that he'd been caught staring at her breasts. She knew he wanted her. Why try and hide it?

He managed to grunt out the word, "Yeah?"

The smoothness of her neck contracted under the strain of a gulp. "Ah—um." She tried to recover from his open appreciation of her body by fashioning a semi-pleasant smile. "Do you?"

Focus, damn it. "Do I what?"

"Want to share my stew?" She'd unpacked a small, lightweight, alcohol-burning stove and a deep-walled stainless-steel travel cup. Everything she needed to prepare her meal had been neatly packed inside the cup she was now using for a pot.

She tore open the packet, dumped the contents into the boiling water, and tried to pretend everything was normal. "It's dehydrated but delicious."

What he wanted to share with her wasn't stew, and he could guarantee that it was damn tastier than dried beef. He lifted the bottle to his lips and killed the contents. Crushing it in his hand, he tossed it back into the cooler and headed towards the stream. "I'm not hungry."

Halfway there, he heard her yell, "Are we going to talk about what happened at the reception, or are you going to stay mad at me forever?"

There was a slight pause in his steps that nearly turned him around. She wanted to talk, and he needed her to understand that he wasn't angry at her for what had happened. But first, he needed to find that stream and take an ice-cold bath.

~

BRODY HAD GONE OFF ANGRY WITHOUT A CHANGE OF CLEAN clothes or a towel. Maybe that's why he was taking so long to come back to camp.

He was air drying.

"Oh, wow," Louisa whispered, licking the ooey-gooey goodness of the toasted marshmallow from her fingertips. That was an image she didn't need in her mind right now.

Brody wasn't the first man she'd caught staring at her breasts. Santa Camino was swarming with cowboys and roughnecks that were prone to ogling, especially when they'd been out driving and working the herds for days or confined to an offshore oil rig for weeks at a time.

Some of those men cleaned up nicely, splashed on a dash of cologne, and managed to say a few words before they started undressing women with their eyes. But others, like Shorty, skipped the bath and went straight for the eyeballing and propositioning. Dirty, smelly men covered in layers of sweat, dirt, and manure…

She fought back a gag.

Having Brody's eyes on her didn't feel like the vulgar gawking of a filthy man. It felt more like a tasteful appreciation, a longing to touch and to please. And oh, what pleasing he could do. Those lips, those hands… that body. It would be sex in its most powerful and raw form. An involuntary shiver curled up her spine, splintering desire and anticipation through her core.

She'd had plenty of time to think about what she might have done differently with the kiss-me-or-I'm-gone situation. She wouldn't have panicked, punched him, or run.

But would she have kissed him?

That question had been running circles in her mind. Right now, all she had were fantasies and notions of intimacy with Brody. If that kiss happened, she'd have a first-hand account. There'd be no way to remove the taste or feel of him from her lips. Sunday dinner at her parents' house would be… different, and intertwining physical intimacy with work would be mentally draining and inevitably lead to disaster.

She reached for another marshmallow to impale. The crackle of the plastic bag rousted Fred's attention. He sat up, alert, and focused on white fluffy confection at the end of her stick.

Brody must have given the dog orders to stay behind

because soon after he disappeared into the darkness, Fred had returned and hadn't left her side. Those big brown eyes of his were trained on the marshmallow, silently begging for a bite.

Although they weren't toxic to dogs, marshmallows had a high sugar content which made them a bad treat. Fred had eaten her leftover stew, so she knew he wasn't hungry. But those eyes…

"You little beggar," she chuckled and tore off a tiny portion of the unroasted treat for him. He devoured the bite and swiped his tongue over his mouth, expecting more. "No. Go and lie down."

Obediently but disappointingly, the dog took a spot near her sleeping bag, lay down, and closed its eyes.

She skewered her fluffy victim onto the end of the stick and held it over the flame. She'd honed her technique for roasting the perfect marshmallow when she was a little girl.

Slow and steady turns over the flame will heat it to just the right temperature without burning it. It was weird that she could remember something her dad had said twenty years ago, word for word, but she couldn't remember the password for her mobile banking app.

Those memories — nights around a campfire, roasting marshmallows, telling ghost stories, and laughing with her family and friends — were something she thought about often. They were some of the happiest times of her life. When she hit her teens, those moments became fewer and farther between. She developed a drive, a need to excel and achieve. Camping and family activities had been pushed aside as sports and academics took over her life. High school had passed in the blink of an eye with her burying her head in books to keep her GPA at a 4.0.

She'd dated, gone to parties and school functions, but

she hadn't been all about falling in love or having a boyfriend for the novelty of it.

In those days, she'd been so driven, so determined, that there hadn't been much that could distract her from accomplishing her goals, and finding Mr. Right hadn't been on her list of priorities. But then she'd met Chris, a smooth-talking, dyed-in-the-wool cowboy who was a little down on his luck.

Sable hair, dark complexion, and eyes that were the color of the ocean. God, she'd been so infatuated with him and hung on every word that rolled off his tongue. She'd been so naive back then and believed every lie he told her, especially the one about how much he loved her.

Chris had been her first lover and it had taken her a long time to get back into dating after the affair ended. Nearly two years passed before she could look at a man without getting nauseous.

Then she'd met Paul, a fellow veterinary student from Oklahoma. They'd had so much in common and had quickly become friends. His parents were ranchers and he'd spent his whole life working cattle. He'd been a quick-witted man with a warm smile and good looks who'd bought her a cup of coffee after class. She spent the first few months of their friendship dissecting him, weighing the pros and cons, overthinking the what if's and wondering if he had a wedding band hidden in his pocket.

Paul had asked her out three times before she said yes. Their first kiss hadn't kindled anything but sexual desire. Her stomach hadn't done summersaults or tied itself into knots. They'd dated on and off for a few months before they slept together. Paul had been a safe way to combat her loneliness. She'd been content with the mediocre sex, but sex alone couldn't hold a relationship together. When he started pushing for more than shallow, physical fulfillment, she'd known she had to end it.

A month after Brody had arrived at the Rescue, she and Paul had gone their separate ways as friends. The last she heard, he was back in Oklahoma and engaged to be married sometime next year.

After classes started, she only saw Brody when she came home on weekends to see her folks. That alone had made her leery. A handsome horse trainer with a sexy smile that she only saw on weekends, dishing out all the right words…

It was like Chris had walked back into her life.

Their short affair had ended six years ago, but the lessons she learned from it would always be with her, throwing guilt in her face and reminding her that love couldn't be trusted.

The marshmallow began to sizzle and caught fire. "Crap." She extinguished the flame with a few quick blows then carefully pulled it from the stick. The paper-thin shell cracked, and hot mallow oozed onto her fingers. "Ouch!"

Fred's eyes popped open and up he came on all fours, watching and waiting for her to give him the word that it was okay to eat the marshmallow.

"You might as well."

While Fred took care of the marshmallow, she reloaded her stick and went back to thinking. Making amends to Brody was only the first step. He deserved to know why she wouldn't give them that beginning, and most of all, he needed to know that there was every possibility that she might let herself fall in love with him if not for the cruel reality of her situation.

She'd lay it all out and be completely honest about everything. She owed Brody that. And after he knew the truth, he might consider staying on at the Rescue because he'd finally see that she wasn't the woman he needed.

But how could she face Brody after he knew the truth about her? With that question looming in her mind, Louisa removed the marshmallow from the stick, gave it a couple of blows, and shoved it into her mouth as Brody appeared in her peripheral vision.

CHAPTER 18

SHIRTLESS AND BAREFOOT WITH HIS FLY UNZIPPED AND HIS jeans riding low around his waist, Brody strode past Louisa, dropped his boots next to the fire, and began rummaged through his bags. The ridged muscles of his back flexed bronze in the glow of the firelight as he stretched his arms through a clean t-shirt and whipped it over his head.

Her suspicions had been right. He had air-dried. There wasn't a single drop of water on his naked torso.

She swallowed, struggling to get the marshmallow down her throat before she choked. With a pair of clean jeans in his hands, he moved behind the rock to change. His silence added to the tense moment of her knowing that his sexy ass was bare and just a few feet from where she was sitting.

When his jeans were up, he walked back to the rock where their supplies were, untied his sleeping bag, and rolled it out beside the fire.

So, he's going to go to bed without saying a word? This is the way it's going to be between us? Long workdays of silence, taciturn brooding, and decrypting facial expressions?

Brody positioned his saddle at one end of the sleeping bag and sat down, relaxing against it with a tired sigh. Minutes passed; the silence felt like a towering wall between them.

Finally, she'd had enough. Holding the bag with the last marshmallow in it, she stood, walked over to where he was sitting, and held it out to him. "There's one left."

He shook his head no.

"You haven't eaten all day, Brody." She snagged her food bag from the rock and started digging. "If you don't want the marshmallow, I have jerky, protein bars and —"

"I'm not mad at you," he said, looking up at her. "But I am furious with myself."

Caught up in the softness of his eyes and the gentle tone of his confession, Louisa crossed her legs and eased to the ground in front of him. "For what? I punched you."

"I told you too." He drew one leg up and rested his elbow on his knee. Curling his knuckles against his lips, he nervously brushed his thumb over his bearded jaw. "I pushed you to do something you didn't want to do. I'm sorry."

Brody was a rough and tough cowboy. She'd seen him get bucked off a horse, tossed into the air, bounce several times when he landed, and come up smiling. But there was another side to this cowboy that made guilt slam into her. The side that held her while she cried and spoke softly to babies. "I'm the one who should apologize. What I did was inexcusable. I punched you and I did it in front of all those people. You must have been mortified."

His bashful grin was unexpected and so sexy. "I might have blushed for a second or two, but I'm hardly scarred for life."

Above his beard line, his cheekbones darkened with a ruddy color. She'd never seen him blush before. It would be interesting to find out how far that shade of red covered his body when he was embarrassed.

"I guess a tough guy like you has had his share of punches."

"More than my share," he admitted, his grin extending to a wide, roughish smile. "I was a rowdy teenager."

Louisa tried imagining Brody as that boy, an unruly teenager, slick-faced, tall, and more lanky than muscular. She wondered if he looked like his dad, Jameson, or his mom...what was her name? She thought, trying hard to recall if Brody had ever mentioned his mother. He hadn't, at least not to her.

The animosity in his voice when he spoke about his dad was another piece of his life she didn't know about. Most teenagers went through a rebellious stage. She had and so had McCrea and Jess. But her parents had been steadfast and patient, guiding them through it with love.

What had those years been like for Brody?

There was so much she didn't know about him, and it wasn't because he'd tried hiding things from her. It was because she wouldn't let him close. She'd had so many chances to know him better and hadn't. And now, he might be leaving because of her. "Are you going to take that job in Colorado?"

He rolled to one hip, shifted his weight onto an elbow, and reached into the bag for the marshmallow. "I feel like we've had this conversation before."

She winced. "We did, with most of the town watching."

He popped the marshmallow in his mouth with a quick lift and fall of his eyebrows. "I wanted to do it over dinner but..."

She thought about the possible outcomes if only she'd had dinner with him. In Augustine, there was a theatre that played old black and white movies on Thursday nights and a quaint little restaurant a few blocks down. Maybe they'd have taken in a movie or gone for a walk through the town park. They might have even held hands and have shared that kiss by now.

But she'd never know how the date would have gone because instead of making a rational, levelheaded decision, she'd bolted like a scared pony. She'd behaved childishly because she was afraid to tell him the truth. "I've made fools out of us."

"Maybe," Swallowing a single marshmallow shouldn't have been hard. But Brody looked like he was choking down an elephant. "You made a choice, and you shouldn't feel bad about it."

"But I do," she said, not able to let him retake the blame. Leaning closer, she ran her thumb over the split on his bottom lip. "Things were getting... intense between us, so I thought if I pretended to be interested in Cord, you'd lose interest in me. It was juvenile, I know, but −"

"I wouldn't take no for an answer," he finished, rolling over onto his back to stare up at the stars.

"You are persistent," she agreed.

He laced his fingers together and placed his hands behind his head. "Damn persistent when I want something."

"And you want me," she whispered.

"In every way a man wants a woman."

The raspy pitch of his matter-of-fact confession vibrated through her, settled in her stomach and stirred those same cravings she'd had while they danced.

"An affair?"

He frowned, offended by the question. "Do you think I

would have invested two years of my life here with you, bought a ranch, and poured my blood, sweat, and tears into it if all I wanted was a woman in my bed?"

His question rousted the sting of tears to her eyes. Brody was saying that the last two years of his life had been an investment in her. "You make it sound like every choice you've made since you came to Santa Camino has been because of me."

"Not every choice," he admitted, shifting his head to a more comfortable angle. "But my feelings for you have played a part in the decisions I've made."

How did she tell him that his feelings towards her, whatever they were, were futile? That he'd spent the last two years investing in something that would never happen? How did she tell him those things without causing more damage? "I wanted to kiss you more than anything, Brody."

"Then why didn't you?"

"Because you were right," she confessed, skimming the surface of the real reason. "I am scared of letting you get too close, so when you asked me to choose, I panicked, and I took the easiest way out. I'm sorry. This whole mess is my fault."

Brody lay staring up at the sky for the longest time before he said anything. "We could spend all night tossing blame back and forth. But that won't get us anywhere."

That "anywhere" was the beginning he wanted, and this conversation wasn't going to get them there either. But at least, he was talking to her.

He rose back to his elbow. "How about we forget everything after I asked you to dance."

There was an optimistic look in his eyes when he'd said that as if forgetting everything after that point would magically make their problems disappear.

Life was not that simple. Relationships were not that simple, and neither was his request. Memories had been made, scored across her heart and soul like the grooves of those old forty-five records her grandma used to listen to. So, even if she could snap her fingers and make their dance disappear, she wouldn't.

The magnetic pull of Brody's eyes, the strong but gentle grip of his hand holding hers, the heat of his body radiating through her clothes, the sway of his hips in tune with the music, the sensual way their eyes connected as they moved around the dance floor… It had been one of the single most moving events of her life and a memory she would hold on to forever.

He reached for her hand, lifted it to his lips, and grazed a kiss over her knuckles, the soft abrasion of his mustache sending goosebumps over her skin. "Can we pretend like we've just met? Wipe the slate clean and start over?"

Start over?

This was Brody, the sweet yet sexy cowboy that she'd been avoiding for two long years. The man with big hands, big boots, and big everything in between. A man she knew without a doubt cared for her, possibly even loved her. She wanted to jump into his arms and say yes.

But starting over would come with a price, not only for her but also for him. "Brody —"

"I know he hurt you," he cut in. "But you can't let what that man did stand in the way of your happiness."

It was on the tip of her tongue to agree and let him think that a broken heart was the only thing keeping her from moving on with her life. But the fact that Chris had hurt her was only one part of the truth. He'd stolen something precious from her, something she'd never get back."

That other part, the one that had shattered her dreams of becoming a mother, was the one she couldn't seem to find the words for. "I, ah, I don't want to forget our first dance."

"You don't?"

"No. In fact, I don't want to forget anything that's happened between us over the last two years." Reaching up, she stroked his beard. "I punched you because I thought ending this thing between you and me was what I wanted, but now I'm not sure."

Shifting his weight from his elbow to his hand, Brody sat up, alert and attentive as Fred had been about that golden treat at the end of her stick. "What are you saying, Lou?"

Oh, those eyes, her heart cried, knowing that if she backtracked and told him the truth, this would be the last time they'd look at her with longing. Once Brody heard the truth, those gorgeous eyes would only pity her. Pain sliced through her. She couldn't bear that. At least, not yet. She needed to hang on to him just a little while longer. Easing closer, she dropped her hand to his chest. "Is it too late for that kiss?"

Even in the dimness of the night with only the fire for light, she could see his eyes change. Dark with desire, the reaction caused a pull in the pit of her stomach that spread lower to form an incredibly delicious ache. "No, ma'am."

BRODY DIDN'T KNOW WHAT HAD MADE LOUISA CHANGE HER mind about the kiss and right now, he didn't care. She was giving a starving man permission to feast, and he was going to gorge himself on those beautiful pink lips of hers.

He shifted around, stretched his legs out in front of him, and reached for her. Palming her head with both hands, he drew her lips to his.

There was no caution, no technique or easing into a moment he'd been waiting nearly two years for. He kissed her the way he had in his dreams, shamelessly and eagerly. The warm sweetness of her mouth intensified his craving to explore other parts of her body. The beautifully mauve parts hidden beneath that thin layer of her bikini bottoms, those lips would taste like honey…

That vision of him pleasing her unabashedly and loving her completely spiked desire through his body. A low, guttural sound gushed from his throat.

Arching closer, she pushed him back until he lay against the saddle. His hands moved to her hips. They were curvy and soft, but he craved to feel her bare skin. She'd traded the beach towel for a long t-shirt that was just long enough to cover her bikini-clad bottom. When he'd walked into camp and saw her sitting by the fire in it, it had added to the temptation. Now, it was a hindrance he wanted to discard quickly.

Moving his hands lower, he found the hem of the t-shirt. Groaning when his fingertips contacted bare skin, he gripped her thighs. The soft whimpering sound she made tightened every muscle in his body and pitched the low-burning fever inside of him to simmering.

God, he wanted her. Here, now, completely. And he was sure she wanted the same. Tonight didn't have to be like one of his dreams where he woke up with a painful hard-on and sweat-soaked sheets. She was responsive in a way he couldn't have imagined.

He could take her right here on this sleeping bag and satisfy them both. His body needed that release, but his heart needed more. Making love to her now might ruin their chances of anything beyond sex.

With that in mind, he pulled his lips from hers. "Louisa?" he whispered.

"Yes?" she answered breathlessly while kissing her way down his neck.

Resisting the urge to reconsider and let her lips go where they wanted, he caught her jaw and drew her head up. "You sure all you want is a kiss?"

Reality plowed through her desire-filled eyes. Still lying intimately against his, her body tightened with a shudder as her head lowered to his chest. Gathering her senses, she pulled away and drew her knees up. She let out a shaky breath. "That was…"

"A long time coming," he supplied, feeling as unraveled as she looked.

She impishly raked her two front teeth over her slightly swollen bottom lip. "Maybe I did the right thing by punching you at the reception."

"Maybe," he agreed, knowing the humor would help ease the aching tension they were feeling. "Imagine doing that with a couple of hundred people watching."

It wouldn't have mattered where they'd been or the size of their audience. That kiss would have been the same. For Brody, it had been phenomenal and ground-breaking. He wasn't sure what it had been for Louisa. Sensual and exciting, he knew that by her body's response. But what was going on in her mind? Her heart? And what had the kiss meant in terms of choices and direction?

Brody stood to his feet. "There's no pressure for me to take the job. It's there whenever I want it."

She let out a small sigh of relief. "That's good to know."

"But I won't wait forever, Lou."

"I don't expect you to."

"I promised Jess I wouldn't decide until he and Mallory came back from Paris. I'll give you that same promise."

After shoving his boots on, he grabbed the flashlight from his bag.

"Where are you going?"

He slid the rifle from the scabbard on his saddle and grabbed his hat. "For a walk. I saw fresh horse tracks down by the creek."

He used the horse tracks as an excuse to leave camp because his body was primed and pumping from their kiss.

"It's too dark to see anything even with the flashlight." She sounded as alarmed as she had yesterday in her office when he said he would find the bay. "There were all sorts of predators roaming around at night. Wait until morning and we can go together."

He rested the barrel of the rifle across his shoulder. "The tracks went towards the clearing, so there'll be plenty of moonlight, and you're safer here with Fred." The dog rose to his front feet, ready to follow, but Brody ordered him to stay. "I won't be gone long. Get some sleep."

CHAPTER 19

THE FACT THAT LOUISA HAD SEEMED RELIEVED ABOUT THE timeframe of Allison's job offer was as encouraging to Brody as them sharing their middle names.

That kiss had been a step in the right direction. But there was a good chance she might turn and run after she had time to think. If she did, there was nothing he could do except pack his bags and take the job at the True Line. There was no backing out now. He'd set his course in stone. Louisa or Colorado.

As he reached the water's edge, he tried concentrating on the bay and the tracks he'd seen earlier. He'd had a sick feeling in the pit of his stomach since he'd spotted them on his way back from bathing. If his gut was right and something was going on at Pinyon Ridge, odds were there'd be more than one man guarding the place. He could do some reconnaissance work, slip closer to the homestead without being seen, and assess the threat. He could even ride and get back up if he saw the bay in captivity. He could do those things.

But once Louisa got her eyes on that horse, there'd be no going for help. She'd be hell-bent for leather.

He might be going into a fight armed with a single rifle, a dog too old to bite through paper, and a woman he'd give his life to protect.

Why had he let her come on this rescue?

He walked along the creek bank until he came to the clearing where he'd first seen the tracks. A clear sky and a nearly full moon washed the landscape cerulean. The contrast of light and dark made locating the tracks easy. He followed them a couple of hundred yards downstream. Judging by the unhurried pace of the animal's steps, it had been foraging for food along the bank. But then the placing of the tracks changed to quick and panicky. Something or someone had spooked the horse, forcing it to bolt into the creek.

He jumped down to the flat creek stones lining the edge of the water and made his way over to where a large pine had fallen across the creek. Hopefully, the soft wood would hold his weight until he made it to the other side. Placing the end of the small flashlight between his teeth, he grabbed hold of a large limb and hoisted himself up. He gained his balance, took four quick strides across the trunk, and landed safe and dry on the other side. There, the horse tracks vanished on the rocky surface of the ridge floor. Tracking the bay was over for tonight. But at least now he knew which direction the horse was going.

In the light of the moon, Pinyon Ridge cast an ominous forewarning over Brody. At daylight, they'd head out and try to make it there by noon. If they didn't find the bay or proof of illegal activity, he'd call McCrea on the satellite phone and report that they'd be home, safe and sound, Wednesday morning.

His gut churned, relaying the message to his brain that

he might not be making that call. He'd been in enough combat situations during his tours overseas to know when something wasn't right, and this whole ghost horse situation had a bad vibe to it.

He crossed back to the other side of the creek. But instead of going towards camp, he continued farther downstream, searching for more clues about what had spooked the horse.

Twenty feet or so past the fallen pine, a portion of the creek bank had washed away, leaving a shallow pool with a patch of sunbaked mud around it.

He didn't see anything out of the ordinary at first, but then his eyes caught what looked to be the faint indentation of a shoe print. The thick grass growing along the bank prevented it from sinking into the mud. But if there was one, there were others.

Brody flashed his light towards the outer rim and spotted another print. He bent to get a better look at what looked to be the left foot of cowboy boot. By his estimation, a size ten, maybe an eleven. The average shoe size for men.

Santa Camino was a small town and strangers usually stuck out like a sore thumb. He thought back to his trips into town this past week — no unfamiliar trucks on Main Street or outside Nash's or the feed store. The only strangers he'd seen were the ones at Jess and Mallory's wedding.

He moved the light down and looked for the right print. He found it near the edge of the water, encased in thick mud. Stamped in the center of the heel cap was the name LaSorona.

Brody's mind automatically went to Cord Watts. The clean-cut, soft-handed man Louisa had been dancing with at the reception.

"Boot Boy," he mumbled.

He pulled his phone from his back pocket and snapped a shot of each print. The uneasiness in his gut tightened when he saw that the boot tracks didn't end at the creek the way the bay's had. Instead, they ventured right and made a wide sweep back towards camp. They stopped near the cluster of shin oaks Louisa had changed behind.

Anger enveloped Brody. The son of a bitch had been watching her. Knowing the guy could still be lurking around, his hand tightened on the stock of the rifle as his eyes scanned the area.

He listened for the sound of rustling bushes or footsteps. But there was nothing. No movement and no sounds other than the night creatures.

He should have asked Finn for a deputy. At least then, Louisa would have had an escort back to Darby's.

Brody kept the flames of the fire in view. He wasn't going to let her get out of his sight again. But he didn't want to go back to camp until he was sure she was asleep. He found a comfortable spot near the shin oaks and sat down. Resting against one of the trunks, he tried sorting out the facts.

The sheriff's department had never found the person responsible for the horse trafficking at the Twisted J. Everyone, including Finn, knew that Tony Chaves wasn't the mastermind of the operation. He'd been a fall guy. Given the Twisted J's proximity to the main highway, they'd all assumed the ringleader had escaped and was long gone.

But maybe the culprit was closer than anyone thought. Maybe he hadn't left town at all, or maybe he was living close by. Maybe he was a local or had ties to Santa Camino. Maybe he knew Louisa.

Maybe it was good old-fashioned jealousy riding his back, or maybe Cord was involved in something more than selling boots. He could handle the jealousy and the thieving if that were the case. What he couldn't handle was someone stalking Louisa.

He asked himself the question he knew Finn would ask. Why would someone like Cord Watts be out here in the middle of nowhere chasing a ghost horse? The fact was those prints could have been made by anyone and there was nothing to connect it to Boot Boy.

LaSorona was a big company with a large distribution base. There were probably dozens of ranches in this part of the county with hired hands that wore LaSorona boots and most of the cowboys at the wedding had LaSorona leather on their feet.

But something about Cord didn't sit right with Brody. He couldn't get Hardin and that phone call the day of the wedding out of his mind.

Hardin didn't keep secrets, especially from his family, but he'd detoured around answering questions about the phone call to Jess and McCrea. Brody didn't believe for one second that Hardin was knowingly involved in anything illegal, and Hardin hadn't referenced horses or anything that might link the conversation to horse thieves.

But he had mentioned Louisa to the person on the other end of the phone. Hardin had asked about the man's wife and son. Had Hardin been talking to Cord?

Damn. Was Cord Watts married? Did Louisa know?

Brody rubbed his tired eyes. He was getting way off target. Whether or not Cord was married had nothing to do with any of this. And Louisa didn't necessarily have to know the man who'd been watching her.

He might be blowing this whole thing out of proportion.

When Brody finally walked back to camp, it was nearly midnight. He hadn't slept the night before and he expected the day ahead would be a long one. But he'd gone longer than a couple of nights without sleep and under worse conditions. He'd close his eyes for a few minutes, drink a strong cup of hot, black coffee and be ready to roll at sunrise.

As he neared the camp, the smell of wood smoke wafted past his nose. The fire had died and was smoldering with low blue flames, shrinking the range of light illuminating the area. He could see Louisa snuggled deep into her sleeping bag, curled in the fetal position with her back to the fire.

Fred was lying next to her. Brody knew if he didn't announce himself, the dog's ears and nose would sound an alarm, so in a low voice, he said, "Asleep on the job."

Guilty as charged, Fred let out a tired sigh.

Louisa stirred and rolled over onto her back. "I was beginning to worry."

Brody sat down and again went about removing his boots. "I lost the tracks when the horse crossed the creek, but," he lay back on the saddle and tried to get comfortable, "judging by the direction it was going when it went into the water, I'd say it's headed back to Pinyon Ridge."

"That doesn't make sense." She rolled over and rose to an elbow to stare at him across the fire. "If it escaped capture there, why would it go back?"

"Maybe it didn't. Maybe it's hiding somewhere between here and there." He laced his fingers behind his head. Or maybe it had been captured by the man at the creek. "We'll find out soon enough, I suppose."

She bit her bottom lip in a worrisome way. "God, I hope it's not injured."

"The tracks didn't indicate anything of the sort."

Her teeth let loose, leaving that delicious bottom lip red and glossy. "Good."

The soft crackle of the dying fire drifted across the silence as Brody thought about keeping the boot prints to himself. He knew better than to mention Cord's name or that the boots had been a LaSorona brand. At this stage of the game, all he had was speculation to go on, and he was too tired to drop hints that might lead to answers. He'd do that tomorrow after he had his coffee.

"Why do you look worried, Brody?"

He didn't want to scare her, but she needed to know the danger of the situation they might be facing when they rode towards Pinyon Ridge tomorrow. "We're not alone out here."

"What?"

"Someone spooked the bay and..." He paused, giving one last deliberation to what he was about to tell her. "I found boot prints that led to that group of shin oaks near the creek."

Her eyes darted in that direction, then widened when she realized what he was saying. "Someone was watching me?"

"Looks that way," he agreed, shifting his shoulders into a more comfortable position. "Don't leave camp without me. Understand?"

She nodded. "Goodnight, Brody."

"Goodnight, sweetheart." He closed his eyes and pretended to sleep.

~

LOUISA HADN'T BEEN ABLE TO SLEEP WITH BRODY wandering around in the dark by himself. Now that he was back at camp, she felt better, but the aftermath of his kiss had her wide-awake hours after they'd said goodnight.

She lay facing the campfire, watching the low-burning

flames dance around the charred wood as the moment of their first kiss replayed over and over in her head. The brush of his beard, the warmth of his breath against her mouth seconds before his lips touched hers, the sweet residue of marshmallow coating his tongue as he tasted her, and that deep rumbling of desire in his chest when he'd restrained himself long enough to ask if a kiss was all she wanted.

Suppressing a moan, she closed her eyes and hoped sleep would come. But it didn't. As it had countless times before, her mind went to Brody. Not the cowboy she steered clear of. But the man who'd just kissed her.

Predictably, the kiss had been ignitable and hot. But it had also been unpredictably more than a fervent encounter fueled by sexual energy and the need for physical satisfaction. When his lips touched her, she'd felt a jolt of electricity and a connection to something deep, something soulful and profound.

Soulful? Profound?

Eleanor, Mallory, and Sage had used those same words when they'd talked about falling in love.

Louisa's eyes jerked open.

Panic peppered her body.

No.

Absolutely not.

This was the second time love had worked its way into her thoughts and it was ludicrous to think she might be falling in love with Brody Vance.

Preposterous.

They'd shared a couple of dances and one kiss.

One.

No one fell in love after one kiss.

No one and definitely not her.

Holding tight to that affirmation, she felt the panic ease from her body.

She was sure sleep would come if she could center her thoughts on something other than Brody, so she closed her eyes again and tried training her ears to the night sounds around her. A hooting owl, croaking frogs, chirping crickets, the crackling fire, and the occasional whinny or blow of Clyde and Stella.

But out here, alone in the dark with Brody, her senses were razor-sharp and unable to catch hold of anything but him. The background noise slowly faded as her ears zeroed in on the sound of his breathing. Numerous times throughout the night, she'd heard him shift restlessly, sigh, and scrub a hand over his beard.

She wasn't the only one who'd had trouble sleeping.

Her focus traveled past the fire to the man. Sometime around midnight, Brody had ditched his t-shirt and was now lying stretched out on his back with his head turned away from the fire. Nude as he was from the waist up, the fire cast bronze shadows across his skin. The arm facing her was thrown over his eyes. The position extended the length of his torso and accentuated those well-used rib muscles.

As much as she loved admiring Brody's bare torso, Louisa found herself drawn to the hand resting across his stomach.

She'd watched those strong, calloused hands tend wounded animals, calm frightened mares, and hold newborn foals. They could be so soft and careful when they were holding Baby Tucker or masculine, tender when they were cupping her jaw for a passionate kiss. They were also more than capable of dealing with trouble if Shorty showed up.

She shifted her hips, trying unsuccessfully to relocate a troublesome pebble trapped under her right thigh.

"Try counting sheep," Brody's deep-voiced suggestion ended with a long sigh.

The pebble moved, allowing her to relax. "I didn't mean to wake you."

"You didn't." He yawned. "But I think you already knew that."

Ah, so he'd seem her watching him.

Wonderful.

She knew her face was blood red like it had been the day the hay bales came crashing down.

"There's nothing to worry about." He rolled onto his side, away from her and the fire. "The guy's probably long gone by now."

"I'm not worried," she assured him, momentarily giving thought to the boot prints by the shin oaks. If someone were out there in the dark, they wouldn't dare get close to her with Brody here.

The quiet returned, allowing Louisa to focus on a question that had been haunting her since the reception. What exactly were his feelings for her?

Sage and even Violet were certain his feelings for her were love, but he hadn't said the words. If he did, she might help him pack his bags. She wasn't ready to hear that four-letter word from Brody. Not yet. Maybe never. Maybe she should tell him to take the job in Colorado and walk away now while they were both unscathed.

But if she did, she'd spend the rest of her life wondering what his answer might have been. But what if he said that four-letter word? What then?

The not-knowing won. "Can I ask you something?"

Scratching his beard, he grunted a "yeah."

"Why would you give up everything you've worked so

hard for here in Santa Camino and leave the Rescue because of me?"

His hand stilled and for a moment, she could have sworn he stopped breathing. "That's something else I think you already know."

"And if I didn't, would you tell me?"

"No."

On the dance floor, he'd been in mid-sentence with what she thought was "I'm in love with you" on his lips when she'd stopped him. Why was he so reluctant to repeat himself? "Maybe that punch hurt more than your lip."

"Maybe," he agreed without hesitation. "A man does have his pride."

So that was it.

"According to Violet and the rest of my friends and family, your motives and feelings for me are blatantly obvious to everyone but me." She paused, thinking it was cruel to press him for an answer when in the end, how he felt about her wouldn't matter. "So I guess you're going to have to spell it out for me."

This time, she was the one holding her breath as the seconds slowly ticked by.

"If I stay, if you give us that chance," he finally answered, cutting into her with a sensual tone that raked across her body with the touch of a lover. "How I feel about you will be crystal-clear and I won't tell you," he went on to say. "I'll show you and it'll take all night long, sweetheart."

Holy Moses.

A woman didn't need an imagination to know what Brody was saying. If she gave them that beginning, that chance, if he stayed in Texas, he was going to make love to her. Slow, satisfying love and that hard body of his would be lying next to her when she woke the next morning.

The explicitness of that made Louisa's body burn. But like she'd told Violet, waking up to that hard body would come with a price. One she wasn't sure she was willing to pay to keep Brody in Texas.

Nothing more was said between them and soon after, she heard the steady rhythm of his breathing as he went to sleep.

Jess and Mallory were due back in town on Friday. He was giving her two days to decide their future. That shouldn't require much thinking. Logic should apply. She should tell him to take that job in Colorado, part with a friendly goodbye, and send him on his way.

Though unintentionally, she had been playing with Brody's heart. He'd bought a ranch and was renovating a house. The man was ready to settle down – with her.

Brody was looking for love. Sadly, he wouldn't find it with her. Her brothers were right. She had to make a choice. Rope him in or set him free.

Louisa rolled onto her back and stared at the night sky. That same sky hung over her little trailer. The same stars, same planets, and galaxies were shining night after night like shimmering glass strewn across the heavens. Nothing astronomical had occurred. The same universe was still spinning in perfect harmonious balance. Yet, something was…different. She was different.

With Brody lying just a few feet away from her, the vast and encompassing darkness seemed smaller and made her feel a little less lonely. A strong feeling of déjà vu hit her. She'd felt the same way when he pulled into her drive.

Enough with the empty acreage, she scolded herself. *Get a dog.*

She and Brody didn't have a future. Nothing good could come of that beginning he wanted.

Nothing.

She plopped over onto her side and yanked the sleeping blanket up to her neck. With her back to Brody, she closed her eyes. She'd made her decision. So why did the prospect of Brody leaving make her feel like a part of her heart was being ripped out?

CHAPTER 20

Louisa and Brody rose at sunup without words and went their separate ways to answer nature's call. Afterward, he fetched water for coffee, and she set up her portable stove for breakfast.

Though he'd tried to hide it, she knew he was worried about the boot prints and about what might be waiting for them at Pinyon Ridge.

She was also worried. After her little excursion into the wood line to pee had her looking over her shoulder at every sound, she began giving some serious thought to whom the boots might belong to.

Shorty was a cowardly man with a deviant personality and a vendetta. No one had seen or heard from him since the incident at the barn. It wasn't too farfetched to think that he was the one who'd spooked the bay or that he was the man lurking in the shin oaks.

With his coffee in hand, Brody sat on the rock where their supplies were packed. He leaned forward, braced his forearms against his knees, and stared at the ground, deep in thought.

Louisa peeled the eggs she'd boiled and wrapped each of them in a paper towel, then handed Brody one. "Breakfast?"

He glanced up to offer her a small smile of appreciation before he accepted the egg. "Thanks."

"I guess Fred spooked more than a rabbit last night," she said, swallowing hard to get the egg past the lump in her throat.

He bit his in half. "There was no reason to think it was anything but a rabbit."

"No, but I shouldn't have been so cavalier about this rescue. Both you and McCrea told me it was dangerous, and I was too pig-headed to listen."

He finished the egg and used the paper towel to wipe his beard. "You can't go jumping at every varmint who crosses your path, Louisa."

Shorty was the only varmint who made her jump, and her common sense was telling her that Brody needed to know why. But to do that, she'd have to talk about Chris. "Who do you think it was?"

There was a look of indecision in the narrowing of his eyes right before he focused them on the ridge in front of them. "I have my suspicions."

Unable to read anything from that, she took a deep breath and said, "So do I."

His eyes remained locked forward. "Who?"

"You said you knew about Chris."

Brody dropped his head with an elusive gesture, agreeing without words.

Why was he suddenly quiet and why was he acting odd? Had Shorty told his version of her affair and breakup with Chris? Or had someone else been talking to Brody?

This town is too small for secrets.

Jesus. Who else knew? Her mom? She closed her eyes, fighting shame. Her dad?

"Hey." Brody's voice jolted her eyes open. He'd shifted his body around and now was watching her. "I'm listening."

He might be, but she wasn't talking. At least not about what Chris had done to her. That pain was so deeply rooted inside that dislodging it would make her bleed and she wasn't going to bleed on Brody.

He didn't deserve messy and complicated. But there wasn't a doubt in her mind that those big hands and tender heart of his would try to mend her if she asked.

That was achingly sweet and touching. "You say that like you're my therapist."

Concern knotted his brows. "Do you need a therapist?"

"Ah, no," she stammered, though sometimes she wondered. Chris hadn't been physically abusive with her, but he'd used and manipulated her like a chess pawn. "And if I did, an associate degree in psychology hardly qualifies."

Surprise relaxed his frown and raised his brows high. "You went through my personnel file?"

"No, of course not," she said, suddenly hit with guilt over the sarcastic insult. "I caught a glimpse of your resume lying on McCrea's desk when he first hired you."

"I see," was all he said.

The sun was rising, but the coolness of night was still holding its own, so why was she sweating?

"I – I shouldn't have said that about your degree. I'm sorry." She stood and shoved her hands into her back pockets. "Shorty told you what happened between Chris and me."

"He didn't go into details."

"But I thought—"

"Shorty included Chris's name," Brody wiped a hand over his beard, his expression tight. "In a derogatory remark about you, sweetheart."

"Oh." She cleared her throat.

Brody's lips wedge into a cruel smile. "He found it hard to say anything after that."

She was reminded again of the altercation with Shorty and the savage way Brody's hand had curled around the cowhand's neck. The fear in Shorty's eyes when he felt the power in that hand and realized it could crush his windpipe helped to soothe her humiliation. "Yeah, I saw that part."

"Do you think the guy in the shin oaks was Chris?"

"No," she scoffed. "He got what he wanted and moved on a long time ago. There's no reason to think he'd be scurrying around in the bushes for a peek at me."

Brody's eyes dulled. "You certain about that?"

"Dead certain. Chris is happily married and living in Oregon."

"Then you think it was Shorty?"

"Maybe. After dad hired Chris, he put in a good word for Shorty. They were friends, so," she lifted her shoulders, "when I ended it with Chris, Shorty did everything he could to make my life hell with the other cowboys around the ranch."

Brody's eyes hardened. "Describe hell."

"It doesn't matter," she said, dismissing his concern. "I handled it."

"Meaning you didn't tell anyone they were harassing you."

"It would have only caused more problems and it was mostly just words."

She'd never seen him look so enraged. "Mostly?"

"My tires got slashed once, but —"

"Fuck," the curse came out harsh and loaded with animosity.

"There's more." Louisa curled both arms around her midriff, feeling frail and naïve in the wake of all that had happened. "I had a bad feeling when my truck wouldn't start."

"Which is why you wouldn't let me look at it."

"Yeah," she winced, knowing now that had been a mistake. "So Violet sent Ty over and he said someone cut a starter wire."

"That son of a bitch," Brody hissed with such venom, she thought he might actually jump on Stella and set out on a manhunt for Shorty.

"The truck was fine on my way into town that morning," she added. "Which means –."

"He was at your trailer."

She'd been lucky nothing more had come of the threats. She could see that now. "Ty made me promise to report it to the sheriff."

"Did you?"

"I was going to on my way to work, but Patty called about Blue Bayou and then Darcy spotted the bay and here we are. I didn't think something like this would happen, and honestly, I was so caught up in what was going on between you and me –"

"So was I," he cut in, scrubbing a hand over his face. "But that cut wire and those boot prints up the stakes. And as soon as we get back to town, we're reporting both to Finn."

This conversation bore a vague similarity to the one McCrea had had with her when he tried to stop her from marching out the door after Brody. Her brother had been right. Now was no ordinary rescue and now wasn't the time to hash out differences or let herself get sidetracked by what might be between her and Brody.

From here on, she'd be more cautious.

Brody snagged his hat from where it lay beside him on the rock and situated it on his head before he rose. "You should have told me about Shorty."

"You have to swear that you won't tell my dad about any of this."

"The only thing I'm swearing to is kicking Shorty's ass and the ass of any man who helped him harass you."

"No," she yelled. "Lining my dad's crew up for a public ass-kicking won't help my reputation with the men Shorty hasn't gotten to. You know gossip travels through Santa Camino faster than the speed of light. I'll never keep a reputable clientele once I go out on my own if you go in there handing out punishments."

"Go out on your own?"

Walking over to where her sleeping blanket lay next to the smoldering coals of last night's campfire, she picked it up, gave it a few good flips and then rolled it up. Sooner or later, everyone would know. "You're not the only one who's had a job offer. Doc Tolbert has asked me to take over his practice."

Brody sat back down on the rock, his large fingers curling around the paper towel in his hand. "Are you doing this because of me?"

She shrugged a shoulder as she tied her sleeping bag. "You're an irreplaceable part of the rescue team."

"And you're not?"

"I have a couple of friends who are more than quali-fied for the position at the Rescue, and if I do take over Doc's practice, it won't happen all at once. Two days a week to start with. It'll be a gradual exit."

"And I don't have a say in this?"

"No," she said, avoiding his searing stare. "Why would you?"

"Why indeed."

Neither of them bothered with small talk after Louisa made her announcement. They worked quietly and efficiently, saddling their horses and re-packing their supplies into the canvas panniers. The silence between them said more than words could. Those taut lines that had crept onto Brody's face as she was telling him about Shorty were now etched deep into his skin, making him appear years older and less and less like the man he'd been before she'd punched him.

Shoving a boot into the stirrup, he hauled himself up and onto the horse. "As much as I'd like to see you out of harm's way, it's too risky for you to ride back to Darby's alone."

"I'm not going anywhere, Brody," she said, assuming the same hands-on-hips stance as she had yesterday. "I came out here to find that bay and that's what I'm going to do."

Irritation mixed with the worry on his face. "I knew you'd say that."

Louisa mounted Clyde and followed Brody towards the creek. With the sun at their backs and uncertainty in front of them, they set a course for Pinyon Ridge.

THE TRAIL HAD BEEN HARD AND ROCKY LIKE THE ONE leading to the west ridge. Covered in dense underbrush and littered with decaying fence posts and rusty wire that were possible hazards to the horses, they'd taken their time. He didn't want to see Stella or Clyde suffer the same fate as Blue Bayou.

By noon, they'd crossed the valley between the two ridges and had stopped on a small incline with a good view. Pinyon Ridge was similar in size and shape to the west ridge, but it was higher with an elevation close to fifteen hundred feet at the top. There was a thick standing of pinyon pines along the east side.

"Pinyons aren't native to this area," he said.

"According to Granddad, the family who owned the land planted them."

"Where's the house?"

"At the top." Louisa pointed towards the ridge. "There's a wagon trail a few miles up ahead. If we follow it right, we can follow it to the homestead. It curves around the base and is a tricky trail to navigate. One wrong move will send you over the edge, and no one will find you out here. But if we get on it, we can follow it to the homestead."

"I thought this was the only way in."

"It is," she said. "Granddad brought us out here years ago, before Darby bought the land. His truck broke down about half-way up the trail. He was so mad." She chuckled. "The county cut through the trail when they built the bypass a few years ago. What's left of the trail is on Darby's ranch and is protected by a fence."

"Unless someone cut the fence and is using the wagon trail to haul in horses," he speculated aloud.

"Well, yeah." She shrugged a shoulder. "I guess they could. But wouldn't someone have noticed?"

"Darby hasn't run cattle on his land in years and most of his fences are rusted in half. Who's going to be alarmed over a portion of missing roadside fence?"

"Okay, so maybe we should follow the wagon trail out to the bypass instead of going to the homestead."

Brody didn't want to be on that trail if a transport

trailer rolled by, and he didn't want her along when he checked the homestead. The only way around that was to make camp and wait until she was asleep.

"I'd feel better if we found a safe place to camp before we do any searching," he said, leading Stella down the incline and towards the ridge.

"I've been thinking," Louisa said, trailing behind him. "You know everything about my family, but I know almost nothing about yours."

He shifted in his saddle. His family. Riley. This was his opportunity. But how did he –

"Is Allison older or younger than you?" she asked, sparing no hesitation with her questions.

"Younger."

"Married?"

"No."

"Your dad's name is Jameson. What's your mother's name?"

Brody hadn't said his mother's name since the funeral. It was a surreal thought that caused remorse to squeeze at his throat. "Katheryn." With a quick cough, he tried clearing his throat before he continued. "Kate to her friends and family."

"Kate," she repeated, testing the sound of it. "I like it."

A long gush of sadness escaped his lugs. "It fit her."

Silenced fell between them and stretched for a few hundred yards before he saw her ride up beside him, a cautious expression on her face. "You said that in the past tense. Did she...?"

"A heart attack in her sleep."

"Oh, Brody," she said, her words low with remorse. "I– I'm so sorry."

"Me too." Crossing his hands over the saddle horn, Brody gazed out over the horizon as he recalled the kind and gentle woman who'd raised him. A soft voice, a sweet smile, and weathered lines of work and worry caused by Jameson's selfishness.

His mother had mended cuts and wiped away tears. She'd made hurts and bruises vanish with a hug, attended every school function and game, and never failed to give him her advice. She'd made every birthday for him and Allison special. Every Christmas, despite her unhappiness, she'd donned a smile and a Santa hat as she handed out presents while his dad had usually passed out in the barn. She'd raised two kids on her own with little to no help from the man she'd loved.

"When I heard the news that El had lost her mother..." Louisa paused to gather her thoughts. "It made me think about how precious life is and about how much of my life I'd miss sharing with my mom if she passed."

The emptiness caused by his mother's death had intensified when Brody brought Riley home to Colorado. Sharing his son with her was something he felt they'd both been cheated out of. She would have been ecstatic about having a grandchild. Her maternal guidance about caring for a newborn would have been invaluable to him and especially to poor Allison, who'd volunteered to care for Riley until Brody was stable enough to take him.

He owed his sister so much. She was a few years younger than Louisa, and on top of running a ranch, she was now a provider for Riley's motherly needs. "Allison is a lot like her. Strong, stubborn, and willing to sacrifice for those she loves."

Another bout of silence fell and Brody knew by the way Louisa's hands tightened around the reins that her next question would be about his dad. He waited, keeping his eyes fixed on the skyline and the dark clouds looming off to the east of them.

"And your dad, Jameson?"

"Died in a car wreck a week before Allison's sixteenth birthday."

"I—I shouldn't have asked. I'm sor—"

"Don't be. I'm not." A faint streak of bright-white lightning cut through the sky. He'd been watching the clouds gather and form for the better part of the morning without much thought other than finding them shelter. Now, amid the pain and bitterness of talking about his mother's death and the wreck that nearly destroyed their family, the clouds reflected his mood. "But there's a part of me that wishes I'd tried harder to stop him from walking out that door drunk. The wreck severely injured one of Allison's classmates."

"Oh, God," she whispered.

"It was a hard time. We nearly lost everything. My mom was a fifth-generation rancher. The ranch had been handed down to her, and she'd had such high hopes for its success. Jameson was never much of a worker. But with him gone, we all had to work harder and do more. No woman should have to work as hard as my mother did and sister did."

Brody thought back to the days after his dad's death, his mother's calloused and sometimes blistered hands working long, exhausting hours. Her eyes had held such grief and loss and not just for her husband but for the ranch she loved. "After I graduated high school, I wanted to stay on and help with the ranch. But Mom wouldn't hear of it. She pushed me to enlist in the Army, said there was more to life than ranching, so I did. I pulled two deployments, came home and enrolled in a local college."

The ghosts of his dad's drunken legacy and the untimely death of a woman who loved her family weren't the part of his family he wanted to talk about.

Brody wanted to tell Louisa about the parts of his life

he was most proud of, Riley and the Twisted J. He wanted to brag about how Allison — through ingenuity and hard work inherited from their mother — had turned the True Line into a sustainable business. But that would be for another time. "After Mom died, I sold my part of the ranch to Allison."

Without warning, more veins of light slashed across the sky, cracking thunder so loud the ground shook.

Louisa jumped with a startled shriek. Clyde let out a loud and nervous whinny and reared back on his hind legs to paw the air.

"Whoa, boy, whoa," she said calmly, reaching down to rub the horse's neck. "It's okay, boy." She patted the horse's neck while giving the area around them a quick once over. "Have you seen Fred?"

"Not for a while." He wasn't worried by the dog's absence, but he knew she was. "You heard Darcy. He may be half-way home by now or off looking for shelter."

"Smart dog," she said, content with his answer about Fred. "I think we should do the same."

Brody had checked the weather forecast before he'd left the Rescue. Only a small chance of rain had been predicted for today. But storms in Hill Country had a way of popping up when and where they wanted. He'd ridden out lesser ones with just a slicker, but the churning energy in the clouds made them sitting ducks for lightning strikes. This storm was building and if it didn't make a swift turn to the north, it would be on them before they reached the ridge.

Knowing they were ill-prepared for the downpour that was coming, he reached inside his saddlebag. "Did you bring a slicker?"

"No."

He handed it to her. "Here, take mine."

Louisa slipped it on without arguing, then balanced her weight in the stirrups, rose to her feet, and scanned the terrain. A few seconds later, she pointed to the ridge. "There. Off to the left of that fallen cedar tree. Do you see it?"

At first, he thought she might have spotted the bay or Fred, but then he saw the tree and the overhang near the base of the ridge. "Good scouting."

Her smile communicated the point she'd made earlier about pulling her own weight in camp.

Shaking his head, he set Stella on a new course towards the overhang. With luck, they'd make it there before the rain hit and ride the storm out, safe and sound. But luck wasn't with them. Fifty feet or so away from the overhang, the clouds burst. Rain and pea-sized hail pelted them. Winds blew and trees swayed under the force of the storm.

By the time they made it to the overhang, runoff from the ridge had formed a curtain of water over the opening. Soaked to the skin, Brody slung his leg over the saddle and dismounted before Stella came to a complete stop.

The overhang was bigger than it appeared from the outside. It extended into the ridge twenty feet or so and provided plenty of room for them and the horses.

Brody gave his hands a fling and wiped a hand over his face. "Damn, this is going to put a twist in our search for the bay."

Louisa joined him on the ground. She shed his wet slicker and loosened the hat cinch from around her neck. "I'm sure it will pass soon. In the meantime, we can let the horses rest and get a bite to eat."

From the way the sky looked just before they'd ducked inside, he didn't think the storm would let up anytime soon. But they could make wise use of the time.

Wincing at his wet t-shirt and jeans, she held out his

slicker. "And you need to dry off. Riding in wet clothes can cause all sorts of unpleasant chafing."

When was chafing ever pleasant? he wanted to ask but took the garment instead.

"Thanks for the slicker," she said, her dark eyes growing soft and warm with appreciation.

The rain had made it past the protective barrier of the slicker and drenched the front of her teal knit top, enhancing the round mound of her full breasts that were nestled snuggly in her lacy bra. In the shadowy light of the overhang, he could see the faint silhouette of her nipples extruding from the undergarment. That aroused his temptation for hands-on exploration and tightened the mounting tension in his groin.

"No problem," he replied coarsely.

Moving back to Clyde, she began untying her saddlebags. She reached inside for a bag of peanuts. "The honey-roasted ones are my favorite, but if you don't like those, I have beef jerky and crackers."

His food bag held much of the same along with a few cans of pork and beans which didn't seem appropriate right now, given their effect on the digestive system.

His stomach made a roaring sound of agreement that caused her to raise her brows.

"Sorry." He rubbed a hand over his abdomen. "Two days of eating sparsely has caught up with me."

"I have more stew," she offered, filling her palm with peanuts.

"Enough for both of us?" he questioned, not wanting her to sacrifice a meal for him.

She popped the peanuts into her mouth and licked her lips. "More than enough."

That innocent gesture sent a hard jab of desire through his body.

Terrific.

He was getting turned on by lip licking. He tried smiling through the gnawing hunger in his gut and groin because he didn't want his earlier assumptions about her misconstruing his sexual frustration for anger. "Great. Ah, I'll get started on the fire."

Limbs of the fallen cedar had landed inside the overhang and were dry enough to burn. He used twigs for kindling and several medium-sized rocks for demarking. While he worked on building a fire, Louisa unloaded their provisions and then set about preparing the stew.

Soon, their small shelter smelled of wood smoke and stew.

Runoff from the ridge above formed a curtain of water Brody couldn't see through. But near the right side of the overhang there was an oddly shaped rock that detoured the water around the opening. Brody could see a dark churning sky and streaks of lightning. They were safely cocooned inside until the storm passed, but they were also trapped if trouble came.

He unpacked the panniers from Milkshake and relieved Stella of her saddle. He bent to haul out a ration of feed from the small sack he'd packed when something nudged him in the ass.

Brody pitched forward and nearly went head-first into a puddle of muddy water that had formed near the edge of the overhang. He caught his balance and spun around to see Clyde standing behind him. The horse's top lip wiggled in a way that resembled a snicker.

Louisa's hand flew to her mouth as she tried stifling a laugh.

Brody kept his cool. This wasn't his first run-in with a young studhorse who wanted a challenge.

"He's a stinker," she said, holding on to her smile. "I'm

the only one who can ride him and he's very protective of me."

Normally, Brody would have climbed on Clyde and gone a few rounds just to show the animal who was in charge. But this was about the horse protecting Louisa. And it was about Clyde paying him back for what had happened at Darby's.

The horse could have easily reared up, freed himself from Brody's grasp, and kicked his ass to the dirt then. But Clyde hadn't chosen to go that route. He'd waited for just the right moment.

Brody reached inside the feed sack for a handful of corn and held it out for Clyde to take. Uncoerced, the horse didn't attempt to eat the food. Instead, he let out a high-pitched whinny.

Brody couldn't help but laugh. He tossed the corn to Stella and leaned over to give Clyde's neck an affectionate rub. "You're a clever fellow, Clyde,"

As if he knew what Brody was saying, the horse lifted his head up and down.

"Oh." Louisa laughed, surprised by the horse's response. "He agrees with you."

Brody leaned lower so that only Clyde could hear him. "I'm looking forward to our next talk."

Louisa stirred the stew, giving it time to rehydrate before they dug in. "Have you always been able to talk to horses?" she asked, one eyebrow lifting high with humor.

"More or less."

She chuckled. "Seriously, though. There's more to Brody Vance than horses. You have a degree in psychology. Why didn't you continue your education and go into that field?"

"I've been around horses my whole life. I learned basic horsemanship from my mom. Like you, I grew up on a ranch and horses were just a basic part of our lives. But when I was old enough, I got a job at a local horse clinic." Brody recalled his years as a first-class shit shoveler. "It was then that I really fell in love with horses. When I started college, I worked at a horsemanship clinic that was close to home. I went to work for them full-time after I graduated."

She studied him with narrow eyes and a whimsical smile. "You're a remarkable man, Brody."

He hardly thought himself remarkable. But it pleased him to know that she saw more than a shallow, simple-minded horse handler.

"I only have this bowl and a spoon," she said, brushing back damp ringlets of hair from her face. They'd swept loose from her ponytail during their ride.

"I'm so hungry. I might just have you put the stew in my hand and eat it with my fingers," he teased and reached into one of the panniers for the coffee cup he'd used earlier and a spoon.

"Two days alone with me and you come back with blisters on your hands and fingers." Chuckling softly, she poured the stew into his cup. "What would people say?"

"You forgot chafed," he said, blowing on the spoon to cool the stew before he tasted it.

She held a hand over her mouth to keep from spewing stew when she laughed. Finally, she managed to swallow.

Smiling ruefully, he handed her his cup to hold and rolled a large log closer to the fire so they could sit while they ate.

She sat down. "Seriously, though. You need to change."

He took the cup back. "After I eat."

It was mostly a quiet meal, like their lunches at work. Starched and stale and as far away from personal as a conversation could get. He supposed, technically, they were working. But this…this didn't feel like work to Brody. This felt more like a dream come true.

Cocooned inside this outcropping by water and stone, sharing a meal with her by the fire. Strangely, he felt at home. There were no Crockpots or fancy kitchen gadgets. They didn't even have the luxury of a table or chairs. But his soul was at ease with her here in this tranquil spot, if only for a little while.

When they finished, they cleaned the bowl, cup and spoons and packed them away.

He returned to the log, wanting more of her company before the rain stopped and they had to get back on the trail. But Louisa didn't resume her spot next to him. Instead, she walked to the edge of the overhang. With her arms hugging her midriff, she stared at the curtain of water.

She was right about the chafing. Though sitting next to the fire had dried parts of his jeans, other parts were still wet and starting to rub him the wrong way. He thought it best if he discreetly changed clothes while she was preoccupied with the waterfall, so he left the log and went to the other side of the overhang where the horses were.

He rummaged through his bag for clothes. With his boots, belt, and socks removed, he peeled the wet t-shirt over his head and quickly exchanged his wet underwear and jeans for dry ones. Grabbing his boots and a clean pair of socks, he snagged his last clean t-shirt and headed back to the fire. He dropped the boots close to the flames so they'd dry faster, laid his socks on the log, and sat down.

Louisa hadn't moved from the spot.

"The rain is already slowing down." The water flowing over the rock in front of them had dwindled, allowing them to see a hint of the world outside through a blurry lens. "We'll be back on the trail soon, and I'm sure Fred will be bouncing along after us in no time."

A slight turn of her head let him know she heard him.

Brody slid to the ground and used the log to lean against. "Please stop worrying about that dog and come and sit down," he said, patting the ground beside him.

With her arms still clamped around her belly, she walked back to the log and eased to the ground beside him. She scooted closer and laid her head on his bare shoulder.

He kissed her head. "What's on your mind, sweetheart?"

"Our kiss."

Her unexpected answer caused desire to surge through him. "What about it?"

She answered by planting soft, whisper-like kissed up his shoulder. "Would it be inappropriate of me to ask for another one?

Inappropriate?

No.

Brutally tempting?

Hell, yes.

Because when a beautiful woman asked a man to kiss her, he didn't turn her down. And when that beautiful woman was Louisa Coldiron, Brody damn sure wasn't going to think twice about how hard it was going to be to stop with just a kiss.

CHAPTER 21

BRODY KNEW THAT LOUISA WOULD BE ONE HELL OF A LOVER by the way her lips moved over his skin. This woman was comfortable with her own sensuality. She could satisfy a man and have him begging for more in minutes. At least, that was his view now that he was on the receiving end of her feminine skills.

His dick agreed, rising to the expected occasion.

"I'm not gonna stop you," he replied, pulling in a sharp breath when her trail of kisses shifted down towards his pec. "Inappropriate or not, we'll take this as far as you want it to go."

"Kissing," she mumbled as her tongue flickered over his nipple. "That's all, for now." Her tongue teased his nipple again. "Is that okay?"

He groaned, fisted the back of her hair and gently raised her. "If that's all you want," he answered, remembering her zeal for more the last time they kissed. "That's all we'll do."

"That's all I want." She gazed down at him, her eyes cloudy and unreadable. "For now."

Brody wasn't going to dive too deep into what that meant because in his present state of painfully aroused, "for now" was enough.

Her lips were sweeter than he remembered. Softly, they grazed over his, tightening the hold on his self-control and building to a moment of earth-shattering satisfaction. But they were only sharing kisses.

Innocent, first base, above the waist – he assumed – kisses. But the longer she kissed him, the more he wanted her naked flesh pressed against his.

Brody didn't remember when she'd eased astride him, only that crux of her hot body was now lying snuggly over his dick.

His hands roamed from her waist to her hips, exploring her soft, feminine curves and deliciously teasing them both with slow, sensual thrusts. The friction caused her to arch into him. She let her head fall back and gave in to a moan.

Watching desire wave across her face, hearing that primal whimper escape her luscious pink lips as he thrust harder and harder had him fighting to hold onto his restraint.

He dipped his head to her breasts and drew in her scent. Cherries. He craved a taste of her, had since he'd caught a glimpse of her damp shirt beneath his slicker. He kissed his way along the curve of her left one, inflicting a gentle bite to the nipple.

Another moan.

Another bite.

Another hard thrust.

The pattern repeated itself, each time building tension and pleasure.

He slid his hand under her shirt and palmed her breast, gently kneaded the mound. When touching her wasn't enough, he raked away the shirt and bra and capped his mouth over the nipple. He sucked gently and teased the bud with his tongue. Her moan catapulted into a cry that was so damn arousing. Brody felt himself nearing the point of no return. "I don't have the willpower to be the voice of reason this time, sweetheart," he whispered against her breast. "So, if all you want is kissing, we need to stop."

Shuddering in his hands, she pulled in a deep breath and eased from him.

The sudden withdrawal of her small body nestled against his made him feel cold and out of sorts. He felt as though she'd taken a piece of him with her, and now there was a giant hole in the middle of his soul.

He'd given her until Friday to make up her mind. He already needed her in ways he couldn't say and fell more deeply in love with her each day. What would be the state of his heart in four days? Could he walk away?

"For now," he growled, so frustrated and hard it hurt to move. "What does that mean, Louisa?"

One of her shoulders lifted as she straightened her shirt. "It means I'm thinking things over and that for now, all I'm allowing myself to have are kisses."

At the reception, the terms of his desperation seemed childish now. End with a punch or start with a kiss. He'd wanted her answer to be simple and quick. A merciful execution, so to speak, of one or the other. A decision that would end his suffering, one way or another. But looking at her now — with her hair hanging in disarray around her face, flushed cheeks, thoroughly kissed lips, and a tight, overly aroused body on the verge of climaxing in his hands, Brody thought about how easy it would be to reconsider those terms. Even if she never committed to their relationship and he spent the rest of his life teasing their temptation. It would be the sweetest kind of suffering.

That, of course, was his body talking. More precisely, his dick. It was ready for aiming and claiming. When he was sober, he didn't let it make choices for him, and he hadn't been wasted since the night Riley was conceived.

"Well, you may be able to stick to a strict, kisses-only diet." Brody's mood shifted from slightly irritated to overly frustrated as he looked down at his crotch. "But I need more, so we can't keep doing this. It's killing me."

Her eyes followed him to where his erection was still blatantly visible under the denim of his jeans. Shock rippled across her face, shading the pink of her cheeks to a crimson red. "Ah, yeah," she said. "I can see how that might be a problem."

"My hard-on, unpleasant and painful as it may be, is not the problem." He rose to his feet and raked both hands through his hair. "The problem is that I need a straight answer from you. I need to know that taking that job in Colorado is the right thing to do. That letting go and moving on is my only choice."

~

LETTING GO?

Moving on?

Yes, that second kiss had been a mistake, but Brody made it all sound so profound and like everything was riding on her giving him an answer right now. "That's not fair. You gave me until Friday to make up my mind. Now, it's like you're placing your whole future at this moment in my hands."

"Not my whole future, just this part. The part that decides if I stay or if I go. And if you really want to give this thing between us a go, then giving me an answer shouldn't take days."

Okay, so he wasn't asking her to have a deciding part in his future. Not that it would have made a difference because she wouldn't, couldn't, be a shareholder in any part of it. But something was bothering him. "What's gotten into you?"

"Nothing. I just want an answer."

"Fine!" she snapped, feeling the heat of his eyes drill into her.

"Fine!" he roared back and stood to his feet.

"I don't want you to take the job," she burst out, feeling that admission snuff out the euphoric feel-good sensation generated by their kiss. "There, I said it, That's my answer. But at the same time, I can't ask you to stay because I can't take our relationship in the direction you want it to go."

"And that's the real problem, isn't it? Not that you can't take our relationship in the direction I want it to go, but that you won't be honest about why you can't." He braced his hands on his hips and looked down at her. His face was grim like it had been when she'd caught him staring out the window at the vineyard. "First, it's your cowboy rule and then you're in love with another man." He held up a finger while one eye narrowed with cynicism. "But then you wanted to sample the goods —"

"Sample the goods?" she seethed.

"So, you caved and allowed us to share a few kisses," he continued, his tone oddly piqued and edging towards bitter. "Now you're back to your usual at-a-distance, uncommittable self and about to dish out some other ambiguous, bullshit excuse as to why you don't want this to work."

Louisa jumped to her feet. "My reasons aren't ambiguous. They're just hard to talk about!"

"Why?" He stood, tossing a big hand up in the air. "If you can't talk about them, throw me a hint, play charades, do something other than blow me off −."

"Jesus, Brody," she yelled, tears welling in her eyes. "You can't expect me to just open up to you. There're things you don't know a−about me and what happened with Chris. Things that are so painful I feel like I'm dying every time I think about them. Things that will most likely destroy our relationship before it even starts."

Brody's hands fell to his sides, the rancor squint of that one eye softening. "You don't know that."

She did know that.

"There's nothing we can't work through, Louisa. Nothing." He poked himself in the chest. "I believe that with all my heart, but there has to be a point when you make a commitment to one another and to the relationship. When you dig your heels in and hold on tight for whatever comes your way."

He didn't have a clue what he was talking about.

"For me, it's not a simple matter of pretending like we just met or − or starting over," she explained, trying to reclaim control over her emotions. "It's me dealing with what happened before we met and then finding the right moment, the right…way to tell you about it. So it's not about us working through something. Maybe it isn't about us at all. Maybe it's about me, just me and," she paused, her words stalled by the pain, "what I can't give you."

He stared contritely at her, taking in all she'd said but not giving up on getting an answer. "All I'm asking for is love and commitment."

"No," she said, jerking her head back and forth. "You want more."

"What? What do I want that you can't give me?"

This was it. Her point of no return. If she was going

to be completely transparent with Brody, she had to dig deeper. Could she do that? Could she reach inside herself and rip out the bitter consequence of what love had cost her and hold it out for Brody to see? Was she that brave?

Summoning all of her courage, she took a deep breath and opened her mouth to speak. But nothing came out. Not a word or a grunt, not even air.

She tried again. "I can't…" Finally. Something. But the words that should have been there, weren't. "The nursery, the – the paint."

He stood there staring at her as confused and clueless as ever.

Jesus! Did she have to spell it out for him or shove one of those infertility pamphlets in his face? "Kids, Brody. You want kids."

His jaw eased open as his brows arched inward, launching a blow-to-the-gut expression. "You don't want children?"

Frustration piled itself on top of the pain and wiggled into a comfortable spot, causing Louisa to grind her teeth. This wasn't about her wanting children. It was about her inadequacies as a woman. Why couldn't he see that?

She wanted children more than anything in the world. Her heart ached to be a mother. Holding that small life in her hands would be a dream come true.

That's what she wanted to tell him. But like before, the words that should have been there, weren't. She would not lie to him. But she wasn't above elaborating on his misconception. "Lots of women have phobias about childbirth."

Brody's eyes went momentarily blank as if someone had unplugged his brain, then he blinked. A slight frown darted across his face before he dropped his gaze to the dirt. Had he taken that little nugget of pretense and turned it into a reason to say goodbye? Or was she going to have to get creative?

She waited for him to retreat and say the words that would secure the end just as she'd predicted. But they didn't come.

Instead, he raked a hand through his ruffled hair and turned away from her to study the rock wall.

Louisa's heart broke a little more. She was getting a taste of her own medicine and karma sucked.

"I guess..." His response started slowly with a hard rub to his bearded jaw. "We both have things that need saying. Things that can't be blurted out."

Louisa had failed miserably to say what needed to be said after days of rehearsing the conversation in her mind. And though she wasn't fool enough to think she'd learned all she needed to know about Brody, she was leery about what it was he felt he couldn't blurt out.

He'd already told her about Colorado and the job he'd been offered. What else was there? Her eyes went to the ring finger of his right hand. Wedding bands were easy to take off and some married couples were happy with only seeing each other on the weekends.

She didn't have any reason not to trust Brody. He'd never lied to her or tried to mislead her in the past. But again, the bruised part of her heart was questioning the real reason behind his weekend trips to Colorado and if the woman who'd gifted him those handkerchiefs was indeed his sister.

He wasn't dating anyone and, to her knowledge, hadn't since he'd been working for the Rescue. But a man like Brody — strong, vigorous, and teeming with sexual potency — had to be getting his needs met somewhere.

But did she think he was the kind of man who'd cheat on his wife?

No, but that didn't mean he wasn't.

"I should have told you sooner," he confessed as he restlessly moved about the overhang. "But as you said, it's about finding the right moment and the right way to say it."

CHAPTER 22

Louisa had been in the middle of pouring her heart out to him, then had suddenly shifted to a phobia about childbirth?

Brody wasn't buying it.

She'd been christened into the glamorous life of a horse rescuer after her third day at Promise Point. They'd been on their way to Odessa to pick up a horse that had been surrendered to the Rescue by a petting zoo when the motor of the truck they were driving threw a rod. Bored with only the radio and a deck of playing cards to entertain them, they'd spent two hours playing poker on the side of I-20 as they waited for a tow truck.

She'd walked away with a hundred dollars of Brody's hard-earned cash that day, but he'd learned two things. Never play poker with a grinning woman who swears it's her first time at cards and when Louisa was losing…she always gritted her teeth.

And something he'd known long before that poker game was this beautiful, intelligent, and headstrong woman standing in front of him didn't let fear get in the way of what she wanted, and she wanted children.

Brody was sure of it.

He could see that loving, nurturing side of her leap to life every time a child came within ten feet of her. So what had caused her to change lanes and veer off course?

Whatever it was, he didn't stand a snowball's chance in hell of finding out now. After that last kiss, it hadn't taken long for his resolve to snap and for him to transform into that irritable bastard he feared he'd become once they were out here alone on the trail.

Predictably and with due cause, Louisa had thought he was angry when he'd demanded an answer about why she couldn't commit, but she hadn't retaliated as he'd thought she would, with brash words and cursing comebacks.

Instead, she'd wept.

Guilt latched hold of Brody's shoulders and climbed on. He hated himself for making her cry and damn inadequate as a man for venting his sexual vexation on her. Now he had to navigate through that smokescreen she'd thrown up as a defense when he'd acted like an ass.

He'd asked her outright if she wanted children and she'd danced around a clear answer. So he had to consider that her confession about childbirth, however odd it may have been, might not be exactly true.

Okay, so what was the truth? Did it really involve that unpainted nursery, or was this another one of her attempts to detour him like her dance with Boot Boy had been?

He hadn't a clue.

The only thing he did know was that the ending to this conversation might destroy his hopes for a life here in Texas with her and his son. If Louisa didn't accept Riley, if she didn't want kids…that beginning he wanted with her would end here and now.

That possibility sent an icy wave of disappointment over him.

"What can't you blurt out, Brody?" Louisa's voice cut through his thoughts. Gazing up at him with suspicion in her tear-stained eyes, she pinned him with another question. "What haven't you told me?"

Dread wrapped itself around his chest and squeezed, but there was no turning back now. "There are parts of my life I've wanted to tell you about."

She sniffed and wiped her face. "Like your sister and the job in Colorado?"

"Sort of," he said, thinking about ways he could ease into the conversation without it blowing up in his face. "You assumed I knew that Tucker was teething because I was an uncle."

She swallowed. "And you're not?"

"No." He took a deep breath. "I know about teething because I have a son."

Her fingers coiled into tight fists at her sides and her spine stiffened. "What?"

He knew he had to explain – fast. "Riley is almost two."

She took a step back. "And your wife? What's her name?"

His wife? The woman she was always taking jabs at him over. The woman he'd supposedly bought the Twisted J for. Brody had never really thought Louisa believed there was another woman until now "I don't have a –"

"The child's mother," she stated frigidly. "Is she why you go to Colorado?"

"What? No," he rushed to say, feeling like he'd just lit the short fuse on a stick of dynamite.

"Don't lie!"

"Damn it, Louisa!" he shouted back. "I'm not lying. I'm trying to be honest with you."

As the rain moved on, the downpour flowing over the ridge dwindled, leaving trickles of water in its place. In the distance, Brody could hear the swollen creek's torrent sound rushing by and the wind as it pushed the storm farther and farther from them.

"Where's the boy's mother?"

The stone-cold way she referred to his son was almost too much for Brody. "My son's name is Riley, and I don't have any idea where his mother is. After he was born, Heather jumped from here to there, doing any drug she could to get high."

A split-second shadow of empathy rippled over the iciness on her face. "She's an addict?"

"She wasn't when we met, but a little while after she gave birth to Riley, she shacked up with this guy, and... Hell," he cursed. He could feel judgment oozing from her every pore. "Why am I explaining what happened to you? You don't give a damn. This is why everyone knows about Riley but you."

"What do you mean everyone knows?"

"Your mom and dad, McCrea and Jess, Eleanor and Mallory..." He raked both hands over his head. "Hell, even Ed Tubs knows I have a son. Everyone knows but you."

She seemed affronted by the news. "If you don't have a wife and you have nothing to hide, then why did you wait until now to tell me you were a father?"

Did he bother with explaining how Riley's conception had happened? She was going to twist the truth and turn it on him no matter what. "I walk on eggshells around you, Louisa. And until the wedding, I didn't think I could tell you. But I knew I had to because I miss my son. I miss rocking him to sleep and singing "Twinkle, Twinkle, Little Star" to him. I miss seeing that sleepy little smile of his after he wakes up from a nap..."

That launched her into a bout of silent tears that rocked her small body so hard, Brody thought she might fall.

"Please, don't," he pleaded, reaching out to hold her only to have her jerk away. "Goddamn it, Louisa," he swore softly as he let his hands fall to his sides. "Don't you see? I had two choices. Bring Riley here or sell everything I own and move back to Colorado."

"And that's where I come in," she hiccupped snidely between sobs. "Deciding if you stay or go. Your future in my hands."

"See," he said, growling in frustration. "This is how I knew you'd take the news, and I knew telling you that my son was the product of a one-night stand with a woman I didn't love would only back up your claim that I'm a man who's only interested in a piece of ass!"

He sat down on the log and slipped his boots and socks on. "It wouldn't matter to you that my mother had just died, and I was looking for anything I could find to ease the grief, that whiskey and sex were my painkillers that night. It wouldn't matter that Riley, though he wasn't planned, though I didn't love his mother, is the best thing that's ever happened to me. And it wouldn't matter that I love my son more than anything in the world or that I want to be the kind of father mine wasn't—sober, loving, supportive, affectionate...present."

Another long sigh found its way up to his throat. He felt so hurt and bruised because he'd just poured his heart out to her and she wouldn't even look at him.

Inside the overhang, the silence between them cast a bleak prediction of the future. Last night, they'd shared their first kiss. This morning, they'd come a step closer to making love and he'd told her about Riley; all had gone the way he'd expected.

Amazingly sweet, simmering hot, and judgmental cold.

"I didn't buy the Twisted J for my wife or some woman I have hidden away in Colorado. I bought it so that Riley and I would have a home, here in Texas, together, with you."

Louisa dropped to the log, a forlorn mien covering her face. With swollen eyes and tear-stained cheeks, she looked as broken as Brody felt. "How can you expect me to believe that? When you've been lying to me from the start?"

"I've never lied to you. Not once and it doesn't matter if you believe it or not. It's the truth. The ball is still in your court. But since you don't want kids, I guess the Twisted J is going back on the market." He whipped the t-shirt over his head. "I can't be in a relationship with a woman who doesn't accept my son."

"I–I," her voice broke. "Want to go home."

Brody gave her a curt nod, agreeing that the trip was over. They'd taken cover here. Their only intention had been to shelter themselves from the wind and the rain, but so much more had transpired here. He felt like he'd ridden out the storm bare-assed and tied to a stake.

He snatched his hat from the log and gave it a hard smack against his thigh as a faint pop echoed outside the overhang. He stopped and listened, training his ears on a sound he knew all too well. The sound repeated itself and was followed by a bark.

Louisa jumped to her feet, alarmed, widening her eyes. "Was that Fred?"

"And gunfire."

"Are you sure?"

"I'm positive." He put his hat on and hurried back to

the horses. Taking his rifle and the satellite phone with him, he strode past her. "If I'm not back in fifteen minutes, get on Clyde and get the hell out of here."

"Brody, wait."

He stopped, suddenly aware of the danger he might be running into and the heaviness in his heart over what had just happened between them. He didn't want to leave this world without having said the words.

Taking three long strides back to her, he grabbed her chin. "Everything I said was true. You're all I've ever wanted." He planted a hard kiss on her lips. "I love you, Louisa. Don't, for once second, think I don't."

Louisa fell to the log with a hard thump. Her head was spinning from Brody's kiss and his unexpected declaration.

I love you. The three words she never wanted to hear had never sounded sweeter.

But Brody was a father.

A daddy to a baby boy.

She cringed and close her eyes as pain echoed through her like it had before when she thought he'd painted the nursery without her. He'd fathered a child with a woman he'd picked up in a bar. How could he have done something like that?

He'd been grieving for his mother and needed something to kill the pain, her heart stepped in to say. It was as simple as that and now he had a son he clearly loved and adored.

A son he wanted her to accept.

Suddenly, the betrayal she felt vanished and all she could think about was holding that little boy.

Another shot rang out, causing her eyes to fly open and

her mind to snap to alert. Brody was headed up the ridge alone in search of the person firing those shots. Two more shots were fired, answered by a different sounding shot.

He was returning fire. She couldn't just sit here and wait. She had to do something.

Though her medical training hadn't prepared her for rushing into a gunfight, it had taught her how to think under pressure. When that part of her brain kicked into gear, she jumped into action. Rushing to Clyde, she pulled the knot loose securing her vet pack to the saddle and headed up the path after Brody. The narrow path was steep, rocky and in some places, muddy from the rain. Scrambling to find footing and keep her balance, she held on to roots and branches until she made it to the top.

Once there, she stayed hidden behind a large mound of limestone rocks as she scanned the ridge for Brody. He was nowhere in sight. Dear God, if something happened to him, she'd never forgive herself.

She listened for any sound that might give away his location. If he was wounded, she needed to find him fast. Her focus went to the ground in search of blood droplets. There were none, so if he had been shot, it hadn't been here.

"Brody," she whispered, not wanting to give her location away to the shooter.

He didn't answer her.

What was she going to do? He had the rifle and the satellite phone. She could ride for help and hope for a signal. If she didn't get one, it would take a day of hard riding before she made it back to Darby's. By then, it might be too late to help Brody.

Suddenly, she heard the sound of boots hitting the muddy ground. She inched up and saw Brody racing towards her with his rifle slung over his shoulder and Fred clutched to his chest.

The front of his t-shirt was splattered with blood.

"Brody!"

"Get down!"

A bullet ricocheted off the rock in front of her, scattering pieces of rock into the air. Startled, she fell backward as Brody jumped behind the rocks.

"You've been shot."

"Not me," he panted. "The dog."

"Are you sure?" she asked, clutching his bloody shirt as she searched his chest and abdomen for wounds.

He grabbed her hand, forcing her to focus on his words. "I'm okay. The shooter missed me, but Fred wasn't as lucky."

The dog, now lying on the ground next to Brody, had a bullet hole in the right lower quadrant of his left leg. Blood oozed from the wound.

Fred whimpered as she inspected it. "It's okay, boy," she crooned. "Did you get a look at the asshole who did this?"

"No," Brody said, sheltering her with his body as two more shots whizzed by them.

"Do you think it's the peeping Tom from last night?"

"He may be one of them."

"There're two?"

"Afraid so," he said, reloading his rifle.

"Open up my pack and hand me the gauze."

He did as she instructed. Louisa capped the gauze over the wound, but the bleeding showed no signs of slowing down. The dog wouldn't make the two-day trip back to town in this condition. "If I don't get the bleeding stopped, there won't be any saving him."

Turning, Brody aimed his rifle and returned fire. "If we don't get out of here, there won't be any saving us."

Fearing another bullet might zip by her head, Louisa hunkered down and stretched across Brody's legs for her pack. She kept it organized and neat, making it easy to reach inside with one hand and find what she needed. She slipped on a rubber glove and used a water-soluble ointment along with a non-adherent bandage to cover the wound and prevent further contamination. There wasn't much else she could do while they were pinned to the ground by bullets. "What are we going to do?"

He dug into his back pocket for the satellite phone and punched in what she assumed was McCrea's number. It rang a few times, and then she heard her brother pick up. "Hello."

Brody flinched as another bullet landed inches from his head.

"What the hell was that?" McCrea exclaimed.

"A bullet," Brody shouted. "We're taking fire. Get us out of here!"

He gave McCrea their location and told him their suspicions about the wagon trail. It wasn't long before they heard sirens in the distance and the faint hum of the county's search and rescue helicopter flying towards them.

Gilmore Dispatch patched the satellite phone into the helicopter com, allowing Brody to talk directly with Finn as the pilot circled the ridge. "The bullets stopped when they heard the chopper."

"Better to be on the safe side, though," Finn said and ordered the pilot to land close to the rocks they were hiding behind so they'd have cover if the shooters were still out there.

Fighting the downward drift of the helicopter's rotor and debris churned up by the wind, Louisa grabbed her vet pack and headed for the helicopter. Brody scooped the dog into his arms and followed her. When they were safely inside the helicopter, Finn handed them each a headset. "How bad is the dog?"

"I didn't find an exit wound," she told him, thinking there was a good chance old Fred might lose his leg or, worse, his life. Bullet wounds were tricky. They might enter at the hip and travel to the stomach or the liver. "The bullet may have clipped an artery, shattered the bone, or be lodged in an organ somewhere. I won't know the extent of the damage until I open him up."

"Shouldn't we transport him to Tolbert Veterinary instead of taking him to the Rescue?" the pilot asked.

Louisa shook her head. "No. We're more prepared to handle this type of emergency."

Promise Point didn't often get horses with gunshot wounds, but the Rescue had the most up-to-date surgical equipment and supplies. Doc was an excellent veterinarian with years of training. But Louisa had seen her share of horses with complex lacerations and joint trauma. She'd even assisted soft tissue and orthopedic surgeries before coming to the Rescue. Fred would need her experience and he was her patient. She wasn't handing him off to another veterinarian.

Brody sat back against the seat and wiped the back of his hand across his sweaty brow. The motion pushed his hat up, revealing deep lines of worry across his forehead. His blue eyes lacked their usual luster as they stared out the window. He looked exhausted and defeated in a way that made her heart ache.

She'd done this to him. She'd finally broken this cowboy and she'd spend the rest of her life regretting it.

Louisa turned her head towards the opposite window and cried.

They arrived at the Rescue fifteen minutes later. The

pilot landed the helicopter in one of the unused pastures located across from the clinic.

McCrea was waiting for them near the fence. His face turned a pasty shade when he saw the blood on their hands and clothing. "Christ! Are either of you injured?"

"No," Brody answered as he rushed towards the clinic with Fred. When they reached the door, he handed the dog to Patty and one of the Rescue's vet techs.

"Get him prepped for surgery," Louisa told them. "I want a CT scan and we need to cross-match him for a transfusion. Call Doc," she told Kara. "He said something last week about treating Lucius Craig's greyhound for a paw injury."

"You got it," Kara answered without hesitation.

"What does a paw injury have to do with any of this?" Brody asked, following her down the hall towards the bathroom.

"There's a shortage of canine blood around the country. Greyhounds have a universal blood type." Using a hip, she pushed through the door and quickly set about washing the blood from her hands. They'd need a thorough cleaning before surgery, but this would keep things sanitary while she changed into her scrubs. "If Doc doesn't have Fred's blood type stored at his clinic, Lucius might sign off on letting his dog be a donor for Fred."

"You are amazing," Brody said, rousting a weak but proud smile through the fatigue as he washed his hands.

The blood shortage was common knowledge in her veterinary medicine field, and the steps she'd taken to save the dog's life were something any well-trained veterinarian would do. They were logical, not amazing. But Brody was always reinforcing her confidence. That was the kind of man he was — generous, thoughtful and, she prayed, more forgiving than ever before.

"Yeah, that's me," she said. "Amazing, with all my cowboy rules and ambiguous, bullshit excuses."

His shallow smile vanished. "I shouldn't have said those things."

"No, you were right," she admitted. "About all of it, except the part about me not wanting kids."

He pumped soap into a palm and began scrubbing the blood from his hands. "I thought the phobia part was a little strange."

"More bullshit." She rinsed her hands and flipped the faucet off. "The way I acted when you told me about your son is unacceptable.

"It was a lot take in." She saw him swallow hard. "I should have told you about Riley sooner.

When Brody told her he had a son, Louisa wanted to crawl under a rock and die. The injustice of it all. Twice she'd fallen in love and twice she'd been betrayed.

But this time wasn't like the last time. Brody hadn't used her. He loved her and he'd sacrificed so much to be with her. "Then you forgive me?"

"What's to forgive?"

Oh, God. There was so much for him to forgive, yet he couldn't recall a single one of her transgressions.

Watching the water and soap wash away the blood and dirt from his hands took her back to the ridge, to the way he'd sheltered and protected her. She couldn't count the number of bullets that had been fired at them, but she could see each one that landed dangerously close to his head.

She'd tried to erase those images from her mind but couldn't. Maybe she didn't need to. Maybe she needed them to remind herself of how foolish she'd been and just how close she'd come to losing him.

That thought made her lunge for him. Wrapping her

arms around his waist, she held on tight. "When I saw the blood," she cried, finally letting the fear she'd felt up on the ridge take hold. "I thought I'd lost you."

If one of those bullets, just one, had hit him, he wouldn't be standing across from her now. Riley would have lost his father and she would have lost the only man she'd ever truly loved.

Yes, she admitted to herself. You are in love with Brody Vance.

What was so complicated to her before was now so simple.

"But you didn't lose me," he whispered against her hair as he returned her embrace. "I'm right here."

"Promise me you'll stay."

"Finn has his deputies combing Darby's ranch for the bay," he said, the vibration of his voice rattling softly against her ear as he spoke. "I thought I'd go back out there and help."

"That's not what I meant." She looked up at him. "Don't sell the Twisted J. Don't move back to Colorado. Stay here with me."

He searched her eyes. "What about Riley?"

Before Louisa had learned of Riley's existence, she'd gone through countless scenarios in her head of how to break the news to Brody that if he married her, he'd never be a father.

That was her biggest obstacle in this relationship. But somewhere in Colorado there was a child, a little boy, with Brody's DNA. Her heart swelled with love for that child. They were starting over, and she was about to be a mother. "I'm sure I'll fall in love with him just like I did his daddy."

Brody's eyes became misty with love and relief. "Sweetheart," he said, lifting her up and around with a spin that left her laughing. "You don't know how long I've waited to hear you say that."

She didn't know the exact time or place she'd fallen in love with Brody, only that she had. And for now, that was all that mattered.

"Does this mean you plan on staying at the Rescue?" he asked.

"I may go out on my own one day," she answered honestly. "But for now, I'm staying right here with you."

"Louisa?" Patty called from the other side of the door.

"Yes?" she answered back as Brody let her slip to the ground.

"The dog is prepped."

"I'm on my way." She dried her hands and tossed the paper towels into the garbage, then stepped outside the door. "I don't know how long I'll be in surgery, but–"

"I'll be here." Brody leaned a shoulder against the door. "Waiting."

She gave him a quick kiss and hurried up the hall towards the surgery. "Promise you won't go back to Darby's." She pointed to the sheriff, who was standing at Kara's desk talking on his cell phone. "Let Finn and his deputies handle it."

CHAPTER 23

BRODY WATCHED LOUISA HURRY UP THE HALL AND disappear into the surgery. There was still an uneasiness looming in his mind about what had happened between them in the minutes before he'd run to the top of the ridge and the bullets had started flying.

She was hiding something from him, and he couldn't figure out why. After all they'd been through together, why couldn't she trust him? He'd done everything he knew to make her see that his love was unconditional, that nothing would ever change his feelings for her. But she was holding onto a secret, a deeply rooted heartache that stemmed from her relationship with Chris.

Her eyes had been filled with pain and betrayal when he told her he had a son, but just now, he'd seen only love and acceptance. Having the man you love say he wanted you to be a mother to his two-year-old son was a lot to process, especially for a woman with a busy career. But it had only taken Louisa an hour or so to go from devastation to love? What changed her mind?

Brody had a feeling that only time would tell. Louisa

wasn't telling him anything until she was ready. So for now, he'd chalk it all up to their near-death experience. Maybe it took something like that to bring people closer and make them realize all the little things they thought mattered really didn't.

He was bringing Riley to Texas and he and Louisa were starting over. She was giving them that beginning.

His heart hadn't felt this light in years.

Trying hard to hide what he knew was a goofy-adolescent grin, he made his way up the hall to Kara's desk.

"Good God, Brody." Kara stopped stacking papers. "What happened out there?"

"I think we got too close for someone's comfort," he said, bypassing all the details he felt like he'd repeated a dozen times.

Finn hung up and joined them.

"Any sign of the bay?" Brody asked, noting the grim set of Finn's jaw.

"Not yet, but my guys are searching the area. If it's out there, we'll find it."

"It's out there." Brody took a small Styrofoam cup from a stack on the counter and filled it with black coffee. "Twenty seconds or so before the first shot was fired, I saw the horse. Fred was chasing it through a patch of prickly pear cactus."

"Did you see the shooter?" McCrea asked, propping an elbow on the top of Kara's standing height reception desk.

"No, I was too far away. But I could see the old homestead. There were two heavy-duty trucks with horse trailers and three high-priced sport utility vehicles."

Finn nodded, agreeing with what Brody had seen. "You were right about the old wagon trail too. The storm made everything a damn mess out there. But my deputies should be able to get sufficient molds of the tire tracks leading out to the main road."

"Shit," McCrea swore. "They've been operating right under our noses."

Irritation hardened Finn's eyes. "Looks that way, but there was no sign of anyone when my deputies arrived. They must have high-tailed it out of there when they heard us coming."

Brody had seen the wagon trail from the top of the ridge. It was only about a quarter of a mile away from the overhang where he and Louisa had sheltered from the storm. The shooters could have been on them in seconds. "How about boot prints?"

"At least two sets. Why?"

"The first night we made camp," setting his coffee on the table, Brody pulled out his phone to show them the pics he'd taken of the prints by the shin oaks, "we had a visitor."

McCrea and Finn came closer to look at the photo.

"LaSorona. A size ten or eleven maybe," Finn observed.

McCrea's eyebrows went high. "Identifying the owner of that boot isn't going to be easy. I own a pair." He pointed to Finn. "He owns a pair. Hell, Jess probably has a half-a-dozen pairs sitting in his closet."

Brody knew the odds of finding the man wearing the boots was slim to none, but he had a gut feeling that the owner was more than a peeping Tom.

"What's that?" Kara rose to her tiptoes and pointed over Brody's shoulder at a mark just below the LaSorona name. "It looks like the letters B and C. Maybe it's a brand of some sort."

"She's right," Finn agreed.

"Maybe we could ask Cord about it," Brody suggested

to McCrea and hit the print option below the picture. The printer behind Kara's desk clicked to life.

"That's a good idea," he replied.

"Who's Cord and why would he know about this brand?" Finn questioned.

"Cord Watts," Kara supplied before McCrea or Brody could answer. "He's the president of the LaSorona Boot Company."

"He was at Jess and Mallory's wedding," Brody threw in. "I figure it wouldn't hurt to ask him where he was the night we were camping."

"He was in Milan, Italy," Kara said, her cheeks tinging pink when the three of them raised their eyebrows, silently questioning how she knew. She smiled sheepishly. "Ivy likes to brag. He left right after the wedding on Saturday."

Brody knew better than to take Ivy's word for Cord's whereabouts and so did Finn. Cord could have easily lied about the trip to impress Ivy or establish a false alibi if he was one of the shooters. Finn would verify Cord's trip before he crossed him off the list of suspects.

"Still," Kara said, shuffling more papers. "It wouldn't hurt to contact someone at LaSorona. Maybe it's a specific brand they sold to a specific region or store like Nash's. If that's the case, the store might have a record of the sale."

"She'd make a great detective," Finn murmured to McCrea out of the side of his mouth.

McCrea grinned. "Don't get your hopes up. Kara's a dedicated employee. Right, Kara?"

Her lips turned down at the corners as she handed Brody the photo and walked past them. "A dedicated employee who needs a raise."

"There's something else." Brody waited until Kara was in McCrea's office and out of earshot before he continued.

"Someone sabotaged Louisa's truck the day of the wedding."

"What?" McCrea blared.

"She didn't file a report," Finn said, looking more concerned by the minute. "I would have seen it."

"There was an emergency here with one of the horses we rescued from Darby's." Brody removed his hat and rubbed his forehead, seeing traces of blood along the outer edge of the brim. "It's not the first time someone's damaged her vehicle. She told me Shorty Turner slashed her car tires a few years ago."

"That son of a bitch," McCrea boiled. "Why didn't she tell one of us? We'd have done more than fire his sorry ass."

"Yeah," Brody said wryly and positioned his hat back on his head. "So would have I. I think that's why she didn't mention it."

Finn helped himself to the coffee. "And you think Shorty was the one at your campsite."

Brody handed him the photo. "We're all thinking the same thing. Am I going to be the only one who will say it?"

"Okay." Finn set his coffee on the table, took the photo, folded it, and slipped into the breast pocket of his shirt. "I'll find Shorty and confiscate his boots."

"I might be able to save you the trouble," McCrea said, reaching over Kara's desk for the landline. "Ed told me Shorty has been in the Roadhouse every day since Dad fired him. He's there like clockwork as soon as the doors are open and usually stays until closing time."

While McCrea talked to Ed, Finn pulled Brody to the side. "Any ideas about who the other shooter might be? Anyone who might have a grudge against you or Louisa?"

Brody rubbed his beard, thinking. "There were a few cowboys who helped Shorty harass her, but she never named names. You might find something there. Have you questioned Darby? This might be about him."

"Questioning Darby will have to wait." Finn sipped his coffee, wincing as the hot, bitter brew made contact with his lips. "I just got off the phone with Deputy Jones. He and another deputy found Darby unresponsive on his kitchen floor. It seems someone got to him before we did."

"Jesus," Brody whispered.

"EMS says he has a concussion and a broken wrist, but should be okay." Finn resumed drinking his coffee. "What I can't figure out is why they'd hurt Darby."

Brody's mind flashed to the camera and map he'd seen sitting on the broken-down table at Darby's house. "Darby had a camera with a high-powered lens. My guess is someone thought he could identify them."

McCrea hung up the phone. "Shorty hasn't been at the Roadhouse since Saturday night."

"Hey, boss," Kara yelled from his office.

"Yeah?"

Kara clamped a hand over the mouthpiece of his desk phone. "It's your mom and she ain't happy."

McCrea shoved his hat up and massaged his forehead. "Shit."

"She's probably heard what happened by now," Finn reasoned.

McCrea headed for his office. "I better go calm her down."

"We made camp Monday night," Brody told Finn, going back to the subject. "It's likely that boot print belongs to Shorty."

"I'll find him, but you stay out of it." Taking his coffee, Finn set a path for the front door. "And don't go back to Darby's.

"What about our trucks and trailers?" Brody questioned, irritated Finn wanted him to drop the matter. "Our horses are still out there."

"I'll take care of it," Finn assured him, pushing open the glass door. "You heard Lou. She doesn't want you out there."

≈

FORTUNATELY, THE BULLET HAD MISSED ALL FRED'S MAJOR arteries and lodged itself in a muscle. But it had hit the femur bone. Louisa stabilized the fracture using a bone plate and screws. Three hours after she hurried into surgery, she tied the last stitch, dressed the wound, and left the dog in the capable hands of Patty and the other vet techs for the night.

As soon as she'd walked into surgery, she'd shut everything out of her mind and focused on what needed to be done. She'd learned to do that early on in her veterinary training. Now that the surgery was over and Fred was in recovery, she could give in to the aftereffects of the adrenaline rush she'd experienced upon the ridge. Exhaustion was creeping into her limbs.

She pushed through the surgery door, rubbing her stiff neck, and gave in to a long yawn. The fluorescent lights of the clinic had been turned off when Kara and the office staff went home. It was almost eight and the facility was eerily quiet this time of night.

She walked down the hall towards her office, noticing that the door was open and the light was on. Given the events that had happened on the ridge today, she was a little apprehensive about who might be waiting. But the clinic was equipped with an alarm, so no one was getting in without triggering it unless they knew the code.

Brody had waited for her.

She smiled and picked up her pace. The quiet soles of her surgical clogs cloaked the sound of her approach, allowing her to peek inside the office without him noticing.

He was sitting at her desk with his legs stretched out and crossed at the ankles. With knitted brows, his focus was locked on his phone. He'd showered and changed into a dark pair of jeans and a baby blue t-shirt. And he'd traded his dirty brown Stetson for the new cream-colored one he'd worn at the wedding.

He stroked a hand over his dark beard, indicating he was deep in thought. She loved watching him and now she didn't have to hide behind a haystack to do. "You waited."

Startled, his head jerked up. He blinked a couple of times then smiled. "I told you I would."

His eyes still looked so tired, but they weren't as dull as they had been during the helicopter ride to the Rescue. That eased her guilty conscious a little. But it would take a long time to undo all the pain she'd caused him.

A lifetime maybe.

She'd never been more ready for that commitment.

"I know, but it's been a long day." She stepped to the cabinet along the wall where she kept her purse, opened it and began rummaging for her keys. "Damn it," she groaned. "I forgot. My truck's still at Darby's."

Brody stood, shoved a hand into his right front jeans pocket, and pulled out her keys. "Finn had our trucks, trailers, and animals transported to the Twisted J."

"Oh," was all she said as she took the keys. She was surprised Brody had her horse and truck taken to his ranch instead of the Rescue where she usually housed Clyde.

Palming the crown of his Stetson with one large hand, he positioned it on his head as he stepped around her desk. "I thought we could pick up some Mexican food and talk at my place. That is," he bent and softly brushed a kiss over her lips, "if you still want to talk."

The near-death experience had saved their tattered relationship and made her realize how precious life was. The words Brody had spoken right before he'd told her about Riley had helped to soothe her fears about her future with him. *There's nothing we can't work through, Louisa. Nothing. I believe that with all my heart.*

The crazy thing was, she believed him. Brody's faith in their love had helped her find the courage and calm her fears about their future together. She was ready to tell him about Chris and the precious gift she'd been robbed of. But she'd do it one step at a time.

This was the first step. Allowing herself more than kisses.

The touch of Brody's lips skimming across hers and the nearness of his hard chest as it brushed against her breasts caused a hot rush of excitement to pulse through her core.

He started to lift his head, but Louisa didn't want the kiss to end. She wanted a foretaste of what she hoped was coming after they had dinner. Curling her arms around his neck, she shoved her fingers into his hair and pinned him to her. He went with her response and deepened the kiss. Her body tightened, rousting a whine from her and a deep growling sound from him. She knew if they didn't stop now, they wouldn't stop until they were both satisfied and exhausted.

"I want to do more than talk," she whispered against his lips.

His eyes were dark with desire and anticipation. "So do I."

"But there are things I need to say before we make love, so we should probably stop now."

"Probably," he agreed, kissing his way to her ear.

She closed her eyes, wanting so badly to give in and let him make love to her here and now. But she refrained. Planting her hands against his chest, she gave him a little shove.

He growled and gave her a sexy grin. "How's Fred?"

"He'll live and might even keep his leg." Reaching into the pocket of her scrubs, she pulled out a small Ziplock bag containing the bullet she'd removed. "He was shot with a 17-caliber rifle."

His eyes told her he was impressed.

"I grew up on a ranch," was her explanation.

He left the bullet in the bag but gave it a close inspection.

She closed the cabinet door and slid her arm through her purse strap. "Varmint guns are a dime a dozen around here. Most ranchers use them to protect their cattle from coyotes."

"That seems to be the way all the evidence is going," Brody said, stepping into the hall so she could lock the door behind them. "But I'll pass it on to Finn anyway."

"There's more evidence?"

Brody wrapped an arm around her shoulders and together they walked down the hall to the main entrance. He filled her in on the talk he'd had with Finn and McCrea about Shorty sabotaging her truck, and he showed her the photo of the boot prints he'd found by the creek.

After she punched in the code that secured the alarm, they exited the building. "You don't think Cord had something to do with Blue Bayou and the bay, do you?"

Brody closed the door and reset the alarm. "Anything is possible, I guess." He escorted her to the passenger side of his truck. Once they were both in, he started the engine and backed out of the parking space. He drove through the main gate and set the alarm on the other side.

On the way to town, he told her about what had happened to Darby.

"Who'd hurt Darby?" she asked, shocked and a little frightened that this sort of thing was happening in her small town. "I mean, Fred got caught in the crossfire, but who'd purposefully harm that sweet old man?"

"Fred wasn't caught in the crossfire."

"Huh?"

"He was trying to herd that bay out of harm's way."

"What?"

"Whoever hurt old Darby doesn't have a conscience. They probably had as much remorse about hitting him in the head as they did about shooting the dog. They didn't think twice about it. Both were a means to an end. Keeping their identity hidden." He pulled into Carlo's Mexican Restaurant and parked near the curb. "I'll be right back."

Louisa tried taking it all in. Could Shorty do something as devious as hurting Darby? And for what? A few horses? None of it made sense. There had to be something more at stake.

Brody had left his phone lying on the dash when he went in for their food. She picked it up and took another look at the boot print. He'd said something about the letters B and C. Using her finger and thumb, she zoomed in on that portion of the photo. She knew she'd seen that brand before but couldn't remember where.

CHAPTER 24

BRODY RETURNED WITH A LARGE CARRYOUT BOX IN HIS hand. In the box were two white paper bags containing their food. He opened the door, placed the box on the middle console, and handed Louisa their drinks one by one. She set them in the cup holders as he climbed in and started the engine.

"Here's your phone," she said, handing it to him, then proceeded to rummage through the box in search of the tortilla chips. "That brand looks so familiar, but I can't place where I've seen it before."

"We'll know soon enough. It shouldn't take Finn long to get the information from LaSorona." He pulled away from the curb and back onto the street. "I called in the order over an hour ago. We may be eating cold fajitas."

"Fine by me," she said, munching on one of the tasty chips. "I'm starved."

Keeping his eyes on the road, he blindly reached into the bag for one. "So am I." He devoured the chip in one bite and went back for more. "That stew we had for lunch wore off hours ago."

The cab went uncomfortably quiet all of a sudden. Louisa guessed it was because they were both thinking about the kiss after that meal and how it had all gone south from there. It set the tone for the next step she needed to take.

"Did you always want kids?" she asked, easing into the conversation.

"Yeah." He chomped on another chip and chewed. "I knew I wanted to be a father at some point in my life."

"My maternal instincts weren't as strong." She broke a chip in half and popped it into her mouth. "In fact, having children never even crossed my mind until I met Chris."

She removed the bag of chips from the box and set it on the dash, so Brody could reach it without digging into the box. It gave her something to attend to while she talked. "When I fell in love with him, I started to see things differently. We talked about our life together after I earned my degree. He said he wanted to marry me and have a dozen kids."

"A dozen, huh?" Brody questioned with a smirk of doubt.

Louisa gave him a wiry smile. "I knew he was exaggerating, but when you're young and in love, you're willing to overlook embellishments. He said he wanted to make something of himself before we settled down and started a family. I admired that. He'd won all sorts of equine competitions and races. He was a good horseman and he'd had experience working at seed stock ranches, so I told Dad that I had a friend who needed a job."

Brody stopped at the last red light leading out of town. "Why did you keep your relationship with this guy a secret? Why didn't you tell Hardin the truth then?"

"Chris wanted it that way. I didn't see any harm in it.

Having secret rendezvous and stealing kisses when no one was looking was exciting and romantic back then."

The light turned green and Brody eased the gas pedal down.

"I was a stupid girl. I didn't realize that one day that secret would come back and bite me in the ass."

"Hindsight is twenty-twenty," he said, his voice cold and low.

Perception after the fact didn't help to console her regret or wipe away the disgrace of her mistakes. "Chris went for the interview and turned on the charm. He made these wild claims about having cattle management experience and ideas about ways he could help the ranch grow and just like that," she snapped her fingers. "The man I was sleeping with was working at my family's ranch."

"Hardin's no fool," he said, scoffing slightly at the notion someone had actually conned Hardin Coldiron. "And he's a shrewd businessman. I'm sure he checked Chris's credentials and saw through the bullshit."

"The credentials, yes. The bullshit, no."

Louisa didn't know if the sound Brody made was a growl or a failed attempt to clear his throat.

"I find that hard to believe."

"You obviously haven't met Chris and if you ever have the misfortune of doing so, you'll understand. Recommendations can be falsified, and certainly were, or Dad wouldn't have given him the job. But Dad did what he always does with new employees. He started Chris out at the bottom, cleaning stalls and running errands. But in three months, he and Dad were going to stock sales together and Dad was letting him bid on horses."

She lifted her drink from the cup holder and took a sip, noticing that they were approaching the stop sign where

Brody would make a right towards the Twisted J. "They still talk on the phone periodically, usually when Chris needs a favor. He's visited the ranch once or twice over the years. I'm never there, of course."

Brody shifted in his seat and tightened his hand around the stirring wheel. "The day you told me about your truck, you said Chris got what he wanted from you and moved on. I assumed you were talking about sex, but that's not what you meant, was it? The man's a con artist."

"That's a nice way of putting it." Louisa was thankful her head was turned away from Brody. Talking with him about having sex with Chris was so uncomfortable. "The man is scum, lower than scum. He – he's like the man that hurt Darby. He has no conscience. And sex—" She tried swallowing the bile that had suddenly hit her throat. "Sex was just a tool for him. We were his pawns, unwittingly helping him climb the ranching ladder of success."

"We?"

This conversation was churning up bad memories that had led to one of the worst days of her life. But she knew she had to keep going. "Dad invited Chris to attend an equine trade show with him. Of course, he said yes. He told me it was his chance to shine in front of my dad and make connections in the industry. I remember we drove to Dallas the day before and I helped him pick out a suit. I even paid for it." She laughed sardonically. "It was my good-luck gift to him."

"You paid for his suit?"

Brody continued to harbor a hard scowl as he drove. She feared those hard lines running up and down his face might be permanently etched into his skin by the time she was finished. "I paid for everything."

Brody had a bad feeling that Louisa was referring to more than material things with that comment. But he wasn't going to ask questions, at least not yet.

These were the things she needed to tell him before they made love, before he showed her what real love was, so he'd bite his tongue and sit through anything she needed to say, even if it was killing him inside.

When he made the turn onto the long gravel drive leading to the house, he stopped the truck. His mind went back to what she'd said about Chris calling in favors to her dad and to the conversation he'd overheard between Hardin and that unknown caller the day of Jess and Mallory's wedding.

I think I can help with that. Yeah. I know she'll love seeing you again. We can all have dinner and catch up.

Chris had called in a favor and intended to visit Hardin soon. Or maybe he already had.

Brody's gut took on that same uneasy feeling as the night he'd found the boot tracks by the shin oaks.

"The trade show was a three-day event, and I was home on summer break, so when I saw Dad's truck pull into the drive, I rushed downstairs to see Chris. But," she gave him a flinty side-glance, "we were keeping our relationship a secret. So there I was—about to go crazy with excitement because I was so in love with the guy —standing in my parents' foyer, waiting for him to walk in." She rolled her eyes. "You can imagine how giddy I was."

Brody remembered the first day he'd met Louisa. She'd sashayed across that same foyer boasting a sexy smile and brimming with sass. That's the moment he'd fallen in love with her. But he knew that hadn't been the woman who'd greeted Chris. The young Louisa had been so in love that she'd been completely oblivious to the ruses of a cunning predator.

"I opened the door." Louisa made a wide sweeping motion with her hand. "And Dad walked in. I asked him how the trip went. He said, fine, blah, blah, blah… I was still waiting for Chris to walk in. But he didn't, so I casually asked Dad where he was. He said Chris had some family business to take care of and that he'd be joining us for dinner later that evening. I didn't know Chris even had a family. He never talked about his parents or siblings."

Louisa stopped, allowing the striking similarities between himself and Chris to align. "I know you're nothing like Chris, but do you see why I held back? Why I was afraid to trust you?"

Brody was a horse trainer, had a close friendship with Louisa's dad, and hadn't mentioned his family to her until just a few days ago. The parallels between his life and Chris's were uncanny up to this point of the story. "Yeah."

She let her head fall against the rest. "Dad said something great had happened while they were at the trade show. Chris had been offered a job as a horse trainer for one of Dad's friends in Oregon. It was a great opportunity, came with a nice house, a handsome salary, and limitless possibilities. I was crushed, completely devastated by the news and heartbroken that Chris hadn't called to tell me himself."

"That's a pretty shitty thing to do to someone you're going to marry and have a dozen kids with."

"You haven't heard the worst part yet," she said, with a dead stare out his windshield. "Dinner time came, and Chris finally arrived – with is family."

Brody had seen that same dead stare in Louisa's eyes when they were under the overhang, after she'd demanded his wife's name, so he knew before she told him. "With his wife?"

"And little boy."

He felt his temper boil over. "That arrogant bastard."

"I was his mistress," she whispered.

There were a hundred ways Chris could have ended their affair without hurting Louisa. A hundred ways he could have slipped away and never come back. But he'd chosen not to. "He knew you wouldn't make a scene."

"If I had, my parents would have known I'd lied to them about our friendship. Not only that, but they'd know that I'd been having an affair with a married man. He used shame to silence me and it's worked for over six years."

Brody had wanted, no, he'd demanded to know why she was afraid to trust him and commit to their relationship and now he knew. Chris had deliberately played her, set her up for a hard fall, stabbed her in the heart and left her to bleed. He'd threatened Louisa's relationship with her parents all for financial gain and the pure hell of it. The man was malicious and three days ago, he'd called in a favor to Hardin. "Christ, honey."

"I later learned that Chris was seeing two other women while we were sleeping together. I always insisted we use protection, but there was one time when we didn't. So while Chris was in Oregon living in his new house with his wife and son, I was getting treatment for a sexually transmitted disease."

She flew through those facts like they were a well-rehearsed script.

"There's more, but that's all you're getting right now because I'm still learning to live with," she wrapped her arms around her belly. "The consequences of his affairs."

Brody collapsed against the seat, feeling like he'd been knocked in the noggin' by a baseball bat. "I don't know what to say."

"There's nothing to say." She bowed her head. "I'm not infectious. I have regular screenings, always use a condom and boil my partners in hot water before we have sex. Can I assume that, except for Riley's conception, you've done the same?"

Sexually transmitted diseases were a serious matter that could cause all sorts of complications, including infertility if left untreated. And after what she'd gone through, Brody understood her concerns about his safe-sex practices. "That's the last time I had sex, sweetheart. Before that, I always wore a condom. You have nothing to worry about."

"So you're okay with making love? I mean, I understand if you tell me to take my cold fajitas and hit the road."

Brody had never loved her more than he did right now. She'd been through a horrible relationship and dealt a shitty hand by a man that was supposed to have loved her. But she was willing to push all that aside and risk her heart for him and Riley.

"Half of these cold fajitas are mine," he reminded her.

He saw a twitch hit one corner of her mouth. "You can keep the fajitas. If you make me leave, my appetite will be ruined."

His lighthearted attempt to ease her anxiety had worked, to a degree. But uncertainty still lurked in her eyes.

Leaning across their box of cold fajitas, he twisted a lock of her hair around his finger. "You are a brave and beautiful woman and I love you."

The insecurity faded from her eyes, revealing that dusky sienna that he loved so well. She propped her elbow on the console and leaned in, her lips edging close to a grin. "Yeah?"

"Yeah, and I really, really want to make love to you

but…" He gave the lock a little tug. "I'm afraid I don't have a pot big enough for you to boil me in."

Giggle's spewed from her mouth. "I guess we'll have to settle for a hot shower."

He smiled. "Now you're talkin'."

CHAPTER 25

A LARGE WOODEN BEAM WITH EQUALLY LARGE POSTS ON each side created a simple but beautiful rustic entrance gate to the Twisted J Ranch. Creek rock had been laid half-way up the posts, which added to the girth and robustness of the structure.

"I was thinking of having one of those custom signs made." After they decided on the hot shower, Brody had driven the truck up the road and stopped a few feet from the gate to elaborate on his plans. "You know," he held up his hands to give her an idea of the size. "The fabricated metal ones Reece Winchester makes."

His enthusiasm was adorable and brought back luster to his eyes. And it wasn't just her finally committing to the relationship that had done it or them making up. It was a combination of all the things Brody had dreamed of and worked so hard to make happen over the last two years. Bringing Riley to Texas and the three of them living here as a family was the key to Brody's happiness.

The road curved and the place Louisa had heard so much about came into view. The light of the moon shone down on the two-story house and illuminated it like a spotlight. Carter's crew had replaced the old gray clapboard siding with modern vinyl the color of wild buttercups that grew along the backroads. The windows and doors were trimmed in white and brown shingles dressed the roof. A porch was centered in the middle and sheltered the front door. He'd planted shrubs and trees along the front and down the sidewalk. "Oh, Brody. It's beautiful."

"It's everything I imagined it would be," he said, smiling wide. He grabbed the box and opened his door. Louisa exited the truck and followed him up the sidewalk to the front door. He unlocked it, pushed it open, and flipped the light on so she could enter first. "Welcome to my humble abode."

As she stepped through the door, she heard the soft sounds of a country music song playing low in the background.

"I leave the radio playing," he said, shutting the door behind them. "It helps with the loneliness."

That, too, was something she could relate to. She kept the radio playing at night to help her sleep. That was probably why she hadn't heard Shorty outside her trailer.

The large room they were standing in doubled as a family room and dining area. It was beautifully designed with cherry floors and light beige paint. There were no curtains on the windows and the sofa and chair were still wrapped in plastic.

"They delivered the furniture yesterday." He shut the door, motioned her towards the dining table, and then hurried to remove the boxes of towels and washcloths sitting on top of it. "I haven't had time to unpack everything."

The living room's ceiling was open, with a balcony that

gave access to the upstairs bedrooms and a small office area that was open.

"It's beautiful. Did you do all of this by yourself?"

"Not exactly." He placed the box on the table and proceeded to unpack the aluminum containers of food. "I knew how I wanted it to look, but Allison helped me pick everything out."

"Wow." She laughed. "She must be some sister. I can't fathom working with McCrea or Jess on something like interior design."

Brody chuckled. "Allison is very patient. She's great with Riley."

"I can't wait to meet him," she said, feeling a swath of nervous excitement swirl in her stomach.

"Good." He reached back into the bag for the plastic forks and knives. "Because they'll be here tomorrow."

Panic and excitement scampered across her nerves. "Tomorrow?"

"I called Allison while you were in surgery." He flipped the bag over and out came the paper napkins. "Are you okay with that?"

"Of course." She waved a hand, signaling it was fine. "I guess I'm just worried about making a good first impression with Allison."

Brody set the bag on the table and hooked an arm around her waist. Bringing her around in front of him, he crooked a finger under her chin and rubbed a thumb over her bottom lip. His eyes were so sincere and filled with adoration. "She's going to love you."

"I hope so. I feel like I have some pretty big shoes to fill as a mother."

"But you're ready for being a mother, right?"

She rubbed her palm over his bearded jaw, marveling at its texture. "More than ready."

The song on the radio changed and the same slow-moving melody they'd had their first dance to started to play.

"Do you remember this song?"

He lay his hands on her hips and began the slow sway that had transformed their relationship. "I'll never forget it."

Their bodies were close, touching hip to hip like they had on the dance floor.

Louisa wrapped her arms around him. "There's something about your body that feels so…"

"Hard," he teased with a grin as the jutting form of his erection grazed her thigh.

She gave him a fake glower.

He chuckled softly.

"I started to say, familiar, like I've known you all my life, like this," she lay her head on his chest and listened to the strong beat of his heart, "is where I belong."

He rested his chin on her head. "This is where you belong."

As the song played on and on, as their bodies moved in time with each other, Louisa felt that same slow tension building in her lower belly.

This night hadn't been planned like the date he wanted. They hadn't dressed in fancy clothes. She wasn't wearing a black dress with high heels, the way she always imagined she would if they ever had a first date. Brody hadn't traded his jeans and t-shirt for a suit and tie. And that Stetson, the one he'd offered not to wear for her sake, was right where it belonged, on the head of the handsome cowboy she'd fallen in love with.

Louisa raised her head to look at him. Staring into those dark blue eyes, she knew she wouldn't have him any other way. From the crown of his dark head to the soles of those size thirteen boots, Brody was perfect just the way he was.

And tonight, he was going to make love to her.

Desire rippled through her. She raked the Stetson from his head and tossed it onto the table. It landed with a *fwap*, scattering the paper napkins and rattling the plastic cutlery. She sank her fingers into his hair and kissed him. It was a feverish kiss that escalated quickly like their second kiss had.

"Shower," Brody mumbled.

"Uh-huh," she breathed.

Not wanting to break the kiss, he planted his hands on her rear and hoisted her up. She wrapped her arms around his neck, her legs around his hips, and held on for the quick trip to the shower.

He opened the door to the bedroom, swung it back, kicked off his boots, and proceeded to the bathroom. Switching on the light, he pinned her to the wall while he blindly fumbled for the shower faucet. Water hiccupped through the pipes, spitting and sputtering, then launched into a warm stream.

He let her slip to the floor so they could undress. Socks and clogs were removed quickly and tossed in a corner. Shirts, jeans, and scrubs lay in a crumpled mess at their feet. But the hurried pace to remove clothing barriers slowed when the only thing between them was underwear.

Bare and beautifully tanned with a dusting of dark hair covering his pecs, Brody was more magnificent than she remembered. The overhang had been dark, and she'd been sitting astride him, so there hadn't been much chance to sightsee.

But there was now. She had all the time in the world to explore.

Her eyes moved to the middle of his chest and followed

the tiger line of neatly trimmed hair from the top of his rippled abdomen to his briefs. Normally, that's where her visual exploration stopped, and her imagination kicked in because everything below that glorious Adonis V had been hidden beneath his jeans.

But with those gone, the only thing between her and his protruding male member were those black, form-hugging briefs.

And what a form it was.

Plowing her fingers beneath his waistband, a fleeting thought skimmed through Louisa's mind. She owed Violet an apology. There was defiantly a correlation between Brody's size thirteen boot and that hard erection she was about to unveil.

She slid the briefs down his muscular thighs until they dropped. Keeping her eyes locked on his, she brought her hands back to his hips, then let them roam inward, across the front of his thighs and down the lower part of his stomach.

His blue eyes darkened with a deep longing that pricked Louisa's curiosity.

Lower and lower she went, sliding her palm over the thickening patch of hair covering his pelvis until she came to the top of his erection. She stopped there, building the anticipation with another heated kiss, then slowly ran her hand down the long length of him.

Brody let out an, "ahhh," and closed his eyes. When she gripped him in her hand, his jaw cocked sideways. His reaction to her touch fueled the fire burning in her core. She shifted her hand up and down, causing him to groan. She repeated the motion over and over until his groans became tight-throated growls.

With a jagged breath and eyes that resembled a starving man's, he covered her hand with his. Uncasing her from around him, he lifted her hand to his lips and gave her forefinger a gentle but firm suck. "My turn."

She considered that a delectable warning of what was to come. He gave her finger one last suck and lowered her hands to her side. The burning coil of desire knotted in her lower belly tightened and threatened to snap as he took the lead in their erotic foreplay.

Hooking a finger through her bra straps, he slipped them down her shoulders. He peeled down the wispy lace of the bra cups but stopped at the top of her areolas.

Brody was unwrapping her like a long-awaited gift, something sensual and promising, but also like something he treasured and wanted to remember seeing for the first time.

He planted his palms on the wall beside her head, securing her in place for his feasting pleasure. He started with a slow, sensual kiss to her lips and moved lower to her jaw. There, he trailed nibbles to her ear and down her neck.

The slow rate of his delicious descent was killing Louisa. She'd never craved a man like she did Brody. The hungry anticipation in his ragged breath as his lips moved across her collar bone made her body pulsate and tighten. Her senses were alive. Every nerve in her body tingled.

She'd never reached this level of arousal.

Never.

And she knew he wasn't going to stop until he'd satisfied every inch of her body.

The soft abrasion of his beard and mustache sent shivers across her skin as he kissed his way down to the underside of her breast.

He was teasing her like she'd teased him. He licked circles around her nipples, heightening her expectations.

Her breath came out as low whines and escalated to a cry when his lips closed over the mauve bud.

The gently sucking motion of his mouth made her tremble. It was the sweetest kind of torture and she wanted more.

He moved slowly and patiently, giving each breast the same arousing attention until her cries grew louder and her fingers fisted his hair.

Catching the waist of her panties with his thumbs, Brody slipped them from her hips. His eyes raked over her naked body, lavishing her with silent praise and approval.

"You're beautiful," he whispered.

She'd never felt so loved or so cherished.

She was only vaguely aware that he'd guided her into the shower or that the water was hitting her skin. She felt immune to the world and locked in this wondrous realm of male magnificence.

He sheltered her from the spray and took a bar of soap from the dish. Water rolled over his body, hitting his shoulders and chest, and cascaded down his flat stomach. He turned her around so that her back was against his chest and glided the bar over her breasts. It was the most sensual experience of her life. The feel of his wide calloused palms coated with soap and suds rubbing across her sensitive nipples caused her to lean against him and sigh.

With his mouth against her ear, he whispered a new proposal. "Will you be my wife?"

There wasn't a doubt in Louisa's mind that this man loved her or that this was where she belonged. Their son would be here tomorrow, and all was right with the world. Brody was her everything and she wanted to spend the rest of her life locked in his arms. "Yes."

Her answer shifted Brody's breath into overdrive. The slow movement of his hands quickened as he rinsed the soap away. He wrapped one arm around her waist, securing her firmly against his body. She could feel his hard erection pushing against her backside. Was this the way he was going to take her? Pressed against the shower wall? It wasn't like she was going to refuse. At this point, she was game for any position he wanted to try.

But he had other plans.

Sliding his free hand past her hip, his fingers skimmed across her belly, then slipped between her legs. Pleasure burst through her body when those fingers grazed her swollen bud. He continued his sweet assault until she was on the verge of a climax.

"That night at the creek," he whispered as she arched against him. "I dreamed about this. Making sweet love to you with my hands."

His fingers continued their gentle assault, tightening that cord of desire inside of her until it snapped. A wave of pleasure rushed over her, catapulting Louisa over the edge. Her body convulsed and shuddered. Trembling and so weak she could hardly stand, he held her in his arms as he switched off the water. He carried her to the bed, laid her down, and then pulled open a drawer from the nightstand. The bedroom was dim, but the bathroom light allowed her to see his face as he rolled the condom on and moved over her.

With eyes so dark they hardly resembled the man's she knew, Brody slowly sheathed himself inside of her. "I love you, sweetheart."

He filled her so completely. "I love you too," she whispered. She'd never felt anything so exquisite.

He drew back and pushed into her, gaging her reaction. She responded with a primal sound that was so unfamiliar, she wasn't sure she'd made it. That was all he needed. He thrust again and again. Over and over, he claimed her body until that fire she'd felt before was raging hot. Soon, she was flying over the edge again and into that bright light of pleasure while he restrained.

"Why?" she gasped against his neck.

"This," he pushed into her, his jaw clenched tight, "is the closest I can be to you. I don't…want it... to end." His release came three hard thrusts later. With a grated groan, he pushed into her and shuddered.

BRODY AND LOUISA ATE COLD FAJITAS AT ONE IN THE morning and crashed on the couch after he'd unwrapped the plastic from it. She'd fallen asleep in his arms and he'd carried her to his bed.

He'd never felt more complete or content than with her soft body lying next to him. But he hadn't been able to sleep. He'd felt that gnawing in his gut again; the one that told him what had happed on the ridge wasn't over.

He didn't know why. Maybe it was because Finn and his deputies hadn't found the bay yet. Maybe it was because Louisa was finally his and he'd do anything to protect her. All he did know was that something wasn't right. He was missing something, and his gut was telling him that something had to do with Chris.

Was it a coincidence that Chris had called Hardin for a favor days before the shootout on the ridge? Or was this Chris guy connected to what was going on at Darby's? Or the horse slaughter operation that had gone on at the Twisted J?

Brody had given up on thinking and fallen asleep around three. Now, at seven in the morning, he was awake with a clear memory of everything that had happened last night. He'd made love to Louisa – several times – and he'd proposed during their steamy shower.

She'd said yes.

As a bachelor, he was used to sleeping alone. He found it strange that waking up without Louisa in his bed made him feel incredibly lonely.

Yawning wide, he used his knuckles to scrub the sleep from his eyes and sat up. He swung his legs around, planted his bare feet on the floor, and stood.

She was nowhere to be found. The coffee tempting his nose hadn't made itself. She had to be here somewhere. Maybe she was exploring the rest of the house. He walked into the living room and saw her standing by the couch. Her head was bent as if she were looking at something in her hand.

The hem on the t-shirt he'd been wearing last night wasn't long enough to cover her hips so, when she shifted from one foot to the other, Brody got a tempting peek of her bare bottom.

"Now that's a sight worth waking up to," he said, crossing the room to stand behind her.

Her laugh was soft like the caress of fingers over his skin.

He slid his arms around her waist and kissed her neck. "You're up early, considering the late night we had."

"I couldn't sleep." She offered him her coffee cup and he accepted it. In her other hand was the silver-framed photo of him and Riley taken last month at the True Line. "He's a mini version of you."

He grinned. "Allison says the same thing."

Taking the photo with her, she moved to the window that overlooked the backyard. Her eyes were fixed on one of his weekend projects. "You built a trellis and planted roses."

He rested his chin on her shoulder. "I saw the one in your front yard. Do you like it?"

"I love it. The house, the yard..." She looked up at him, smiling like she did in his dreams. Sweetly. Lovingly, like everything in the world was right between them. Rubbing a hand over his beard, she sighed. "It's all so beautiful."

"You haven't seen the rest of the house. There are the two upstairs bedrooms and a bedroom across from the kitchen."

If she heard him, she didn't respond. Her hand slipped from his face and she went back to looking at the trellis.

Her behavior bothered him. Or rather, the mystery of it bothered him. The love they'd made last night was phenomenal. She'd been so happy, all smiles and laughter. But now she seemed so numb, so out of touch and so lost. It was like her heart was in a different universe and he couldn't reach it.

"I'll give you the grand tour," he said, hoping to spur a little happiness. Lacing his fingers through hers, he led her towards the small room adjacent to the master bedroom. "It's a little small, but how much room does a baby need?"

When she figured out that he was referring to the nursery, she stopped.

"After you proposed, I'd lie awake at night, thinking about that room, the paint colors we would have chosen, the furnishings..." Her voice drifted lower. "How it would feel to hold our baby in my arms, to nurse it and watch it grow."

He'd had those same thoughts, those same restless nights of wondering what could have been. But why did she sound like those experiences were lost? They were engaged and married soon if he had his way, and Riley was coming to live with them.

Her feet moved hesitantly towards the room as if she feared what was inside. Confusion and apprehension cast a dreary glaze in her beautiful brown eyes as she scanned the unpainted walls and empty space. "I don't understand. Why haven't you finished it? Why aren't the walls painted little boy blue? W–why hasn't Riley's bed been set up?"

"Riley's almost two," he said, sipping his coffee. "And like I said, it's a small room. He'll need more room as he gets older, so I didn't see the point of moving him into the nursery. His things are in the bedroom across from the kitchen."

"You've thought of everything."

It suddenly hit him that all of this might be a little overwhelming for her. She was standing in a house he'd designed without her input and he sounded like a dictator. "I've had plenty of time to dwell on the layout and where I think everything should be. But this is your house too. Feel free to change anything."

Her focus moved back to the picture of him and Riley. "Did you mean what you said? About there being nothing we can't work through?"

"I did."

"So, if I really did have a phobia about childbirth, if," she lovingly placed her hand over the photo, "Riley was the only child we ever had, you'd be okay with that?"

The tearful expression on her face twisted his heart. "Louisa, sweetheart, where are you going with this?"

"Please," she pleaded. "Just answer the question."

Brody thought, wishing he knew the reason behind the question before he tried answering it. "I'd be fine with that."

Louisa stared at that picture, unconvinced by his words. "You say that now, but…"

He understood why she'd guarded her heart and had

been afraid to love him. But her questions and odd behavior this morning had him completely baffled. It was a new fear and one that seemed to be more deeply rooted than her inability to trust him. Why was she so fixated on their future children?

He eased an arm around her waist and kissed her softly on the lips. "I say that now and I mean it. It doesn't matter to me if we christen it pink or turn it into a game room or a—"

A shard of pain sliced through her eyes, causing her to push him away.

Coffee sloshed over the rim of his cup, covering Brody's hand. It burned like hell, but he hardly noticed. Louisa's sudden one-eighty had him at a loss for words.

"I— I'm sorry. I'm late for work."

It was only seven-thirty. They had plenty of time before they were expected at the Rescue.

He followed her into the bathroom. "Is something wrong?"

She gave him a smiling frown. "No, why do you ask?"

The dichotomy of those two facial expressions and her abrupt about-face added to his suspicions that something had gone astray between them falling asleep on the couch and that scalding-hot brew dripping from his hand. "You seem… a little out of sorts."

She picked up her clothes from the bathroom floor and headed back to the bedroom. "I am just nervous about tonight."

Tonight? He didn't want to talk about tonight. He wanted to talk about what had just happened in the nursery. But she obviously didn't.

He set the cup on the bathroom sink and watched her slip on her panties and scrub bottoms. "I told you, Allison will love you. Don't worry."

"That's easier said than done," she said, whipping his t-shirt over her head.

If the circumstances of their morning-after sex had been different, if she wasn't behaving so…out of sorts, Brody would have stopped her right there, relieved her of those panties and scrubs and tossed her back on the bed for more lovemaking. Standing there bare-breasted with her long hair a mess and lips that begged to be kissed, she was a tempting morsel he wanted a taste of.

But he refrained.

Her phone buzzed. She snatched it from the night-stand, hit the mute button on the ringer, and flung it on the bed.

It wasn't like her not to take a call, especially since Fred was recovering and the bay was still missing. "Spam?"

"What?"

"The call. Was it spam?"

"No," she huffed. "It was Dad. He's been calling all morning."

McCrea had probably given their parents the G-rated version of what happened on Pinyon Ridge and left out parts about them being shot at. Since Louisa was okay, there was no need to go into details that might worry them.

He would have done the same thing.

But Mike Warner had called Brody yesterday, wanting details about what happened on the ridge. Rumors about another horse slaughter operation were already making their way around town.

Brody had declined to say anything, but the incident was probably front-page news by now.

"You should call him back. You know they're worried about you."

"Put yourself in my shoes," she continued, ignoring

what he'd said. "What if you'd met my family first, as my boyfriend?"

Her boyfriend?

"Not as an employee of the Rescue. Well, my dad and mom. Yeah. Imagine meeting them. Not McCrea and Jess…They don't count." She spun around, searching the floor. "Where's my bra?"

Brody had never heard her ramble like this and that scrap of lace she referred to as a bra was lying next to her left foot. Plain as day.

Something was amiss.

Stepping over to where she was, he picked up the bra. "If I were meeting your folks for the first time, it would be as your fiancé, not your boyfriend. Or did you forget that you accepted my proposal last night?"

"I didn't forget," she whispered in a faint voice, not like a woman who was excited about marrying the man she loved.

"Turn around."

"I can do it—"

"Around," he said, and she did, with an eye roll. He was more accustomed to removing women's undergarments than he was at putting them on. But he managed the task quickly and efficiently. And without letting his hands wander south.

"This is awkward," she told him. "I've never had a man dress me before."

"Get used to it." He slipped his arms around her again, trying to cuddle her into a good mood. "If," he put an emphasis on the word, "we decide to start a family, there'll be a lot of things I'll have to help you with. Remember when El was pregnant with Tucker? McCrea had to tie her shoes that last month."

Louisa jerked loose and grabbed her top. "I've got to

go. I—I'll see you later," she said, looping her arm through her purse as she headed for the front door.

Brody listened as she started her truck and drove away. She'd been gone for a total of two minutes, but he already felt so alone, and he knew that if he didn't find a way to reach her, he'd lose her.

Forever.

He started pacing the floor, replaying what had happened over the last couple of days. His mind regressed to the overhang. Louisa's odd behavior had started after their second kiss when he'd morphed into that irritable bastard.

He closed his eyes, remembering the mournful expression on her face. *Maybe it isn't about us at all. Maybe it's about me, just me and what I can't give you…*

The tremor in her voice… *The nursery. The paint.*

Her desperate outburst to make him understand what he should have figured out days ago…

His eyes opened and suddenly, it was all crystal clear to him.

Kids, Brody! You want kids!

"Oh, Christ," he whispered, as his legs gave way and he dropped to the bed. He now understood why every reference she'd made to their children was accompanied by a deep sadness that always triggered her withdrawal.

The way she'd cradled that picture of Riley. Her questions about their future children. *What if Riley was the only child we ever had; you'd be okay with that?*

The way she'd stared at that empty nursery. *I'd lie awake at night, thinking about that room, the paint colors we would have chosen, the furnishings… How it would feel to hold our baby in my arms, to nurse it and watch it grow.*

His mind went farther back to their past conversations. Her words echoed through his mind like ghosts. *So while*

Chris was in Oregon living in his new house with his wife and son, I got treatment for a sexually transmitted disease... I'm still learning to live with the consequences of his affairs.

Brody did what she asked. He tried putting himself in her shoes. What if he couldn't father a child? How would he feel? How would he tell her?

The emptiness and pain that consumed him made him grab his chest and fight for a breath. He loved Louisa and would die before he hurt her. But he had. The reference he'd made to the nursery, the comments he'd made about them starting a family...

He propped his elbows on his knees, dropped his face to his palms and cried.

CHAPTER 26

LOUISA MANAGED TO MAKE IT THROUGH THE MORNING medical staff meeting with a marginal amount of professionalism. She'd laughed away everyone's concerns by explaining that her red eyes and sniffs were from a bout of hay fever.

No one had questioned her.

With everyone caught up on their patients' status, it was time to roll up their sleeves and go to work. Patty was an excellent equine nurse who'd started out as a vet tech when the Rescue opened. She usually accompanied Louisa on her rounds and was a tremendous help. But Patty had called in sick this morning.

Louisa didn't mind. She needed time alone to think. She was a firm believer that horses were good for what ailed you. They helped heal a person's heart and soul, and over the years, she'd taken comfort in many of her equine friends. Nothing soothed her like the company of a horse.

But this morning, she was finding solace in another four-legged friend.

Fred.

The dog was still lethargic from the surgery and a tad disoriented from the anesthetic. But his vitals were good. Overall, his prognosis was good, and Louisa anticipated a full recovery.

She rubbed his scruffy ear while she tried sorting through the mess she'd made. Yesterday, she'd been so overwhelmed by the bullets and the adrenaline rush, she'd convinced herself there really wasn't anything she and Brody couldn't get through as a couple. She'd been on a lovemaking high, certain that love could bind them together and see them through any obstacle.

He'd asked her to marry him again, and she'd been so caught up in the pleasure of his tender lovemaking that she'd let her heart override her mind.

She'd said yes. She was engaged to Brody Vance. "Oh, Fred. What am I going to do?"

The dog cracked an eyelid open but then drifted back to sleep.

Added to her engagement complication was her commitment to Riley's future, a precious little boy arriving with his Aunt Allison this afternoon.

Brody had thought of details like that silly rose trellis. This morning, he'd tried calming her nerves and taken such tender care of her by helping her dress.

But waking up next to that hard body had indeed come with a price.

When we start a family…

Those consequences she'd warned Violet about were beating Louisa's heart black and blue. And the misery she'd made for herself wasn't going to end anytime soon. The electric chime had just gone off, signaling Brody's arrival to work.

She took a deep breath as she prepared for him to enter the examining room where they were keeping Fred.

When the door opened, she cast a glance over her shoulder, expecting to see Brody.

"Dad?"

"There's my girl," Hardin beamed.

She wanted to groan. "What are you doing here?"

A familiar yellow beard and dirty pinch front hat appeared in the doorway beside him.

Hardin gave her a wink. "I brought Fred a visitor."

"Hey, Darby." The sight of the old man hobbling across the floor made her smile. "How are you feelin'?"

"This doesn't hurt at all." He held up the cast covering his right wrist, then yanked off his hat and pointed to the bandage that covered the left side of his forehead. "This hurts like I've been kicked by a mule."

"I'm sorry," she crooned, stepping to the side so he could see Fred.

"Oh, I'll live," he said grumpily.

Now that Darby was himself, Louisa wondered if he could shed light on what had happened. "Did you get a look at the person who hit you?"

He shook his head. "It all happened so fast. The only thing I saw was the butt of that Henry long rifle."

Darby had just identified the other rifle, and it was just as common as the rifle that had been used to shoot Fred. Brody was right. The evidence was going nowhere.

The old man sniffed back tears as he gingerly stroked the dog's head. "How's this scamper doing?"

"He's seen better days, but I think he'll make a full recovery."

Tears of relief flowed down his weathered cheeks. "Good." He sniffed again and made another swipe across his face. "Doc, I have a favor to ask."

She couldn't think of anything she could do to help him, but she was willing to try. "Anything, Darby."

"I've decided I'm too old for ranching." He capped the hat back in place. "I'm going to live with my sister Gladys in Florida. She has a condo down there and I'm afraid Fred would hate it. Would you take him?"

Oh, lord. "Take him?"

"He's took a real likin' to you and he's a good dog."

How was she going to get out of this? She loved Fred, but her life was in such a state of mayhem right now. "Darby, I…"

"We'd be glad to take him," she heard Brody say from behind her.

Louisa looked around to see that he had entered the room quietly and was now standing beside her dad. He had a peculiar expression— red, puffy eyes with a touch of regret and sadness mixed in.

Maybe Brody had regrets too. About last night. About her…

Darby bent to plant a kiss on the dog's head. "You'll do good with these two. Good people. Fine couple. I expect soon, you'll be herding kids around the yard."

"I expect you're right," Hardin said, boisterously, as only a proud granddad could.

The weight of her dad's expectations saddled Louisa's shoulders, and today, she wasn't strong enough to carry them.

"Well," Darby shuffled around and started his trek back to the door. "I best be getting home. Gladys will be here next week and I have a lot of packing to do."

Hardin shoved a hand into his jeans and bowed forward as he scratched his jaw. "Darby, do you mind waiting for me? I'd like to speak to Louisa before we head back."

"I have some errands to run in town," Brody cut in.

"The refrigerator is empty and with Riley coming, I need to stock up on supplies. I can take Darby home."

"I'd appreciate that." Hardin held the door open for Darby. "I hardly see my little girl anymore."

His little girl had been purposefully avoiding him since Jess and Mallory's wedding. But thanks to Brody's generosity, she was being forced to spend the better part of an already long morning entertaining her dad's curiosity about her love life.

This day just keeps getting better and better.

Brody stepped across the room before leaving, produced her phone from his shirt pocket, and reached it to her. "You left it on the bed this morning."

She glared at him, her eyes communicating a silent message. *You just told Dad we slept together.*

His mouth skewed to one side in a way that said she was acting childish, and though she hated to admit it, he was probably right. Her parents and everyone else in the county thought she and Brody were already lovers. He leaned over and gave her a chaste kiss on the cheek. "Allison and Riley will be arriving at the house around seven. Don't forget."

Not likely.

Brody exited the room, leaving her in the company of Hardin Coldiron. In the past, spending time with her dad hadn't been such a task. She couldn't blame him. He was the same loving father he'd always been. Her guilt was to blame, but if she thought too long about that, she'd have a full-blown meltdown in front of him. So she sucked it all up and pretended she was fine.

Hardin motioned towards her phone. "I guess that explains why you didn't pick up when I called."

"Yeah," she said, laying it on top of the clipboard she carried with her when doing rounds.

Hardin rubbed his booted toe over a blemish in one of the cream-colored floor tiles. "How long have you been here?"

"A while."

Rounds at the clinic began at eight and, sparing rescues, emergencies, and setbacks, ended at five. Her days were usually longer and sometimes when it was hectic, she went without breaks or lunch. Normally, she didn't mind the overtime. But she wanted to shower and change before she met Allison this evening.

That wasn't happening now. This talk was going to throw her whole schedule off.

Oh, well.

Louisa smiled through a sigh and adjusted the stethoscope around her neck. "What's on your mind?"

"Why does anything have to be on my mind?" His brown eyes were a picture of innocence as he opened his arms. "Maybe I just stopped by for a hug."

"A hug, huh?" She couldn't help but be a little amused. "Those six missed calls on my phone were because you wanted a hug?"

"If your phone was on the bed this morning, how'd you know I called six times?" One dark brow raised high. "You didn't so much as glance at it when Brody handed it to you."

Damn.

He dropped his arms and moved a finger back and forth in a shaming way. "You've been avoiding your old man."

Louisa let her head fall forwards in a dramatic manner, knowing she was busted. "Okay, Dad. You got me. I didn't answer your calls this morning because I was busy."

This time, both brows went up.

Louisa felt her face burn. "Don't tease me."

"Who's teasing?" The question came with a jerk to his shoulder. "I'm happy as a lark you and Brody were busy this morning. After you socked him in the mouth at the wedding, your mom and I were worried the two of you might never reconcile your differences."

The heat in her cheeks went up a notch. She and Brody had done a lot of reconciling last night. Their love-making had been the sweetest and most tender moments of her life. But how long would that last once Brody knew the truth?

Hardin moseyed over to where she was standing, his eyes still on his boots. "I see he told you about Riley."

"Mm-hmm."

"Has that… caused some friction in the relationship?"

"Dad," she complained, feeling herself one step closer to tears. "I appreciate that you're trying to help, but there's really…" The words she'd been thinking all morning rolled to the tip of her tongue. "No hope for us."

Hardin ran a hand over his jaw, generating a brushing sound as his palm met whiskers. "Does Brody know that?"

She managed a wobbly, "No."

The long rush of disappointment expelling from her dad's lungs blew straight through Louisa's heart, piercing old and new mistakes. Suddenly, the emotions she'd been trying to hold back escaped, propelling the floodgates open and her into tears.

"Ah, honey." Hardin wrapped her in his arms. "Love ain't easy. You have to work at it."

She cried hard and long like she had under the over-hang when Brody told her about Riley. She cried because her heart was breaking, and no one understood why. She cried for all that could have been and all that had been lost. "There's no amount of work that can fix what I've done, Daddy."

He set her down on a stool and knelt to one knee. "Tell me what's wrong, Pinto."

In between the sobbing tears and the hiccups, Louisa told him about Chris, about the way he'd manipulated and used her. And with her last bit of courage, she told him the secret no other living soul knew.

The lines of time that were usually sketched across his face disappeared. Anger took hold of him, yanking him to his feet. He walked to the window. "Why didn't you tell me, then, Pinto?"

"I was too ashamed. And after it was all over, I convinced myself that everything would be alright. I didn't need children to be happy. But then, Brody came into my life. I fought so hard, Daddy." Tears dripped to her lap. "So damn hard not to fall in love with him, but did, and now he wants to marry me and have babies."

"Sweet Jesus," she heard him whisper.

She was a mature woman, a doctor who was about to have her own practice. But right now, she felt like that shattered nineteen-year-old. "Please don't be disappointed in me."

Hardin spun around, his eyes wide and glossy. "I could never be disappointed in you. You're my little girl and you've grown into a beautiful, strong woman." He went back to a knee and tenderly took her face in his hands. "Brody loves you. Tell him. Don't close him off and don't throw away what you two have because you think he can't handle what you just told me. You two can work through this."

She pushed his hands down and rolled the stool backward. "No, I won't deprive Brody of children. He'll move on."

"And what will you do, Pinto?"

Wither away.

THE GRIEF AND REGRET HE'D EXPERIENCED THIS MORNING hadn't smothered out that bad feeling in Brody's gut. It'd made it worse because all he could think about was Chris, the pain he'd caused, and how malicious the man was. Those thoughts led to another alarming thought he couldn't get out of his head.

The boot prints.

The prints of the boots that had been on the feet of the man watching Louisa. He was willing to bet a year's wages that those same boot prints were around her truck. But after the storms, any evidence would have been washed away.

After he drove Darby home and made sure he was safely inside, he drove back into town and found a parking spot close to the sheriff's office.

"LaSorona's a big company," Finn said, closing a file drawer before he sat behind his desk. "It may take a while before they get back with me."

Brody removed his Stetson and dropped into the seat across from the desk.

"But," Finn flipped through the paperwork on his desk until he found a photo, "those letters B and C, the ones we thought looked like a brand. They showed up again."

Brody scooted to the edge of his seat. "Where?"

Finn handed him the photo. "On the butt of a Henry rifle."

The black and white image taken of Darby's concussion wound bore the same marks Brody had seen on the boot print.

"This guy's arrogant," Finn declared, hitting a raw nerve in Brody's spine.

An arrogant, boasting bastard who liked leaving his

mark on things. A mark that had robbed Louisa of something precious.

"There might be a new suspect," Brody said. "A man named Chris. I don't know his last name, but he was an employee of the Coldiron ranch six years ago."

Finn leaned back in his seat, his eyes narrowing as he thought. "Have you asked Hardin about him? That was before my time."

Brody knew Finn had worked for Durant Resources in the oil fields before he was elected sheriff. "I'd rather not get Hardin involved in this. I thought maybe someone here might remember him."

Finn gave him a tired once-over. "Most of the deputies retired when I took office, but I'll look into it. Why do you think this guy might be a suspect?"

"It's just a gut feeling. I can't prove anything, but he and Shorty were friends."

"Shorty has a lot of friends." Finn started rearranging papers on his desk. "I'm not going to send my men out on what could be a wild goose chase because you have a hunch, Brody."

"I was told, in confidence, about Chris. I can't say any more than he may be one of the shooters."

"May be." He huffed in a way that was uncharacteristic of the normally calm Finn Durant. "Just like you may be wanted by the FBI?"

"Goddamn, it, Finn," Brody shot out, drawing glances from outside the office. "This is more than tall tales started by gossip. I'm worried about her. If I'm right, this guy's not done, and I won't sit by and let him hurt her again."

Finn chucked his pen across the desk and sighed. "Fuck me. They were lovers."

"I was told in confidence," Brody re-stated. "This Chris guy is arrogant and doesn't have a conscience."

"That doesn't mean he committed a crime."

"He fits the profile of the man who hurt Darby."

Finn scratched his ear, irritated he had to have this conversation. "You've been watching too many movies. We don't have a profile and the only evidence we have is that brand."

"Which links this guy to two crimes."

"This guy?" Finn asked. "We don't have any proof the perpetrator is a guy. It could have been a woman. There are plenty of women ranchers around the county who own a Henry rifle."

"True enough. But there are not many women who wear a size eleven men's boot."

Finn stood and straightened his duty belt. "I've been on the phone with LaSorona twelve times since you showed me that boot print. Now, I can haul my ass across the street and spend half the day kissin' Judge Butler's ass to get a warrant, so I can climb my ass into that cruiser and spend more time going through Hardin Coldiron's employee files. But we're a small department with more than this case to investigate."

"So we sit here and do nothing?"

Finn walked to the windows that separated his office from the rest of the offices and closed the blinds. "This is my county. These people elected me to protect them. I'm doing everything I can to do that. I'm chasing every lead I have in this case, but finding answers takes time and I have to find them while operating within the boundaries of the law."

Brody knew when someone was throwing him a hint, but he wasn't quite sure what Finn's was. "What are you saying?"

Finn reached into his shirt pocket for a cigar, then he raked it under his nose for a long sniff.

CHAPTER 27

"I DON'T HAVE A SHADY DICK," DEAN INSISTED, SLIDING AN arm into his suit jacket.

"That's a matter of opinion," a short, slim-built redhead mumbled under her breath as she strode past Brody and out of Dean's office.

Brody hadn't driven all the way to Austin, a forty-five-minute trip from Santa Camino, to be brushed to the side. "But if you did have one," he dodged an older blonde woman as she delivered a stack of files to Dean's desk. "You'd help me, right?"

Dean took the top file and flipped it open. "That all depends."

"There was some trouble out towards Pinyon Ridge the other day concerning a bay horse," he explained. "Louisa and I were –"

"Caught in the clutches of dangerous horse thieves," Dean finished for him, checking his wristwatch. "I believe that's the way Mike phrased it. I have an online subscription to the Tribune."

Brody raked his Stetson off and scratched his head. He

hadn't gotten a chance to read the paper. No wonder Hardin was so worried. "We weren't exactly caught in the clutches."

"What? No." There was a dry undertone to Dean's voice. "Don't tell me Mike embellished the story."

"Anyway," Brody continued. "I need help finding a guy I think may be connected to what went on out there. Chris something or another. He worked for Hardin about six years ago."

"You're the second person I've talked to today about Chris Keegan."

"Keegan?" Brody was shocked to the boot heels the man he was after was Chris Keegan, the cowboy host of a half-hour horsemanship show that aired on major networks. "The guy on television?"

"The one and only," Dean answered, unimpressed. "In my opinion, he's an asshole. But most people call me an asshole too, so…"

"Imagine what those people would call you if they had to work with you," the older blonde said as she handed Dean another file.

Dean didn't look up. "You're such a sweet woman, Deloris. Always feeding my self-confidence."

Brody twisted the Stetson around and capped it back on his head. "You said I was the second person asking about Chris. Who was the other?"

"Since my uncle isn't normally a vengeful man, I can only assume the rage in his eyes was because he found out about Lou's involvement with Chris."

Rage? Hardin?

Holy shit.

Brody ran four fingers across his forehead. Louisa must have told Hardin about the affair. Had Louisa stopped there, or had she confided in her dad about what Chris had robbed her of? "I don't understand. You knew?"

"Yeah." Dean glanced up at him for a second. "The five of us were close at one time."

Brody had heard plenty of stories about Dean, McCrea, Jess, Louisa, and Eleanor's childhood shenanigans.

"So I knew something happened when she suddenly went from the sweet girl I grew up with to the cowboy-hating sarcastic sass she is today." After he had what he wanted from the file, Dean tossed it to his desk and grabbed his briefcase. "I'm late for an appointment. If you want to talk, you're going to have to walk with me."

"Lead the way."

Dean straightened the collar on his jacket as they headed out the door and down the sidewalk. "Hardin wanted me to dig up anything I could on Chris. His finances, land deeds, who he does business with. Hell, he wanted to know what the man had for breakfast this morning."

"And what did you find out?"

They stopped at the crosswalk and waited for the light to change.

"Breakfast is a mystery. No one's seen him in weeks." Dean rechecked his watch. "But thanks to Hardin's generosity and connection, Chris was able to establish himself as a respectable horse breeder and cutting horse trainer. His horse King Jupiter Green won the National Cutting Horse Championship two years in a row with earnings well into the millions."

Brody whistled. "Remind me to buy your shady dick a case of whiskey."

"She prefers vodka."

The orange hand on the crosswalk flashed, signaling it was safe to cross.

"Chris was living on easy street, but then everything fell apart."

"What do you mean?"

"His wife got tired of his shit. She divorced him last year, took the kids and his money. Networks dropped his show and he put Blue Creek on the market two months ago."

"Blue Creek?"

"His pride and joy," Dean said, twisting his mouth into a disapproving frown. "It's a huge ranch in Wheeler County, Oregon, with temperature-controlled barns and training paddocks…"

The letters B and C.

Blue Creek.

The brand.

"That high-priced, over-decorated arena you see in the background of his television show," Dean continued. "It's at Blue Creek. The man has his own line of boots some boot company."

"LaSorona," Brody said aloud, knowing he had proof that tied Chris to the evidence at both crime scenes.

"Yeah, I think that's the name. Why?"

"Nothing. What else did you find out?"

"Chris owes his balls to some of the heaviest hitters in the horse industry. Some of those hitters are on the opposite side of the law. King Jupiter Green sired a bay Chris named Easy Come, Easy Go. This where it gets good. Three weeks ago," Dean gave Brody a seldom seen grin, "Easy was stolen from Blue Creek."

"Shit," Brody hissed. "A horse like that has to be insured."

"You can bet your sweet ass he is." Dean frowned. "But

if you're going to steal a horse for insurance money, you better damn well have a way of getting rid of it."

"Getting rid of it," Brody repeated as his mind shuffled through bits and pieces of evidence. "But why bring a horse all the way to Texas to do it? Why not just kill it and dispose of the body?"

"And take a chance on getting caught?" Dean shook his head. "Too risky. Chris is broke and suddenly his high-priced horse is stolen? Any insurance investigator worth his salt would see through that."

"But if your horse is stolen and then rescued from rustlers…" A cold chill ran over Brody.

"And has to be put down." Dean's face went white. "Where's Lou?"

"WHERE DID YOU FIND IT?" LOUISA ASKED, RUNNING alongside Deputy Jones to the horse trailer that was parked outside the clinic.

"He was about half a mile from Pinyon Ridge."

The deputy accompanying Jones had the horse unloaded by the time they reached the trailer. The deputy scratched his head. "The strange thing is we searched that area high and low."

"Horses roam, especially when they're hungry," she said, dismissing the oddity as she placed the stethoscope over the animal's heart. Strong heartbeat. She slid it around. And his lungs sounded clear.

This horse wasn't like the others. His shiny coat and trimmed mane and tail were signs he'd been well cared for. "Any word from the sheriff?"

"No," Deputy Jones answered. "Carly B says he's in a

Tri-County Planning meeting over in Augustine. She left him a voice mail but doesn't expect him back until later."

Carla Beasley had been with the department for more than thirty years. She would have given the young deputy's ear a good ringing if she'd heard him refer to her by that nickname instead of her professional title of administrative assistant.

Looping the stethoscope around her neck, Louisa straightened and took a step back to assess the horse's stance. He was standing with his left hoof tipped up to the toe. "His leg looks lame."

"Yeah," Deputy Jones agreed. "I pulled prickly pear needle from that leg before we loaded him."

The bay had been out there on his own for well over a week. Cacti needles could be dangerous to a horse if left unattended. "Let's get him inside."

It was twenty past five and the medical staff had gone home for the day, so Louisa was on her own. Her dad's talk had left her emotionally drained, and she still had to greet Allison and Riley with a smile.

"Thanks, guys," she said to the deputies once the horse was in the exam room. "I can take it from here."

They said their goodbyes and walked out the door. A few minutes later, she heard the truck and trailer drive away.

"He looks good, considering," Kara said, gently grazing a hand over the horse's neck. She'd stayed after the call came that the bay had been found.

"Thank God." Louisa ran her fingers along the horse's neck, feeling for the juggler groove from which she could draw a blood sample.

"Do you want me to try the sheriff's cell?" Kara asked.

"No. There's nothing to say other than they found the bay, and I'm sure Carla included that in her voice mail."

After the needle was in, she placed the Vacutainer tube onto the bottom and watched it fill with blood. "I'll examine the horse and give Finn a call in the morning. You should go on home."

"Are you sure?" Kara glanced around the large empty room. "Brody's truck isn't at the cabin and I hate leaving you here all alone."

"The horse seems fine. I'll finish my exam and be out of here in no time." Kara was a young woman, who was just old enough to drink, worked three jobs, and helped care for her ailing mother. "Now, go on." Louisa shooed her towards the door. "Get out of here."

Chuckling, Kara exited the exam room and went to collect her purse.

Louisa waited until she heard Kara walk out the door and set the alarm before she continued. She hadn't seen Brody since he walked out with Darby earlier this morning. He'd left her a voice mail. He had something to do in Austin and would be back by seven.

Taking her phone from her scrub pocket, she punched out a quick text message to him saying the bay had been found and was at the clinic with her. She wouldn't be able to make it to meet his sister.

Feeling guilty but relieved, she turned the ringer off and laid the phone on the counter. Brody would call when he received the text, but with Allison and Riley at the Twisted, he wouldn't be dropping by the clinic tonight.

Louisa moved on to examining the horse's hoof. She started at his shoulder and stroked downwards to his knee. Then she grasped the cannon bone firmly and gently pulled the leg backward while she pushed against his shoulder with her other hand.

The hoof was healthy with a supportive heel buttress and had recently been shod. Satisfied that the cacti needle removed by Deputy Jones was the reason for the lameness, Louisa examined the other hooves.

They were also in good condition. The horse seemed to be mostly unscathed by his time in the backcountry. She'd order diagnostic testing in the morning to be sure.

The clinic was usually filled with the hustle and bustle of noise and chatter as the staff moved about the building. She'd learned to tune out the sounds and concentrate on her job, so it took a second or two for the noise to register as something alarming.

She rose from her crouching position beside the horse and listened.

Tap. Tap. Tap.

The hair on the back of her neck stood up.

Footsteps.

Booted footsteps.

Brody?

The large, analog clock above the counter read sixforty so maybe he had dropped by, explaining why the security alarm hadn't gone off.

Relief relaxed her shoulders. Shedding her latex gloves, she tossed them in the trash and pushed open the door. The lamp in her office was on and projected a square light into the dark hallway.

The shadow of a large man wearing a Stetson passed by it.

Damn it.

Why couldn't he have waited until morning?

Stepping from the exam room, she let the door swing shut and set a path for her office.

Louisa wanted the ending to their love story to be less painful than the beginning had been. She'd thought all day about how to make that happen, how to soften the blow and the words she could say to relieve the sting. But there were no easy endings.

She knew that now.

She paused for a sigh and stepped into the light, expecting to see Brody. But the blue eyes looking back at her weren't that warm metallic blue she loved so much. They were an arctic shade of stone-cold blue.

Her stomach heaved.

The man sitting in her chair behind her desk was someone she never wanted to see again. "Chris?"

He smiled. "Hello, Lou."

Her mind stalled but then kicked into gear. Why was Chris Keegan in her office? Sitting in her chair? The chair that Brody had sat in just last night. That thought appalled her. "Get the hell out of my chair."

Chris didn't move. "Now, is that any way to treat an old friend."

"Friend, my ass." An old ghost was more like it. "The clinic is closed. How did you get past the alarm?"

He winked at her. "I have my ways."

His ways involved lies and deceit, so why was he here? She crossed her arms and leaned a shoulder against the doorframe. "What do you want, Chris?"

His smug smile faded, and his lids lowered a fraction, giving him a snakelike appearance.

Appropriate.

How had she fallen for this guy? How had she been seduced by that smile and those cold, cold eyes?

Chris propped his elbows on her desk and brought his fingertips together, forming a triangle. It was something he did when he wanted to look studious and authoritative.

Louisa wanted to vomit.

What a jackass.

"You have my horse," he announced.

An uneasy feeling marched up Louisa's spine as the image of those boot prints on Brody's phone flashed in front of her.

Oh, God.

B and C.

Blue Creek.

How could she have not remembered his ranch? Because layer by layer, kiss by sweet kiss, Brody had all but wiped those memories from her mind. If not for her infertility, Chris Keegan would have been just a speck of dust on her past.

But she didn't have that luxury and Chris was here.

In the flesh.

He'd sabotaged her truck and been one of the shooters at Pinyon Ridge. Fred. Poor Darby. And he'd been the man at the creek—the man watching her undress.

But why? Why had he done all those things? Why was his horse in Texas? Was Chris was the man behind the illegal horse operation? The man Chaves answered to? She'd keep that theory to herself until she knew where this was going. "What do you want?"

"A favor."

She shuddered.

Scoffing, Chris stood and hooked a thumb into the back pocket of his jeans. Walking around her desk to a bookshelf, he trailed a finger across a row of equine medical journals. "Don't worry. It's not that kind of favor." One side of his smile lifted like a theatrical curtain, revealing perfectly veneered teeth. "I'm not much on indulging in second-hand snatch. I like my women young and innocent." With a sling of his hand, the journals flew from the shelf and scattered across the floor.

Louisa jumped and stepped back, preparing to spin and run. But a set of arms clamped around her shoulders.

"Hold on there, Dumplin'," Shorty said, his breath hot and rancid against her ear. "We ain't done with you yet."

"The sheriff knows I'm here," she announced, her voice raspy and weak. "It was two of his deputies that found the bay."

Shorty pushed her into Chris's arms. "Took 'em two damn days to do it too."

Chris clamped a hand around her wrists and yanked her to him. Her attempt to jerk from his grasp failed. He was too strong. "The horse's name is Easy Come, Easy Go," he said. "I named him after you."

Anger cut through her fear. "Go to hell."

A hard and unexpected slap knocked her eyes out of focus. "Shut up," he ordered, gripping her arm tight as he dragged her up the hall to the exam room.

Louisa was too addled to fight back. Her cheek hurt and her vision was coming and going. Chris had never shown the slightest hint of aggression while they were together. So what had changed him? And what was she going to do to protect herself from him? Brody wasn't coming to her rescue this time. She'd made sure of that by turning her phone off and leaving it on the counter.

She and the bay were at the mercy of this predator.

Chris pushed her through the door. She lost her balance, stumbled and hit the floor. The horse whinnied and jerked his head back in a panic to free himself. But the lead rope hooked to the wall held him in place.

"He's lame," Chris observed.

Louisa managed to get to her feet. "A prickly pear needle was in his hoof."

Chris went to a supply cabinet and began rummaging through it.

"What are you doing?"

"The horse is lame and suffering, so you had to put

317

him down." He coldly glanced her way. "That's what you'll tell the insurance company."

Insurance company. The answers to her questions hit Louisa like a ton of bricks. This was all a scheme, a well-thought-out plan for the money.

Sweet Jesus.

That eeriness returned to his eyes and was accompanied by a perverse smile. "Is that little brain of yours finally connecting the dots?"

"You let Chaves take the fall, didn't you?"

"Tony was a greedy fool who almost ruined the entire operation for few pottery shards," he said before turning his attention to the locked cabinets on the opposite wall. "Where are the goddamn keys?"

"You're not getting them."

Clamping his jaw tight, he strode towards and she knew another slap was coming.

"I'm not putting him down," she shouted, putting herself between Chris and the horse. "He's strong and healthy and the lameness can be treated with rehabilitation."

The slap knocked her sideways. Clutching the lead rope, she tried keeping her balance. But the room was spinning.

"We're wasting time." She heard Shorty say. "I'll look in her office."

"You will put him down." Chris fisted a handful of her hair and yanked her forehead to his. "Or Daddy will know what a tramp his little girl is."

This time her anger was projected in the form of what her brothers would call a perfect loogy.

Chris recoiled and raked a hand over his face.

"My dad–"

Another slap stopped her words.

But she wasn't giving up. The horse's life was a stake. "I'm not killing him." White-hot anger spread over Chris's tanned skin and Louisa knew another slap was coming. She closed her eyes and held on to the lead rope.

Louisa prayed she was strong enough to take it. But his fist was no match for her. Everything went black and she fell to the floor. She couldn't see but she could hear everything. The clamoring of keys as Shorty returned and Chris telling him to finish it.

"You said she'd be easy to control," Shorty said, his voice spiked with fear. "But you heard her. She ain't going to go along with the story, and when Brody finds out you beat the hell out of her, we're as good as castrated."

Louisa felt herself go up and over. She forced one eye open. Chris had thrown her over his shoulder.

"He won't find out."

She raised her head and saw the bay drift farther and farther away.

The bay.

She had to save the bay.

CHAPTER 28

"Something's wrong," Brody slammed a hand over the horn as the car in front of him slowed to change lanes. "I can feel it."

They'd made it to Santa Camino in only thirty minutes and had just passed the city limits sign.

"Slow down," Dean ordered. "She's probably just busy with the horse. The deputies said she was fine when they dropped it off."

When Louisa didn't answer her phone, Dean had Deloris cancel his appointment, and he and Brody had spent the drive back to Santa Camino calling people they knew.

No one but Carla Beasley picked up. She'd put a call into the deputies, who assured her everything was fine at the Rescue.

But Brody knew better. He could feel it in his bones — in his heart. This morning he'd been so afraid of losing Louisa. He'd put off facing her because he'd felt guilty about not seeing what was right in front of him. Now, he might lose her forever.

He should have manned-up and told her he was sorry. He should have listened when she tried telling him about those babies and that unpainted nursery.

Damn it.

He should have known.

"Let's be calm and rational," Dean said. "Is there any other reason Louisa wouldn't answer you back? Did you two have an argument before you left?"

"No, but," he gripped the stirring wheel with both hands, "I have a feeling that today was a hard day for her. And she was supposed to meet my sister and Riley tonight."

"So it's possible she might just need space? Time alone?"

God, he hoped so. "Maybe. But I called Allison. Louisa never made it to the Twisted J."

"She could have gone home," Dean suggested. "Let's check there first."

Brody felt like it was a waste of time, but if Dean was right, he was blowing things out of proportion. He flipped his signal light on and headed in the direction of Louisa's Airstream.

Ten minutes later, Brody turned into her drive. There was a little light burning in the front window. But her truck wasn't there. He parked, hurried up the steps, and opened the door.

Dean came in behind him. "It looks like it's been a while since she was here."

Brody moved to the small dinette table near the window. Scattered on top were a dozen or more infertility pamphlets and two empty wine bottles.

"What the hell," Dean whispered, picking up one of the pamphlets.

Brody snatched it from his hand and shoved it into his back pocket. "No one knows. Okay?"

"Yeah." He swallowed and nodded. "Sure, man."

On their way out, Brody's phone rang. "It's McCrea," he told Dean before he answered. "Tell me Louisa is with you."

McCrea didn't answer and Brody felt his heart stop. "What's wrong?"

"I'm at the Rescue. You better get over here."

By the time Brody and Dean arrived at Promise Point, Finn's cruiser and three other sheriff's cars were sitting in the parking lot. Those silent blue lights flashing in the darkness caused Brody to lose his breath.

He shoved the truck into Park before it came to a complete stop and jumped out. His eyes skipped from here to there, looking for McCrea.

"What happened?" he asked, running towards the police car nearest to the clinic when he spotted Finn.

Finn held up his hands. "Calm down."

"What happened?" he repeated.

"We don't know," Finn answered, his face grim as the Reaper. "After you called Carla, she had the deputies do a drive-by. Called it woman's intuition."

Brody's blood ran cold. "And?"

"They saw Shorty's truck in the parking lot," McCrea answered for him. "Found him inside, but Louisa is missing."

"Goddamn it, McCrea," Finn swore.

Brody's eyes zoomed in on the police car and the man sitting in the back.

Shorty.

Shoving his way past Finn and another deputy, Brody opened the door, latched onto Shorty's collar and pulled him out. "Where is she, you son of a bitch?" He punctuated his question with a hard punch that knocked Shorty to the ground.

With his hands cuffed behind him, he couldn't do anything but roll over and groan. "I don't know."

Brody was about to go for another question when Finn grabbed him. Two more deputies took hold of his arms. "You can't beat the hell out of a man who's handcuffed and in my custody."

"Uncuff him and watch me. Where is she?" he yelled.

Shorty drew his knees up and rolled to a sitting position. Both eyes were blue and puffy.

"I asked him the same question," McCrea said, rubbing his knuckles. "Several times before he was taken into custody."

Brody lunged for him again but was restrained by the deputies.

Shorty reacted on instinct, curling into a ball. "I swear I don't know. He said he was going to make sure no one found her. That by the time they did, we'd be long gone. But I didn't sign on to kill her," he cried. "A horse? Sure. But not her. I knew I was as good as dead if I helped him, so he left me here to finish the horse."

"They found him before he could administer the lethal injection," McCrea said.

Brody jerked free and spun around, feeling like he might lose his mind. "Christ!"

"We've put an APB out on Chris and are setting up roadblocks on all roads in and out of the county," Finn said. "They won't get far."

"Why?" Brody asked Shorty. "If he wanted the horse found, why did the two of you two shoot at us?"

Shorty scooted up against the car and rested against a tire. "Chris wanted to expand the business."

"From a slaughter horse operation to insurance fraud?" he asked, and Shorty nodded.

"But Easy got away," Dean stated.

"Chris knew you were coming," Shorty continued. "He'd followed you from Darby's. We thought the storm would slow you down, and we could get out of there before you saw us. But then..."

"Those heavy hitters paid you two a visit," Dean surmised, casting Brody a smirk. "They wanted their money."

"But when Chris didn't have the money," Brody said, "he offered them a cut of the new business."

"He told them he had a vet that would help. She was a sure thing. That it was a fool-proof plan." Shorty closed his eyes and let his head fall against the car. "Then that damn dog came along and started barking. All hell broke loose. Easy."

With everything explained, Finn helped Shorty up and back into the car. That was it—the end of the story.

Brody had set out to prove Chris was behind it all and he had.

But Louisa was gone.

"Maybe that old jalopy of hers will break down," Dean told them.

Break down...

Break down...

Pinyon Ridge.

The wagon trail.

"Make sure no one finds her... I know where she is!" Brody launched into a dead run for his truck.

≈

THE WORLD SHIFTED, BUT THE BLACKNESS REMAINED. Louisa wasn't sure if she was dead or alive.

But if this were the afterlife, if Chris had killed her, then she was in hell.

Heaven couldn't be this dark and painful. She tried recalling something that might birth light in the nothingness.

Something that might kill the pain throbbing through her face and body.

Brody was her first thought.

Riley was her second.

Their faces faded in and out of the darkness like scenes from a movie. Flipping and spinning until they merged, and she found herself staring at that silver-framed photo.

There was the light emanating from behind the photo shining in a thousand different directions. It was so beautiful.

They were beautiful.

Oh, how wonderful life with them would have been. Brody and his little boy. They would have filled that emptiness inside of her.

But they were gone.

All gone.

The hope.

The possibility.

Gone.

Brody would never make love to her again, and she'd never hold that little boy in her arms. Their faces started to fade and the blackness returned.

But the world shifted once more, harder this time. Her body went up and landed with a thud. The impact caused her to roll over and cough.

Forcing her lids open, she focused on the blurry object in front of her.

She wasn't dead and this wasn't the afterlife.

This was the inside of her truck.

Ha! Her mind laughed—she'd been kidnapped. Why did she find that amusing? Because Chris had used her for face as a punching bag and knocked her sensless.

Yeah, that was it.

She groaned and tried sitting up. But her arms wouldn't work. They wouldn't move. She wiggled her fingers. They worked. She tried again to lift her arms and determined that they were bound behind her back.

Figures.

She wiggled her toes and shifted her feet. When she learned they weren't bound, she drew her knees to her chest and sat up.

Chris was behind the wheel.

"If you're going to kill me, do it now." It hurt when she moved her jaw. "I'm tired of looking at your face."

"I'm not going to kill you," he assured her, that cold, angry mien was still plastered across his face. "I'm going to let gravity do it for me."

She was too woozy to think about that or care. "You really are a son of a bitch."

"Still pissed about that nasty little infection, I see."

If she'd had any spit left, she would have given him a good shower. But her mouth was so dry.

She was so thirsty.

She wished she were back at the overhang with Brody. The rain, the campfire, the love she felt when he kissed her…

"You really shouldn't be so devastated," he continued his rant. "Kids are a pain in the ass."

That caused her eyes to sting as tears filled them. "You have no idea how much I want a baby."

"Spare me," he said, shifting the wheel around, so the

wheels caught traction. They did, shifting the truck side-ways and back on the trail.

Louisa scooted to the passenger door so she could see out the window. They were going up a hill, a steep hill. A ridge. She lifted her gaze up and saw pinyons.

Gravity.

He was going to roll her off the Pinyon Ridge.

Tragic and effective.

Unless she could find a way out of this mess, she'd be maggot food in the morning.

But even if she could escape Chris, how would she find her way to the road? In the dark?

It was hopeless.

She leaned back against the seat and turned her head to look at the moon. It was beautiful. It was a gorgeous night to die.

Her gaze drifted farther and farther until she saw tiny blue lights flashing in the distance.

Like the wheels on her truck, something in her foggy brain caught traction. She blinked again and again. Each time she did, the lights looked bigger and bigger.

Snap! Her brain clicked.

Those were police lights.

"You'll never get away with this," she jabbed, hoping to distract him.

"You euthanized the horse because it was lame," he shot a blood-curdling smile her way. "I'm sure there'll be a search party and I'll be a part of it. Don't worry. When the sheriff finally finds your body, I'll console Hardin and Belle. And after they've had time to grieve, I'll convince him to help me invest my insurance money."

"No, you won't. I told Dad everything. He knows all about how you used me."

Chris's head jerked around.

She laughed. "Now that face, I like. Blue Creek. B and C. The brand is on your boots and the end of your Henry."

His face lost all expression.

"Is that little brain of your starting to connect the dots?'" she mocked and then laughed again. "You thought you had it all worked out, but your arrogance has pinned your ass to all of it."

A familiar hum started in her ears. At first, she thought it was from the slaps, but then she saw the flashing lights of the county search and rescue helicopter above them.

A spotlight targeted the truck and the whole world went bright. They knew she was here.

"Goddamn it," Chris belted out, stomping the gas pedal.

The truck spun and shifted to the left then to the right. Each time it did, it threw her against the door. They were almost at the top. If she could just get the door open...

She grabbed the handle and held on, waiting for the next shove. He turned the wheel again and out she went. She landed on her side and rolled. The impact blasted the air from her lungs. She couldn't breathe.

"Louisa," she heard Brody call and knew she wasn't hallucinating. He was here, searching for her. But how? How had he made it up the ridge? The helicopter. He'd been in the helicopter.

She tried answering him but couldn't. Finally, she coughed, and the air rushed back to her lungs. "H–here. I'm here."

"Oh, God. What did he do to you?" The last thing she remembered before the darkness crept back in was the wonderful feeling of Brody's hands holding her face.

∽

LOUISA FADED IN AND OUT OF CONSCIOUSNESS. McCREA'S voice merged with Finn's, and the sirens fused with the helicopter blades' whooshing sound.

Other voices, unfamiliar voices, scattered through her ears with noisy static.

The perpetrator is in custody...

The woman has been found...

The only sound that remained clear was Brody's voice.

She woke up once at the hospital but quickly closed her eyes. She was so tired. She remembered the ride to the Twisted J and Brody carrying her inside. But after that, everything was blurry.

"Are you sure she's okay?" she heard a woman ask. "Those bruises on her face "

"Will heal," Brody replied, his voice low. "Nothing was broken and she doesn't have a concussion. The doctors said she was fine. She just needs rest, Allie."

Allie.

Allison.

Brody's sister, she thought before everything faded to black.

When Louisa opened her eyes again, she had a clear picture of reality. Nothing was blurry anymore. She wasn't staring at the inside of her truck or the dark and dusty surface of the ridge floor.

She was in Brody's king-sized bed. The forest green comforter she'd slept under the night they made love was covering her. The soft pillow that smelled of his cologne was beneath her head.

She was safe.

She was home.

If only for a little while.

Wanting nothing more than to snuggle under the covers and stay in this moment forever, she rolled over. But she wasn't alone. Sleeping soundly beside of her was a beautiful little boy.

Riley.

A mini version of Brody.

Dark hair and lashes. Chubby cheeks and full baby lips that were parted in slumber.

Tears sprang to her eyes. Was he really here, or was this a dream? She slowly lifted her hand. She wanted to touch him, feel his breath, and know that he was real.

A flesh and blood child.

Her child.

Their little boy.

She hesitated, thinking that if she touched him, he might vanish. She couldn't bear that. But if this were a dream, she couldn't live in it forever.

Carefully, gently, she placed her palm over his chest. The soft rise and fall of his breath caused her to smile. Laying her head beside his, she pulled in a deep breath.

He smelled wonderful.

She saw Brody enter the room and knew the happiness she felt was about to end. He eased into the bed beside Riley and stretched out. Propping his head on his hand, he reached across the boy to brush back a strand of Louisa's hair. "There you are."

She licked her bottom lip. "Here I am."

Dark red veins webbed through his rheumy eyes. Pain tore through her when she realized he'd been crying. Those tears would only get worse once she told him the truth. But she was tired of keeping secrets, tired of knowing she'd never be enough.

"I can't have babies," she blurted out and let the tears come. "What Chris gave me... there was too much scarring. The doctors say it would be a miracle if I were able to conceive."

The somber reality of what she'd said melted Brody's smile and her heart felt like it might break in half.

God, she hadn't meant to hurt him. "I'm so sorry I didn't tell you sooner. But I just wanted to hold on to you for a little while longer."

A large tear spilled from his right eye and rolled down his cheek . "You can hold me for as long as you want, sweetheart. I'm not going anywhere."

She was sure shock was preventing him from grasping hold of what she'd just confessed. "You don't understand. If you marry me, that nursery will never be pink or blue or–"

"I understand perfectly," he said, producing one of her infertility pamphlets from his pocket. He held it up for a second then tossed it over his shoulder as if it meant nothing to him. "It's just a room, Louisa."

"It's not."

"Yes, sweetheart. It is," he insisted. "And our relation- ship—our marriage—won't be contingent on how many children you can give me."

She had to be dreaming. This couldn't be real.

"I love you and I want you to be my wife, my partner, and a mother for Riley. That's all that matters to me. The children we might have... are like the next breath we take. Neither are promised."

She didn't know what to say. All she could do was cry.

Brody leaned across Riley and planted a soft kiss on her lips. "And if that miracle doesn't happen for us, I won't stop loving you." He smiled as his eyes roamed over her face. "You'll always be enough. Always."

Not one man looked at her that way.

Not one.

"Oh, Brody, are you sure?"

"I'm positive, sweetheart."

Louisa wrapped her arms around his neck and cried.

She cried for all that had been gained and for the love bursting inside of her.

Mina and her husband live on a farm in the beautiful Appalachian Mountains populated with rescue dogs, miniature horses, and donkeys.
Life in her corner of the world consists of long winter nights curled up by the fire, cheering on her favorite football teams in the fall, enduring March Madness in the spring and walking barefoot through her garden with a cold jar of tea in the summer — fireflies at sunset accompanied by a serenade of crickets and frogs, and lazy nights in the porch swing.

Books by Mina Beckett

Coldiron Cowboys series
The Cowboy's Goodnight Kiss
(ebook prequel novella only available on Mina's website)
The Heartbreak Cowboy
The Fallen Cowboy
Breaking the Cowboy

Rough Creek series
A Cowboy Charming Christmas

Coming soon

Hollywood Cowboy

A Cold Montana Christmas: a Coldiron Cowboys inspired novel

For more book news, visit minabeckett.com